"Turn it and turn it again, for everything is in it. Contemplate it, grow old over it, and never depart from it, for there is no finer pursuit."

Rabbi Ben Bag Bag,
Pirke Avot (Sayings of the Fathers)
on the Torah

"Learning is a treasure that will follow its owner everywhere."

Chinese proverb

The
Lost Torah
of
Shanghai

To Renée Powell, Many thanks. Linda Frank

The
Lost Torah
of
Shanghai

Linda Frank

To Eli, who makes sure I'm never lost,
wherever we go!

The
Lost Torah
of
Shanghai

Contents

PROLOGUE
Bombay, India
December 1918   1

PART I
New York City and San Francisco
January 1991   5

PART II
Shanghai, China
January–February 1991   33

PART III
Jerusalem
January 1992   139

PART IV
Bombay, Shanghai, Hong Kong
1919–1949   147

AUTHOR'S NOTE: THE TRUTH
BEHIND THE FICTION   195

GLOSSARY OF FOREIGN WORDS USED
IN *The Lost Torah of Shanghai*   203

ACKNOWLEDGMENTS   205

PROLOGUE

Bombay, India
December 1918

THE THREE YOUNG women drank tea and nibbled *machboz,* a pastry—filled with cheese, walnuts, and dates—indigenous to the Sephardic Jewish heritage of Miriam Ezra, the hostess. Their rattan chaises cushioned in ivory canvas were positioned on the stone terrace like spokes of a wheel against the hub of a small round white marble pedestal table that held a blue-flowered bone china teapot and the platter of sweets. An arrangement designed, despite the stretch to replenish plates and cups, to capture every smile, frown, and raised eyebrow of their conversation. In short, to not miss a moment of their limited time together as best friends soon to be parted. While many of their peers and certainly their elders would have spent this stifling afternoon lying in solitude in draped and darkened rooms under newly installed whirring ceiling fans, napping was the furthest thing from the minds of Miriam and her Indian girlfriends, Maya and Mena. Eighteen years old, they were newly minted graduates of Bombay's elite Queen Mary's School, where they were known by their classmates and instructors alike as "the three M's." Each was soon to embark on a separate journey: Maya to marriage arranged by her parents, Mena to medical studies in London, and Miriam on a mission accompanying her widowed father, an attorney assigned by his older brothers to tidy up a family legal mess.

"I don't know how I will manage without you two," said Maya. "It scares me to think about it. Living in Anil's parents' house and not even having my dearest friends around?"

"I am not going away until summer," said Mena.

"And by summer I should be back in Bombay," Miriam said.

"You will be sure to write to us, won't you, Miriam? I will, too, once we are settled after the wedding. I hope I can . . . " Maya was nearly in tears.

Miriam reached over and took her friend's hand. "Of course, I will write, and you two must keep me informed about everything here."

They sipped their tea and gazed toward the parlor just inside the terrace doors. There, four steamer trunks were squeezed among substantial pieces of furniture draped in white muslin sheets that appeared to be ghostly puffs of meringue made limp by humidity. One of these puffs engulfed a large sofa, and nestled on it was a four-foot-high cylinder of hammered sterling silver, bedecked with jewels and clasped in the middle with a shiny Star of David.

"Miriam, do Jews always take a Torah with them when they travel?"

Mena's question made Miriam laugh.

"I really don't know about other Jews. But my grandfather brought this Torah from Baghdad. Father refuses to leave it. You see that steamer trunk over there, the biggest one right behind the settee? It's specially fitted out with a raised bottom and sides, so that the Torah will never touch the ground."

"But," countered Maya, "if you're only going to be away for a short time, isn't that a lot of trouble? Surely, your houseman would keep it safe."

"Father insists we take it to Shanghai. He wants me to continue to read Torah with him every Shabbat. The family there would disapprove; they firmly adhere to the belief that women are too unclean for Torah. Anyway, Father says, 'Wherever this Torah is—is home.'"

PART I

New York City and San Francisco

January 1991

Chapter 1

"Lily Kovner . . . Nothing to declare?" The customs officer with the Brooklyn accent arched his eyebrow as he scrutinized my form.

"Nothing to declare," I said.

"Classy lady like you didn't shop in London?"

"Too busy visiting my new granddaughter."

"Welcome home, and mazel tov!"

An only-in-New York moment of universal Yiddishkeit, worthy of submission to the Metropolitan Diary column in the *Times*. I made a mental note to write it up and send it in.

The remark put a smile on my face as I made my way out of the dingy JFK customs hall. It was usually easy to spot my driver, Yossi, uniquely clad in black leather jacket and jeans amidst a row of black-suited chauffer types. But, in scanning the arrivals area for this outfit and the familiar bright blue-lettered sign saying "Mrs. Lily K," I spotted one of his liveried competitors reading the *New York Post*. Its headline screamed, SCUDS ATTACK ISRAEL. My mood changed instantly.

Yossi stood three persons to the left of the newspaper reader. Yossi is Israeli. He is a partner in one of New York City's ubiquitous Israeli-owned car services named for cities there (Tel Aviv, Carmel . . .). I'm not sure why so many *yordim* (Israelis who live outside Israel) got into this business here. Or why, considering that it's taking your life in your hands to ride with an Israeli driver in Israel, I and their other clients patronize them. One thing I knew for sure on this particular morning—Yossi would be able to fill me in on the news. As soon as he commandeered my luggage cart, I peppered him with questions.

"What's going on in Israel? What are Scuds? When did this start?"

"Ah, Mrs. Lily, Scuds are missiles. I worry about my family."

"Missiles? From where?"

"Iraq. That *mamzer* Saddam Hussein." Yossi used the Hebrew pronunciation of the epithet for bastard.

Saddam Hussein? Attacking Israel? In the middle of Operation Desert Storm? After Saddam had attacked Kuwait the previous summer, we Americans had launched this retaliation to support Kuwait in driving out Saddam's forces. And now he had turned on Israel. Yet another tyrant joining that notorious club founded by Pharaoh.

"This started when? Overnight?" While I was 37,000 feet above the Atlantic, in a flying cocoon.

"Yes. To everyone now in Israel there's a gas mask. Already these Scuds have fallen on Tel Aviv."

"Oh, my God. I hope your family will be all right. Everyone there . . ."

Everyone there—in Israel—included *my* family: my cousin, Ruth Sofer; her husband, Boaz; and their two children. And Simon Rieger, the man in my life, though also a Manhattan resident was spending that week in Tel Aviv on business.

The ride, even in off-peak traffic by New York standards, should take at least a half hour. Yossi possibly set a record from JFK to Central Park South, and twenty-six minutes later, Victor, our genial weekday doorman, greeted me. More warmly than I deserved as I rushed into the building barely uttering "Yes, nice trip" and "thanks, Victor," as we rode the elevator and he deposited my luggage in my entry hall. My silence didn't go unnoticed.

"Take care, Mrs. K, hope you feel better," he said on the way out.

I couldn't get into my apartment and pick up the phone fast enough. My home phone, that is, what's come to be called a landline. Simon was way ahead of me both in his embrace of the future and his willingness to pay for it. He already had a mobile cellular phone equipped for international calls. He picked up after five rings that seemed as long as my flight home. Between static on the line and a cacophony of shouting in the background, I tried to piece together what he was saying.

"Scuds. Ruth, Boaz, kids . . . Mossad . . . special shelter . . . overnight. Tel Aviv. Fine, fine . . . you're home? Good. Don't worry . . . interesting story . . . Ruth . . . Torah . . . China . . ."

The line went dead. Ruth . . . Torah . . . China? What was he talking about?

Well, at least he was alive and well, and it sounded like my cousins were, too. It was nearly noon in New York, about seven o'clock in the evening in Israel. Apparently, he was spending the night in a bomb shelter.

That thought made me shiver with memories—of shivering. When I was a little girl in London during the Blitz, I had spent so many nights in the frigid Underground. No matter how many layers of clothing and blankets were piled on me, the penetrating chill precluded any possibility of resting comfortably. Falling asleep was out of the question, between the whimpering babies, the ale-fueled card games, and the constant whirring overhead that might or might not culminate with an ear-popping, wall-shaking bang.

How long ago that seemed, compared to the glamour and liveliness of the rebuilt London where Simon and I had just spent a week visiting my daughter, Elizabeth; her husband, Jonathan; and their two-month-old daughter, Charlotte Ann. Like most Jewish children of eastern European Ashkenazic descent named after deceased relatives, Baby Lottie-Ann honored the memory of two of the most cherished—her first name after my aunt who'd died at 90 the previous summer. This was the aunt who raised me in England after, at age eight, I escaped Nazi-occupied Vienna on the kindertransport, a special evacuation of Jewish children to England—the same aunt who tried to keep me warm and lull me to sleep throughout the Blitz. The baby's middle name, Ann, commemorated my husband, Arthur, who'd died nearly two years before he had a chance to be her grandfather.

As much as I missed Arthur, it was very special to see Simon, not yet a grandfather himself, playing surrogate to this smiling and cooing infant who had already grown so much since I had first seen her as a newborn in October. Simon and I tore ourselves away from this precious bundle for a romantic New Year's sojourn to Paris. From there he had left for Tel Aviv, where his jewelry business had an office in the Diamond Exchange, and I had returned to London to savor another week with the baby and her parents.

My suitcase lay on the bedroom floor challenging me to pay attention to it, but sinking onto the bed was more my speed at the moment. The view of Central Park from my apartment across the street was appropriately hazy and gloomy, but I never took for granted my good fortune to occupy this perch atop one of the most sought after real estate locations in the world. Even so, just then, my home and, certainly, the tranquil pleasures of the past few weeks seemed flagrantly luxurious and self-indulgent as people and a country I loved faced the murderous ambitions of a maniacal despot. Again.

Uncharacteristically for me during the day, I flipped on the television. At least there would always be news on CNN. On the screen the skies of Tel Aviv were punctuated by what looked like shooting stars or firecracker duds falling to earth. So, these were SCUDS. How could Simon have sounded so calm and soothing?

Despite the explosions, I felt myself dozing off. Fear of jet lag roused me. Enough, I said to myself—they have to be fine. One thing my life had taught me was to try not to drive myself crazy over what I could not control. In the meantime, I was home and needed to return to my own routine. Since I left the set on, it was hard to avoid glimpsing the continuing flashes or hearing the crackling sounds that accompanied them, audible even over the news correspondents' commentary. I forced myself to make it background noise and unpack and check through my accumulated mail, mostly bills.

Eventually, motivated by a need to replenish my barren refrigerator, I turned off the set and bundled up for a bracing walk from Central Park South up the West Side to the Fairway Market at Broadway and West 74th Street. But there was no escaping the nerve-wracking news from the Middle East. Whispered conversations, overheard as I edged my cart through the store's aisles, only increased my anxiety.

"I talked to my daughter in Israel today."

"Is she coming home?"

"No, she insists on staying. What can I do?"

"I saw pictures on the news—the gas masks . . . "

"Why doesn't Bush bomb that Saddam Hussein to hell?"

"Oil. It's always oil. What has Israel got? No oil. Just Jews."

Exchanges of nods and shoulder shrugging "what can we do?" expressions signaled tribal sympathy and solidarity, albeit anonymous, that provided a level of consolation, if not reassurance. For more tangible comfort—and to ward off the sore throat and sniffle that had just cropped up—I laid in supplies of soup and orange juice. Suddenly weary, I sure didn't feel like cooking for myself.

As soon as I got home, I clicked on the television in my study. CNN's around-the-clock coverage alleviated the need to wait for the evening network news programs. I sat down and really watched this time. The live shots from rooftops in Jerusalem and Tel Aviv fascinated as much as frightened me. As a print journalist, I've always pooh-poohed the glib and abbreviated news coverage of the younger medium. But I had to admit these onsite reports in real time were mesmerizing. Alerted by the wail of sirens seconds ahead of those now familiar bursts of light, I witnessed an entire enemy attack on screen. The missiles exploding over downtown Tel Aviv and over ships in Haifa's port may have sparkled on first glimpse. But these explosions ignited real fires and giant puffs of smoke that lingered ominously. The correspondents speculated that anthrax or other chemical toxins could be attached.

All I could think about was Simon and my cousins. It was frustrating not to be able to talk to them. Perhaps in the morning. In the meantime, CNN reported that the United States was urging Israel to not retaliate but to let us take care of it. If this warning exasperated me, I could only imagine how it was playing with the Israelis.

I stayed up as long as possible, until ten o'clock, but slept restlessly. Every time I woke up, my head felt more and more stuffed and my throat was sore. In case that wasn't enough to keep me from sleeping, I'd switch on CNN again and just lie there watching Scuds showering down on Tel Aviv and Haifa. Finally, at four—11 a.m. in Israel—I picked up the phone and dialed Simon's office.

"Lily, what are you doing up? It's the middle of the night there. I was going to call you about seven o'clock your time."

"I've been watching CNN on and off all night. Are you all right? What were you saying when I talked to you before? Where were you?"

"In a safe room."

"You mean a bomb shelter?"

"Right. People here are making them at home, even if they don't know what they're doing or have the knowledge or experience to seal them properly."

"So, was this at your house? Was Ruth there? Everything was garbled on the call."

"No, I haven't had time to do anything at my house. This was a special Mossad safe room at headquarters in Tel Aviv."

Simon and I had met nearly a year before at an auction where my family's antique Seder plate reappeared in my life fifty-two years after the Nazis

11

stole it—and vanished again moments later. At that time Simon Rieger was a name I'd only read about on the society pages. I figured he was too much of a player for me, but our relationship evolved to an intimate affair during the course of my search for the looted treasure. Along the way, actually on the day I got the Seder plate back, yet another surprise about Simon came out— his job moonlighting with the Mossad. He was an expert on precious Jewish texts and books, and served as a consultant to Israel's legendary spy agency.

"And Ruth was there?"

"Yes, when I heard from Avi"—Avi Ben-Zeev was Simon's closest colleague in the Mossad—"that I should get over to headquarters, he asked if there was anyone else I wanted to bring, up to six people. I called Ruth, and she and Boaz and the twins came. I also took Shoshana from my office and her husband."

He couldn't see either my smile or my eyes welling up with tears of gratitude for the generous and considerate gesture of reaching out to my family and inviting them to what was probably the safest place in Israel at the moment.

"Thank you, Simon."

"Nonsense. Your family is my family. Plus, it turned out to be a very interesting evening . . . "

"I'll bet, sitting there listening to how close to you the Scuds were landing."

"Well, that, too. But didn't you hear what I told you about the Torah that was stolen from Ruth's aunt and uncle in Shanghai?"

"Her aunt and uncle had a Torah stolen? In China? All I heard, was Torah . . . China. What were they doing with a Torah?"

"I'm still not entirely sure, but it has to do with a family her father was close to during the war. Ruth didn't want to talk about it in too much detail in the safe room. I think she didn't want to upset the twins with talk of her going away. She wants to go to China as soon as possible to help her relatives. And she wants us to go with her."

Incredible, I thought. Another lost treasure! But a Torah in China?

Finding my cousin Ruth was a bonus benefit of Afikomen, my code name for the previous year's search for the Seder plate. The hunt ended up in Israel; I met Ruth in Tel Aviv at the Mosaica gallery of Jewish ritual objects, where she worked as curator. Her boss, a former Nazi officer named Rudolf Bucholz reinvented as Israeli gallery owner Eliezer Ben-Shuvah, was the devil in a deal with my late surrogate uncle, Nachman Tanski. Uncle Nachman had conspired in an arrangement in which Bucholz had secured his new identity and business after World War II. In return Uncle got some fine specimens of art that Bucholz had looted as a Nazi officer. But the real prize, and Uncle's ostensible rationale for partaking in this diabolical transaction, was a stash of usable German war materiel that Uncle and his Zionist cohorts procured for Israel's War of Independence.

Before I encountered Ruth at Mosaica, I didn't even know she existed, never mind that she was my cousin. Her father, Erich Heilbrun, was my mother's twin brother who had fled Vienna for Shanghai before I left on the kindertransport. My parents didn't survive the war, and my aunt and uncle in London lost contact with Uncle Erich after the Communists took over China in 1949. All we knew then was that his Chinese wife was pregnant and couldn't travel when they were supposed to leave Shanghai for Hong Kong. Ruth was the half-Chinese product of that pregnancy. When we met, in Tel Aviv in 1990, she wore a locket around her neck similar to one I wear. Our mutual grandmother had bought both of them, and the same family photos were inside.

Ruth's odyssey from China to Israel wended from her parents' deaths—Uncle Erich in 1960, her mother during the Cultural Revolution—to study in the Soviet Union and the United States, places where she established relationships with Jewish *refusniks* and an American lawyer advocating for them. Along the way she developed an interest in Judaism, met Boaz—an Israeli in graduate school at MIT when she was at Harvard—and officially converted to Judaism to marry him and join his Egyptian Sephardic family.

"So, that's all you know, just that a Torah was stolen?" I said.

"No, she called me this morning with more details. But it's a long story, and I don't have time to go into it now. It's not just any Torah—it's old with a pedigree and a very valuable case. Originally from Baghdad."

"Baghdad?" Visions of cocky, gun-toting black-mustached Saddam Hussein rushed through my head. I looked up at the TV to see CNN panning over a line of his tanks grinding through the desert. Baghdad, where this Torah was from, now the launchpad for missiles aimed at Tel Aviv.

"Yes. You know the Sephardic community in Shanghai—Sassoons, Kadoories, Hardoons—they were originally from Baghdad."

Of course, I'd heard the name Sassoon. "You mean the poet, Siegfried Sassoon? In England, when I was in school, we read his anti-war poems, but his Jewish roots weren't advertized. And the hairdresser, Vidal . . ."

Simon's chortle crackled into the static already on the connection. "Siegfried and Vidal. I love your frames of reference," he said. "I suppose they were all related. But the group that settled in Shanghai first got there in the 1840s."

"Right," I said. "Mainly to trade opium, as I recall."

"Yes, but to their credit many stayed to build the city and even provide some social service benefit to the indigenous Chinese, though Shanghai was a famously international city. Of course, they became fabulously wealthy until they had to hightail it out of there when the Communists took over. Apparently, Ruth's father worked for one of those families."

"It's always fascinated me to find pockets of Jews in unexpected places. But it's comforting to know that Uncle Erich lived among them when he made his way to China. If only my mother and I had gone with him, my grandparents . . ."

Simon didn't answer but steered the conversation back. "You heard me tell you that Ruth wants us to go to China with her, didn't you?"

"Yes. Why?"

"Me, I think, because of my background in texts. This Torah dates back a long way and might be a famous one. Not that I'm an expert on anything Baghdadi or Sephardic, but I have a bit of an eye. You, because you're family—her cousin and kindred spirit. She loves you, Lily, and respects you so much. But I also know she wants you along because you're a great detective. A regular Jewish Miss Marple!"

Now *I* laughed. Of course, I loved the books and those films with the doughty—and dowdy—Margaret Rutherford playing Agatha Christie's character. But I didn't think my brief Afikomen "caper" put me in her league.

"Me, the Jewish Miss Marple? That's funny," I said. "Was that Ruth's description, or yours? The Miss Marple part?"

"Hers. She loves Agatha Christie."

"Back in London, we all thought Agatha Christie was a flaming anti-Semite. I wonder if Ruth knows that or what Miss Marple looks like in those movies? Bassett hound face, figure the width of a picture window dressed in those voluminous suits and capes, the old schoolmarm sensible shoes."

"I think Ruth has just read the books, not seen Margaret Rutherford."

"Okay. I'll go. Of course. I must support Ruth. I can only imagine how torn she feels between her concern for her family in China and this attack on Israel. When does she want to take this trip?"

"Not for at least a week or so. She'd like to wait until things quiet down here . . . "

"Do things ever quiet down in Israel?"

"Well, at least until the family is back to sleeping at home. But Boaz told her she should leave as soon as she can, that he and his parents can handle the kids and the home front. He's very concerned about her relatives. This aunt and uncle and their daughter and her little boy are the only family she has left on her mother's side."

That was a feeling I understood only too well. By the summer of 1945, I knew that Aunt Lottie and Uncle Arnold and their sons, Julian and Daniel, in London, and Uncle Erich, in faraway Shanghai, were my only remaining close relatives. I could hardly know then that forty-five years later I would find another, much younger, cousin, Ruth.

"We need visas to go to China, don't we?"

"Yes," said Simon, "You can go to the Chinese consulate downtown and get one right away. Here in Tel Aviv it's not so easy—China and Israel still don't have diplomatic relations. There's a Chinese tourist office here, but I don't think it issues visas. Ruth and I are going to have to fly to Hong Kong and get them there."

"Okay, I'll at least get a visa photo taken today. Maybe I'll stop in San Francisco for a day or two to break up the trip and see the kids on the way."

My son, Jacob, a pediatric oncologist, lives in that breathtaking city with his wife, Amy, and their twins, Gabriella and Joshua, four years old. Their life is hectic, and I'd just been there, with Simon, for Thanksgiving. But you can never see your grandchildren too much, and I try to go along with their plans and help out—even driving the city's hills—when I visit.

"Good idea," Simon replied. "Listen, I've got to go. Everyone's working at breakneck speed all day to get things done before going to the safe rooms at night. I'll keep you posted. By the way, have you given any more thought to what we talked about in Paris?"

"Here and there."

"I hope more 'here' than 'there.' Okay, Lily, go back to sleep, for God's sake. I love you."

Going back to sleep would not be easy. It was hard to turn off the unrelenting news coverage, especially now that I'd heard from my personal correspondent in Israel. Even though everyone was all right so far, the constant barrage of blasts and flames was terrifying, and updates on diplomatic efforts did nothing to relieve the tension.

What Simon meant—what we'd talked about in Paris—was also unsettling, in a different way.

We had acknowledged being in love with each other. We'd shared intimacy, commitment, and companionship. I could see living like this forever and I thought he could, too. Yet, in Paris, from out of the blue came an age-old question.

"Why don't we get married?"

I didn't laugh it off but didn't answer seriously, either.

"And give up my remote control?"

Lying there watching CNN in the wee hours was a poignant reminder that maybe my flippant answer spoke more truth than I let on. If Simon were lying here with me, would I be watching the war on TV right now? Possibly, if we were both awake and jet-lagged. Not the best example, as certainly he'd be as concerned about Israel from afar as I was. But on a typical night together, sometimes I wanted to watch "Nightline" and he preferred to relax with Johnny Carson, at least for an instant, until he'd click through to the next channel and then the next and the next . . . surfing, sampling, driving me nuts.

How superficial! That's a reason not to get married? After all, there's more than one television set in both of our apartments. And we don't even watch them much. But the remote control has become a universal symbol of male influence, because men just click up and down and never settle on anything to watch, unless it's sports. Such an annoyance, especially now with cable.

I find our life of being together often, but not all the time, perfect. Before Arthur's death two years ago, I'd never lived on my own. Few women of my generation did. I like it. It's nice to have a man around the house—or be the woman around his—but it's nice to be a woman on my own, too. For now, at least.

I drifted in and out of slumber until seven and debated with myself about my usual morning swim. I felt chilled, drowsy, and lazy but decided it would be good for me. And it was—in a way that both energized me and provided a sense of accomplishment, whatever else I might or might not get done that day. That's fundamentally why I swim almost every day when there's a pool handy.

Home from the athletic club, with CNN and exploding Tel Aviv still dominating my sensibility, it was hard to focus on China or anything else. But the day was surprisingly warm and sunny for January, my budding head cold seemed to have abated, and I decided to walk downtown. With plenty of time, I ambled all the way to the Lower East Side, stopping at a small photo shop for visa pictures, en route to a one o'clock lunch date that had been on my calendar since before I left for Europe.

Marty Zuckert, my longtime friend and sometime editor, stood at the head of a ridiculously long line waiting for tables at Katz's Deli, which had become a tourist destination since Meg Ryan's onscreen orgasmic reenactment in the film *When Harry Met Sally* two years earlier. Everyone wanted to have what she had at Katz's. But for me eating here with Marty was a tradition that preceded by three decades the deli's newfound status as a culinary destination. And no one would have mistaken Marty for a Meg Ryan groupie! The Dashiell Hammett shock of white hair, the ground-sweeping tweed great coat, and the long Burberry scarf wound tightly around his neck made Marty an even more flamboyant persona in his early seventies than he was thirty years before, when, still dark-haired, his was the first Jewish Afro among my acquaintances.

Bronx-born and a New Yorker to the core, the now Washington-based Marty embraced me in a bear hug, and we followed a waiter to the same two-top where we'd sat for years. Typically, the monologue started gushing out before we even sat down.

"Lily, how are you? You look fabulous! I'm so glad we could do this. You're just back from Europe, right? How was it? The new granddaughter? Catch me up! When did you get back?"

"I got back yesterday, and all's well. Except for what's going on in Israel, of course. I was up half the night watching CNN."

"Me, too. Don't you have family there? Are they safe?"

"I talked to Simon . . . "

"Ah, yes. Simon. The swain," Marty said. "If I didn't check out Bill Cunningham's pictures every Sunday in the *Times*, I'd never know what my fancy society lady friend is up to, now that she's got Simon." He raised his water glass in a mock toast.

17

I ignored the tinge of sneer. "Simon is in Tel Aviv right now, too, and he had my relatives in a safe room, which is what they're calling shelters there. But who knows how long it will go on?"

"Indeed. Saddam Hussein is a real *meshugenah*, to be charitable. One good thing is so far the reports of chemical warfare aren't credible. But it sure is disturbing. Here I came up yesterday, a day earlier than I needed to be in New York, thinking it would make the trip more restful. All night in the hotel I couldn't turn off the damn TV."

"Remind me what you're doing in New York, Marty. Just craving a pastrami fix? Work?"

"It's so good to be in New York again. DC's such a wasteland for deli. Among other things. How I'd love to move back here. But what can I say? That's where the job is, and at my age I'm lucky to have any job, let alone the *Smithsonian Magazine*. Yeah, I've got a few people to see here for work, but mainly I came in for my nephew's wedding this weekend. Big extravaganza—at the Pierre, no less."

Marty took a breath long enough to stab at the ubiquitous plate of pickles.

"That kind of wedding can be fun," I said, "especially if you're not the one paying for it."

"I don't know," he said, "since Nancy died, I feel like a fifth wheel at big social events. But my son and daughter-in-law will be there, thank goodness. And I figure they'll seat me next to some woman on the prowl. Too bad you're already spoken for, Lily."

That really shocked me. Marty and I went back thirty-five years as friends and colleagues. I was married to Arthur for all but the last two of them, and Marty was either married or living with someone. Nancy was a lovely long-term companion who had passed away several months before. Was this a romantic overture?

"I don't know that I'm spoken for, but Simon and I have a nice relationship going. Kind of a side benefit of finding my Seder plate."

"Well, if you ever . . . no, forget it."

"Let's not spoil a wonderful friendship," I said, patting his hand.

"So, are you working? Another mystery on the horizon?"

My foray to the Judaica auction where I'd discovered my family's Seder plate began on assignment from Marty to write about antique Jewish ritual items and the market for them in light of the recent fall of the Soviet Union.

The personal story that resulted turned out to not be what he and the *Smithsonian Magazine* envisioned, and they'd given me a "kill" fee. However, the *New Yorker* picked it up, and the reaction to my piece shocked me. Besides significant news coverage, Holocaust survivors all over the world immediately began writing and calling to ask me to find their looted family treasures—ranging from cheap, commercially produced silver Kiddush cups to priceless Rembrandts.

Using some money left to me by Uncle Nachman, I'd established a global foundation to be based in Israel and headed by my art historian cousin, Ruth. Her first goal was to set up a registry of art still sought by pre-war owners or their heirs. So, despite the fact that I hadn't personally taken on another Afikomen-style quest or even another free-lance assignment since then, I was "hot" by editor standards. Marty was still kicking himself for not accepting my story as it evolved, in spite of its ultimately personal nature—and the expenses incurred along the way.

"A new mystery? Funny you should ask. As of today I'm preparing to leave for Shanghai to look for a stolen Torah."

"A Torah in Shanghai? You're joking?"

"No. If you read my *New Yorker* piece, . . . "

"Yeah," he grumbled, "Who didn't?"

"Then you know my cousin in Israel is half-Chinese and half-Jewish. Her aunt and uncle in China have just had a Torah stolen. On the way here I had photos taken for my visa to China. I can get quick turnaround from the Chinese Consulate and leave in a few days."

"Wow! Maybe I could snag the story this time?"

I hadn't even considered the professional possibilities this trip could afford.

"You had your shot last time," I said.

"Yeah, I know. We blew it. Are you going to talk to the *New Yorker*?"

"Honestly, Marty, this just came up overnight. I'm not going to pitch it for an assignment. I have neither the time nor the energy to do it right now. You know I don't need the *Smithsonian* or the *New Yorker* for an advance or expenses. Let's see how this turns out."

"OK, but please don't talk to anyone at the *New Yorker* until I call you. Maybe I can talk the *Smithsonian* into it this time!" he said, slathering brown mustard on a piece of rye bread and plopping it onto a piping hot mound of peppery sliced meat.

19

"In your dreams, Marty."

"I guess I shouldn't be so surprised about a Torah having been in Shanghai, but now? So many years after the Jews left? You know, I had an aunt who lived there. Married to my mother's brother. Her father worked for the Trans-Siberian railroad in Russia, and he was transferred to Harbin, when the czar wanted to extend it there. A whole Jewish community sprung up that was happy to be free of pogroms. My aunt was born there, I think, but she and her mother moved to Shanghai after the father died. Some other relatives had gone there after the Russian Revolution. My aunt and her mother left China long before the war—in the late twenties. They had relatives in Montreal, who sponsored them out, and my uncle was working there—running bootleg booze during Prohibition—as a young man. And the rest is history. But Aunt Teddy was quite a character . . . "

"Aunt Teddy?"

"Yeah. Her real name was Theodora. Her parents were *ferbrente* Zionists. They had a thing for Theodor Herzl and named her after him. Aunt Teddy was really something. Even though she left China at something like nineteen, her tiny little apartment was full of all sort of Chinese *tschotchkes,* and she would wear those skinny little Chinese dresses . . . "

"*Cheongsam* they're called."

"Right. Really cheesy ones she had probably had made in a little Chinese tailor shop three blocks from here and, believe me, she didn't have the figure. But she was our own Jewish Anna May Wong from the Bronx at every bar mitzvah and wedding."

"That's a riot. She must have stuck out like a sore thumb."

"Well, she sure added a little exoticism to the family. My mother and grandmother laughed and talked about her behind her back and didn't treat her very nicely. But Aunt Teddy was a good lady, and I had a nice relation-ship with her. She loved me, because I'd sit and listen endlessly to her stories about life in China. She'd haul out a scrapbook she'd kept since she left. We'd pore over it page by page as she explained the postcards and pictures in it. She started collecting as a young girl before she left and added to it when she received letters and cards from girlfriends who stayed longer."

"Wow, I'd love to see that."

"When are you leaving?"

"Probably the end of next week."

"When I get back to DC Monday, I'll send it overnight on Federal Express."

"That would be great, Marty. Thanks. Look at that."

At that moment an elderly Chinese couple accompanied by a little girl of about ten sat down at the table next to us. All three were elegantly dressed in beautifully tailored clothes—the man in a camel hair coat over a grey flannel three-piece pin-striped suit and conservative tie, the woman's black cashmere coat topping a black St. John suit, the child in a red wool coat with navy velveteen collar and cuffs over a red party dress and tights. Elegant by Katz Deli standards, for sure, they looked like escapees from lunch at the Four Seasons.

"Ha!" Marty said, "Finally, some payback for the Jewish infatuation with Chinese food. Maybe they could give you some advice about going to Shanghai to find a stolen Torah."

"Not so loud," I said under my breath. "The man turned this way when he heard Shanghai. Can't be too careful."

"Oh, sorry. I forgot how experienced a sleuth you've become. The Jewish Miss Marple."

I laughed. *"Et tu,* Marty?"

After lunch I hugged him and said goodbye. Although the family next to us was an incongruity at Katz's (and probably in Chinatown), nominally that district lay several blocks south of East Houston Street. But it had begun to meld with the Lower East Side. The prospect of my forthcoming trip made me more attuned to the Chinese businesses and their indigenous clientele I passed before turning uptown. Also more dubious about the likelihood of succeeding on the upcoming quest. Would this be a ridiculous wild goose chase? The Miss Marple epithet notwithstanding, my credentials as a private detective were nil; with *Afikomen* at least I had connections and referrals to initial contacts, as well as both personal and historical context to start with. China was so much more obscure, foreign, and—well—mysterious. But I was a journalist and, after picking up my visa photos, I realized the discussion with Marty had stimulated my professional instincts. With or without an assignment, I needed to do some research so on the way home I stopped at one of my favorite haunts, the New York Public Library.

Baghdadi and Russian Jews in China? The card catalogue yielded practically nothing—just a few mentions I quickly jotted down, including a smattering of references to the Europeans, like Uncle Erich, who settled there to escape the Holocaust. But a book on the Jews of Kaifeng piqued my interest enough to check out. It was odd to page through illustrations of Torah scrolls being read by men with distinctly Asian physiognomies who did so clutching a traditional *yad* pointer. These were the so-called "real" Jews of China, as the preface described them. Newspaper microfiche from 1938 to the war yielded more. Stories about Jews arriving in Shanghai from Europe. This was familiar, of course, because of Uncle Erich. Going back to 1918, I found a small piece about Jews leaving Russia for China. Although I could sit reading old newspapers nonstop for days, I found little to enlighten me on the forthcoming mission to Shanghai and I was anxious to return to CNN. I went home, acknowledging I clearly had a lot to learn.

The arrival a few days later of Aunt Teddy's scrapbook took me into a Jewish world in Shanghai I would have never expected. Marty had truly provided a treasure trove of background material and orientation for my trip.

Theatre programs from Yiddish productions, snapshots of young people at dances at the Jewish Club. A photo of the club's exterior looked like a shiny white embassy in Washington set on landscaped grounds. Wedding couples and their families. Young boys wearing the uniforms of Betar, a Zionist youth organization. A bar mitzvah boy holding a Torah. Every photo was labeled on the back with names Aunt Teddy knew and where the people moved after leaving Shanghai. It was remarkable she'd kept up so assiduously with friends, considering she herself had left China so young and so long before the mass exodus of Jews and others that accompanied the Communist takeover.

But they had, indeed, taken over—more than forty years before my quest. Aunt Teddy's Shanghai Jewish world was long gone. Interesting, yes, but unlikely to point me toward finding a stolen Torah there.

Chapter 2

My husband Arthur was an economist, and he called children the "dividends" earned through marriage and grandchildren the "big pop, tax-free capital gains." Remarkably, these were among his final conscious pronouncements. The time allotted him to spend with our first two grandchildren, twins Gabriella and Joshua, was negligible—they were only a year and a half when his pancreatic cancer was diagnosed a mere five months before he died. But he made the most of it.

Within days of the fatal news, our son, Jacob, wangled a research exchange between the University of California-San Francisco (UCSF) Medical Center and New York's Sloan Kettering, and his wife, Amy, who had derailed herself off her former law firm's "mommy track" since the twins' birth, took a leave from her job at a legal services nonprofit. A week later the young family arrived in New York for the duration. A neighbor in our building, leaving to open a new Singapore office for his banking firm and not permitted by our co-op by-laws to rent out his apartment for less than a year, was only too happy to have it lived in. It was something of a workaholic bachelor pad—with few fragile possessions yet acquired—so we made short shrift of childproofing. Our daughter, Elizabeth, and Jonathan, then her husband of only six months, somehow managed to fly in from London at least every other weekend and for longer chunks of time over holidays.

Looking back, I try to focus on the family around the dinner table eating, while he still could, Arthur's highest cholesterol menu treats and, while he could still get out, on walks through the Park. I remember the movies we all watched together, the singing we did to his favorite Broadway show albums,

the block buildings and zoo-animal games he played on the floor with the
twins, and the bedtime stories he told them from his hospital bed crammed
into our bedroom. There's a lot about that time I try to forget. But, as neither
Arthur nor I would have ever asked the kids to alter their lives as drastically
as they did, the joyousness of it overcame Arthur's initial fury over his fate,
and I can honestly say he died smiling.

Ten days after arriving back in Manhattan from London, I touched down at
San Francisco International on a Saturday noon and saw the four-year-old
twins holding up a crayoned construction paper "Welcome Gram" sign. I
bent down and swooped them into a dual hug.

"Did you bring cookies?" Joshua asked, eyeing the large Bloomingdale's
Brown Bag I was carrying.

"Chocolate chips for you and Gabrell, 'rocks' for your dad," I said.
Somehow, even with getting the visa for China, packing, and putting my
business and household affairs in order for a second overseas trip within two
weeks, I'd managed to whip up a batch of the kids' favorite. "Rocks" were the
hardened date and nut cookies adored by Jacob. At heart I'm more your basic
Jewish mother and grandmother than Jane Marple.

Amy rolled her eyes as she reached out to embrace me. "One of these
days, I will have to start baking," she said. "Between your cookies and my
mother's chocolate cake, how can I compete? To say nothing of finding the
time."

"Honey, you cook great. Competing with my mother—or yours—forget
about it. A non-issue," said Jacob, brushing my cheek.

"You have to see the doll I got for Chanukah," Gabriella said. "It's my
own baby."

"Tell Gram the baby's name," said Jacob.

"Charlotte Ann—like our cousin, Auntie Elizabeth's baby."

"Well," I said, "when we get to my hotel or your house, wherever we're
going first, I will show you the new pictures I have of Baby Charlotte Ann."

San Francisco real estate prices, despite the physical and economic devastation of the Loma Prieta earthquake and the Oakland fire within the previous two years, compared to Manhattan's. The kids' Forest Hill house, while

more than adequate for a young family in the City, was just the size they could (barely) afford but desirable because of the eight-minute commute time for Jacob from that leafy neighborhood to the Parnassus campus of the UCSF Medical Center. A guest room might come with a later addition, when the financial coffers refilled. And, devoted as I am to these precious children, a hotel mattress and swimming pool would prepare me better for the long plane trek over the Pacific than a night with them squirming in with me in the extra twin bed in Gabriella's cramped room.

The flight had transformed my universe from grey, snowy New York to the sunny City by the Bay. But almost six hours in the air was more time than I'd spent news-free since the Scud attacks had begun nearly two weeks earlier. I didn't want to alarm the children but murmured a quick question to Jacob as he hoisted my suitcase off the carousel.

"What's happening in Israel?"

"Another attack at sundown," he said. "No new casualties, though."

Joshua grabbed my hand to walk to the parking lot. "First, we're going to the park," he announced. "We're having a picnic."

Golden Gate Park was cloudless and bursting with pink magnolia buds and green leaves. It was hard to believe this was still January. Amy and Jacob, despite her protests, were no slouches in the kitchen, and they unpacked a lunch worthy of *Bon Appétit* both in presentation and taste: cold rosemary chicken, cucumber and tabouli salads, fruit, and the locally ubiquitous sour dough baguette. Two hours of swing pushing, jungle gym climbing, seesaw patrol, and a walk to Stow Lake followed. It all seemed so normal I almost forgot I didn't do this with them every week and I was starting a trip to China the next morning. With the kids along, the subject didn't even come up.

But that evening, with the exhausted twins tucked in with a beloved babysitter at home, it was just the three of us out to dinner at Vanessi's, our favorite Italian formerly in working class North Beach transplanted to upscale Nob Hill. As soon as we sat down, I could sense Jacob reverting to earnest persona and settling in to confront a burning question in characteristic scientific inquiry mode, delivered staccato in a tone more suited to Grand Rounds at UCSF than to Saturday night dinner.

"Mom, your life—what are you doing? You're running all over the world with these cockamamie mysteries with that guy, Simon, and this co-called cousin, Ruth. Are you becoming some sort of Jewish Jane Marple?"

Despite the seriousness, I could only laugh, which they didn't understand. I didn't bother to explain that the Agatha Christie reference was becoming a trademark—or a cliché.

My daughter-in-law shifted uncomfortably in her seat and made a point of looking at a party being seated three tables away from us. It seemed to me she didn't agree with Jacob, which heartened me as much as my son's outburst nettled. Who the hell did he think he was? What was behind this eruption?

Which is exactly what I asked.

"So? What's wrong with that?"

He adopted a softer pitch in answering.

"I'm worried about you. You can't settle down. I think all this picking up and running around means you're avoiding staying home to face your life without Dad."

"Worried? I'd think you'd be thrilled that I'm so busy and not leaning on my children. I've been home plenty. I still see my friends and I go to concerts and theatre with and without Simon. I entertain, Simon helps me, sometimes we cook together . . . "

"Yeah, he makes that yucky Rumanian stuff, what do you call it?"

"Gvetch," I said.

"It's like ratatouille," said Amy. "I think it's delicious. You just don't like eggplant, Jacob. That's not Simon's fault."

"Listen, Jacob," I said, back on topic, "You really think I haven't faced my life without your father? I have. It's been almost two years. Believe me, I have no illusions about being alone or loneliness. They can be two different things, by the way."

"So, what about Simon? What are his intentions?"

I could only laugh out loud.

"His intentions? That's pretty old-fashioned. Who do you think you are? My parents agonizing over my virtue?"

"I don't know," Jacob said. " You travel all over the world together, you're together a lot in New York—I know he's there most of the time when we talk late at night."

"And this is a problem for you? Why? You think your generation owns the exclusive rights to co-habitation or sex without marriage?"

At this point I thought Amy would fall off her chair laughing before she launched into a defense that fulfilled a mother-in-law's fantasy.

"Jacob, your mother is fabulous. She's as loving and caring a mother and grandmother as anyone can be, but she's doing incredible things and having wonderful adventures that, at least with the Seder plate, gave her a huge professional coup—that *New Yorker* piece."

"Yes, I know. It's great that you're working again, Mom. But Simon . . . "

I didn't let Jacob finish the sentence, if there was more to come.

"For your information, Simon is begging me to marry him. He proposed while we were in Paris for New Year's. I told him I thought things were fine the way they are, but he's continued to bring it up—even on the phone from Israel."

"Oh," said Jacob. "Maybe I've got him wrong."

"Yes, maybe you have."

"Sounds good to me," said Amy.

"Okay, okay. But, if he wants to marry you, why are you backing away and giving him a hard time?"

"I'm not giving him a hard time. I just don't see any reason to get married. We love each other, we feel committed to each other. Until your father died, I'd never lived on my own. I kind of like it. Look at Uncle Nachman— he had all those women friends over the years that he never married. You didn't think there was anything wrong with that, did you?"

"Yeah, right. Uncle Nachman," Jacob grunted. "What a fine example he turned out to be—supporting an old Nazi in Israel, no less. Plus, he carried the torch for my grandma his whole life."

"Uncle" Nachman Tanski had been my mother's platonic lover before and during her marriage to my father. The infamous Seder plate from the Afikomen search had been his gift to her that last glorious Passover in Vienna, in 1937, the last time I celebrated the holiday together with the intact family of my childhood—parents, grandparents, aunts, uncles, and cousins. Nachman took on the role of surrogate father to me and grandfather to my children after the Nazis murdered my blood relatives. I learned the full story of his involvement with Bucholz, the war criminal turned Israeli art dealer, only hours before Uncle's death in Israel. As much as that final betrayal hurt, I still tried to view him from the perspective of the many positive years we considered him an adopted family member.

"You're right. Uncle was hardly perfect. But, don't forget, he was the closest thing you had to a grandfather most of your life, after your Grandpa

Kovner died when you were ten. And, God knows, Uncle Nachman had his faults, but loving my mother wasn't one of them. Maybe that was the reason he didn't marry; I really don't know. Uncle had a lot of interests, business and otherwise, and he had a full life. He always said he just didn't get around to marrying, and he had his nieces and nephews, as well as us, and it must have been enough."

"How can you continue to defend him after all you found out last year?"

"You know, Jacob," I said, "it's not easy, but I can't forget all the wonderful things he did for us and all the good times. Look, even what he did with the Nazi Bucholz, he did to help to get Israel going—the deal secured desperately needed arms and equipment for the War of Independence, which no one in their wildest dreams imagined Israel could win. Maybe it was the wrong thing for the right reasons, but I believed Uncle when he said he didn't know Bucholz still had the Seder plate and was trying to prevent me from getting it back. Uncle loved us all. Anyway, that's water over the dam. You should try to take a more forgiving and long-term view about him, too."

Jacob sighed, took a sip of wine, and visibly relaxed. Amy patted him on the hand. But the storm hadn't totally passed. He took a deep breath and tackled another subject.

"Now this Ruth person," he said. "She tells you her aunt and uncle in China have a Torah in the house that's gone missing, and it's a reason to run there with her?"

"Ruth is family, Jacob." I was getting really annoyed. "A blood relative, my uncle's daughter. That makes her my first cousin and your second cousin once removed, or something like that. And, she's doing an incredible job in running the foundation for finding looted Nazi art. So, even in the wake of all that mess, more good is coming. Ruth is very highly respected in the Judaica academic world and she gets a lot of attention, not only because of her skill and reputation, but also because she's Jewish and Chinese. It's really good for the work we're doing. I don't know yet the whole story of why or how her aunt and uncle had a Torah, but she wanted Simon and me to help, and we're going. You met her and her family at my house for Passover last year. Didn't you like her? 'This Ruth person'? Shame on you, Jacob, that's just not nice."

"Sounds like another great *New Yorker* piece to me," said Amy.

"Marty, my friend from the *Smithsonian Magazine*, is hot on my trail after that. Kicking himself for rejecting the last one. We'll see. These hunts are fun and stimulating, and, don't worry, Jacob, there will still be enough money left for you and your sister and all your kids."

"You think this is about money?" Now Jacob took on the mantle of the offended party. "Jeez, Mom, no! I'm just concerned about you. I don't want to see you hurt. No doubt, my sister is all for this adventure, of course."

"I've barely had time to discuss it with Elizabeth. She and Jonathan went away for a few days to Morocco before she goes back to work after maternity leave. Her in-laws took the baby to let them have a little vacation. In general, you're right. Elizabeth has told me she's very pleased to see me happy and busy."

"As we all are, right, Jacob?" Amy squeezed his hand now, and I suspect a simultaneous kick under the table accompanied that gesture.

"Yes, okay, okay. I give up. When the women gang up on me, it's time to fold," Jacob said, finally laughing. "Maybe I'm getting to be an old fuddy-duddy before my time." He raised his wine glass. "Cheers, Mom, *l'chaim*! Have a great time, but be careful, please."

In the morning I shared the hotel pool with three courteous generations of a Chinese family. The elders and one child reminded me of the trio I'd seen at Katz's Deli, but that would be too much of a coincidence. After a good swim, I returned to my room to find a note under the door. It was a crude hand-lettered script on lined paper ripped out of a notebook.

"Lily Kovner, don't go to China."

And there was a large Chinese character:

I was stunned.

I'd encountered no one—not even a hotel maid—in the corridor between the elevator and my room then or at any other time since I'd checked in less than twenty-four hours before. Hotel security regarding releasing room numbers was getting more and more scrupulous, so I had no idea how anyone who might have delivered this would have obtained my room number, other than by following me.

Having been threatened throughout the previous year's Seder plate caper—in addition to confronting the murder of a contact and a violent, thankfully thwarted, attack on me, personally—I didn't take this lightly. But, as before, I wasn't going to let it stop me.

I called the hotel desk immediately to report the note and said I would bring it downstairs shortly before checkout time. When I arrived in the lobby, I was greeted by the on-duty manager and a San Francisco police detective. The manager, a wiry and very nervous middle-aged man named Thomas Sinclair, gushed, "Mrs. Kovner, I am so sorry you have had a problem. We hope it hasn't spoiled your stay at the Palace. As a token of our regret, we will not charge you for your stay."

"That's not necessary at all," I said. "In fact, I insist on a regular bill."

"As you wish," he said, "but perhaps the next time you come . . . "

"Mr. Sinclair, we have greater concerns than her bill to discuss with Mrs. Kovner," said the solidly built San Francisco police detective in snug navy blue uniform pants and shirt, policeman's cap, and protruding gun. Had the detective not spoken, I wouldn't have expected to be introduced to a Jennifer.

"Detective Jennifer Wong, SFPD, ma'am. Morning," she said, removing the cap and revealing a short haircut with Buster Brown bangs. "Come with us." She pointed to Sinclair, who led the way to his office.

Detective Wong's appearance and initial outward toughness betrayed her when she blanched and looked visibly stunned as she read the note.

"This character—it means death," she said, pocketing it before making notes in a little spiral bound notebook. "Mrs. Kovner, why are you visiting San Francisco?"

"I'm only here to see my family," I said. "Son, daughter-in-law, grandchildren. But I'm leaving this afternoon for China to meet a cousin whose relatives there have had a precious possession stolen."

"China? How unusual. Your cousin has relatives in China? Why are you involved in this situation?"

"My cousin is half-Chinese. It's a long story, but her aunt and uncle in Shanghai somehow had a Jewish Torah in their home, and now it's gone. I've had some experience looking for stolen Jewish objects, and she wants me to meet her on this trip. "

Sinclair had kept quiet and looked truly mystified. Finally, he spoke.

"What can you do to investigate, Detective?"

"I guess we can go over your hotel register, but there's no actual crime here, at least none I can discern so far. Mrs. Kovner, are you sure you want to leave this afternoon?"

"Of course. I've been threatened before, and it didn't stop me. I just thought I should report it, so the hotel would know that maybe its security isn't as airtight as it should be. I can't figure out how somehow got my room number. I assume you don't give them out to just anyone who asks, right, Mr. Sinclair? And yet I don't think I was followed at all."

The manager straightened up and said, "Our procedures are very strict about that, both for telephone inquiries and face-to-face at the desk."

"Which isn't to say," Detective Wong replied, "that an operator might not have slipped just once—or a desk clerk perhaps persuaded by a crisp bill?"

Sinclair's face reddened. "I will interview every relevant staff member. Mrs. Kovner, I apologize, if a security breach led to this dreadful experience here at the Palace. Our history speaks for itself, but our continuing reputation depends on the safety, satisfaction, and enjoyment of our guests."

I stood up.

"Thank you both. Mr. Sinclair, I'm sure you will take adequate measures to prevent something like this from happening to anyone else. Fortunately, no true harm came to me. And thank you, Detective, for coming over and interpreting the Chinese character for me. But I must be going. My family is picking me up for brunch before my flight."

"I will keep the note," Wong said, "if that's all right with you."

"Absolutely," I said. "But Mr. Sinclair, can you Xerox it for me? I'd like to keep a copy."

Obviously, I deliberately avoided mentioning the threatening note to my family before I said goodbye at the airport a few hours later. The last thing I wanted to do was worry Jacob any more. Or provoke another battle royal.

As my son gave me a last hug, he looked uncharacteristically sheepish.

"Sorry for last night, Mom. Even though we had our bump in the road, it was terrific seeing you, and I hope you have a great trip and good results."

"If we didn't have our bumps now and then, we wouldn't be us," I said. "That's part of what open and loving family relationships are all about—in our family, at least."

"Right," he said, "Give my best to Ruth and Simon. And be careful. Please?"

PART II

Shanghai, China

January–February 1991

Chapter 3

Taking off to the west from San Francisco International Airport that clear Sunday afternoon afforded a view that would put postcards to shame. It refreshed my enthusiasm for this magical landscape after a scant twenty-seven hour visit one could only describe as bittersweet, with my son's eruption and the Chinese death threat casting a pall on the maternal and grandmotherly pleasure I normally take for granted. Although I had had little time to read or watch news, events in Israel remained a source of angst. But on the plane I could settle into the nest that a long flight provides, fully relishing the isolation from reality—both personal and the one broadcast around-the-clock—that went with it. I had newspapers, magazines, and a few good-sized books with me to pass the time. Although this flight would see mostly daylight as we crossed the International Dateline, my brief San Francisco sojourn had been wearing, and I had no trouble dozing off several times.

Changing planes at Tokyo's frenetic Narita airport rocked me back to reality. Screens along the concourse showed bright bursts of gunfire at night. I hoped it wasn't Israel—maybe just Iraq or Kuwait? The Japanese reporters kept me blissfully in the dark. But within minutes that illusion was shattered, as CNN in English blared from a bar. Scuds were indeed still plopping onto Tel Aviv. By now Simon and Ruth were heading eastward to China, but I worried about Ruth's husband and young family, to say nothing of the entire country, left behind to deal with nights in the safe rooms. Normally, I didn't think much about mine, fifty years earlier in the London Underground. But the memory revived with visceral effects every time I pictured the Sofers and other families burrowed together underground in Israel.

Boarding my flight to Shanghai, I wondered whether I'd be able to keep up with the news. I remembered CNN had been banned in China, penance for broadcasting the Tiananmen Square uprising almost two years before. A CNN crew in Beijing, ostensibly assigned to report on then Soviet Premier Gorbachev's visit, scored an unexpected scoop that exposed the protests and the Chinese government's ignoble response in real time around the globe. I figured no such blast of current events in English would welcome me to Shanghai. Despite my reporter's instincts and hunger for information, perhaps a news vacuum, even cutting me off from the grim news from Israel, would be a welcome respite.

When my plane did land at Honqiao airport in Shanghai, TV screens were hardly the only amenities lacking in this barren terminal devoid of shops, restaurants, and bars. A sign saying "Lily Kovner" led me to my ride, a hotel-dispatched taxi pre-arranged by my travel agent. It was a lurching, seat belt-less trip weaving through narrow streets lined with buildings as grey and murky as the air and sky, which soon merged into drizzle weeping down a windshield lacking wipers. However did all that laundry dry? The garments that hung obtrusively outside most upper windows bridged, in some places, an entire lane, with lines strung from one building to another. At least they provided some color.

This was my first visit to Shanghai. The city's skyline was only a few stories high, its skyscraper building boom still only a pipedream. It was not only depressing but reinforced an increasing sense of isolation from my personal world. I longed for the arrival of Simon and Ruth a few hours hence. Maybe Jacob had a point. Was I really the intrepid, independent woman I purported to be?

The Jin Jiang Hotel anchors a walled-off compound clustered around a grassy rectangle in the French Concession area of Shanghai. The hotel's off-street setting made it look like a quiet rural haven in the middle of the city. I had read that its buildings had been luxury apartment houses built in the 1930s by the Jewish Sassoon family. The Jin Jiang's more recent, Communist-era, claim to fame was as the site of a meeting of Mao Tse-tung and President Richard Nixon that resulted in the 1972 signing of the first of what became known as the Three Joint Communiqués.

I'd bickered with Simon about the choice of this hotel. His preferences run to modern convenience, and his first choice was the nearby Hilton. But I'd read about the Jin Jiang's pedigree and lobbied for the history, character, and charm I associated with it, despite the prospect of an indoor swimming pool at the Hilton. To compromise he suggested the Garden Hotel, Japanese-owned with a sleek modern tower. Located across the street from the Jin Jiang, the Garden's older wing had been the French Club, another relic of Shanghai's flamboyant pre-Mao heyday. Plus, it had a pool. Perhaps irrationally, I'd held out for the Jin Jiang and hoped to buy my way into swimming in the Garden's pool.

My arrival at the Jin Jiang somewhat deflated that resolve, as the drab reception lobby and shabby sitting area up a cracked marble flight of stairs didn't offer a hospitable welcome, and the outdated and bulky furniture in my large, tired room looked like nothing had changed since long before Mao and Nixon met. None of this cheered me up, but the room's chief amenity—a constantly percolating hot water machine—and the one-channel option afforded by the remote control poised atop the television were bits of uncolored local color worth noting. I don't back down easily so I decided to make it work.

Once unpacked, I went downstairs and found an English-speaking female concierge from Australia, Christina Jones, who accompanied me across the street to the Garden Hotel's pool and served as translator for me to negotiate a daily swimming deal. Swimming forty minutes in the sterile, but clean, white tile facility restored some energy and enthusiasm for this adventure by providing uplift not only for my body but also for my psyche. And my appetite.

I emerged from my dip ready and committed to take on Shanghai. I walked out of the Garden Hotel through its older section, the white mansion formerly known as Le Cercle Sportif Français. The large lawn was a vacant oasis, enclosed by wrought iron fence, in the crowded city, and, as I walked down the sidewalk just outside it, I spotted a commercial area a block away. Crossing at the next intersection entailed dodging my way through clusters of bicycles whizzing by in both directions and then leaping onto the crowded sidewalk on the other side. The lack of motor traffic made it an eerily quiet walk for someone used to the cacophony of New York. An occasional public bus, spewing visible and malodorous fumes, overtook and cleared the bike packs, as did the very rare cars.

I certainly didn't blend in. And not just because of my western face. I'd thought my down coat looked very Mao until I waded into the sea of olive green padded jackets and realized black was not Shanghai chic. Trousers, skirts, and scarves didn't necessarily match, but the point was to ward away the damp chill. I tried to respond with a smile to the unabashed stares at me.

The noxious bus smell competed with a pervasive aroma I identified as a blend of sesame oil and garlic. Now that I'd navigated crossing the street, I could refocus on my primary mission—finding a place to eat. Fortunately, there was a decent-looking small restaurant on the first block, alleviating the need to cross the street again for a while. By pointing to a noodle and vegetable dish at a neighboring table, I managed to order a delicious lunch. After the waiter plunked my plate down in front of me, he hung around watching me, as did other patrons, until I started eating. Their subsequent grins and thumbs up made me grateful I could use chopsticks.

Forty minutes later I walked back up the Jin Jiang's driveway and spotted Ruth and Simon alighting from a taxi.

"Lily!" The moment he saw me, Simon dropped his briefcase next to his bag and ran to over to take me in his arms with a big kiss on the lips. "Lily, you beautiful person, you're here, even before us!" The physical stirring I always experienced in his arms never ceased to delight and surprise sixty-one-year-old me.

I loved the way he kissed me but felt the need to extricate myself quickly, with Cousin Ruth and the Chinese hotel staff watching our every move.

"And Ruth," I said, turning towards her. "I apologize for this guy's bad manners. What a trip here you must have had." I gave her a more restrained hug and kiss on both cheeks.

I hadn't seen Ruth since the previous summer, when she'd come to New York and then I'd gone to Israel for legal meetings establishing the foundation and looted art registry she was now running. In the year since we first met, I'd finally gotten over the initial shock of realizing that this sleek now forty-two-year-old woman with predominantly Asian facial features was my first cousin. Only blue eyes and a slight waviness in her coal black hair were evidence of her connection to her father, my Uncle Erich Heilbrun, and to the European—and Jewish—side of her family.

But at this moment the normally radiant Ruth looked exhausted. The trip, the strains of life in Scud-weary Israel, and anxiety over the lost Torah had taken their toll. Her accustomed graciousness, though, surfaced intact as always.

"Lily, I'm so glad to see you. Thank you for coming. After Simon checks in, you must both come with me to my aunt and uncle's, where I'll be staying."

"Ruth, you haven't seen your family here in such a long time. Don't you think you should have some time alone with them first?"

Simon looked tired, too, and I could tell going with her was not what he had in mind. Nor did I.

"You're right," Ruth said. "Of course, I must go myself. But they'll want to meet you soon. Probably dinner this evening. I'll call you later this afternoon in your room."

She asked the doorman in Chinese to signal a taxi hovering in the driveway, then gave us both a little hug, hopped in the back with her bags, and was gone.

Upstairs I watched Simon pick up the lame remote and try to flip his way through nonexistent channels, his thumb hitting the single key over and over. When I laughed at him, he pulled me down on the bed. Clearly, going to Ruth's relatives' house had never been his choice.

"Umm, you smell good," he said. "You've had a chance to shower, haven't you? Did you swim? I shouldn't inflict my smelly self on you. I need to clean up. But I just missed you so much."

"You're fine. Yes, I had a great swim. The pool across the street is gorgeous. But I want to know about the Torah. It's not fair. You've had all this time to get the whole story from Ruth. How did her aunt and uncle come to have a Torah lying around their house?"

Simon ran his right hand—the one that wasn't stroking my neck—through the fringe of hair that remained on his head. He sighed and audibly exhaled with forced exasperation.

"Okay, okay, here's what I know."

I listened intently as he repeated everything Ruth had told him. The tale began with the arrival of my Uncle Erich, Ruth's father, in Shanghai in late 1938. Almost immediately after disembarking, he was hired as an attorney by a company owned by one of the wealthy Sephardic families that had founded a Jewish community in Shanghai after the end of the Opium War in the 1840s.

"He got a job right off the boat? Did this just happen to people?" I pressed Simon rhetorically—after all, this was just an incidental detail. "Uncle Erich just up and left Vienna," I said. "As I remember, he didn't even tell my mother and my grandparents that he was going until the day before he left. You can imagine the screaming that went on. My father was in Dachau, still

39

alive as far as we knew then, and my grandparents were clinging to the belief that everything would be okay. It was right before Kristallnacht. If he had a job waiting here, maybe it wasn't such an impetuous decision, after all. I suppose it took a while to book passage, but getting a job in advance . . . "

"Guess who made contacts for him?"

"No idea."

"Nachman Tanski."

"Uncle Nachman? I don't believe it."

"None other."

I thought for a moment and realized it had to be true.

"Of course. But did Ruth tell you this, too? How would she have known?"

It shouldn't have surprised me to hear that Nachman Tanski, my surrogate "Uncle," had business connections among the successful Sephardic Shanghai Jews. But Ruth had never met Uncle, and I'd only had a brief conversation with him about meeting her just before he died.

"She told me that Bob Igra, Tanski's attorney nephew, sent her a packet of letters he'd found in Nachman's belongings. One from her father, Erich himself, soon after his arrival here, thanking Nachman for the opportunity. And one from Erich's employer—I can't remember the name, not Sassoon or Kadoorie or Hardoon, a lesser known one—thanking him for recommending Erich. There were a few more from that fellow related to mutual business they had."

"I wonder why Bob or Ruth didn't tell me about these letters," I said, slightly miffed.

"I think this just happened fairly recently," Simon replied. "Anyway, it's not important to the story, the Torah . . . "

"You're right. Sorry. Please get back to that."

"So, Erich goes to work for this company, and the owners are very fond of him. He almost becomes part of the family. I can't remember if I've already told you that some of these families were so *frume* they owned Torahs and kept them in their homes to use during floods or other times when they couldn't get to the synagogue."

"No, I don't think you did tell me, but no matter. It's all unbelievable—on so many levels."

My short foray in the neighborhood made it hard for me to imagine a time when this drab city was home not only to a vibrant Jewish community but also boasted the nickname "Paris of the Orient."

"This Torah," Simon continued. "It was in this family since they lived in Baghdad. It's supposed to be very old. Ruth says her aunt calls it the Ezra Torah."

"As in Ezra the Scribe?"

"I can't imagine a Torah attributed that far back would have physically survived. It would be the same vintage as the Dead Sea Scrolls, which were untouched and kept for thousands of years. Hermetically sealed in a cave. But that's what Ruth says her aunt calls it."

"After looking around Shanghai a little today, I can't imagine anything in China being so well preserved. You're an expert on old scrolls and manuscripts. Aren't there ways of proving how old such a Torah is? This could be a giant hoax. A fake."

"The Torah's exact provenance is open to question. But it's still likely to have some historic worth. Especially the case. You know Sephardic Torah cases can be very elaborate. This one is supposed to be silver and jeweled. But aren't we getting ahead of ourselves even discussing age and value? We have to find it first, remember?"

"How did Ruth's aunt and uncle come to have it in their house?"

"It's complicated. First, it's important to remember what happened here during the war," Simon said. "Most of these Baghdadi Jews were British citizens, so the Japanese interned them in camps after Pearl Harbor."

"Camps? Concentration camps? I didn't know that."

"Prisoner-of-war camps. They weren't death camps, per se, though the conditions were not good, and certainly many people died either while they were there, or later as a consequence of internment. Of course, the Japanese already occupied Shanghai and most of the rest of China, but World War II in the Pacific didn't really start until December of '41. Remember that Spielberg movie a few years ago—*Empire of the Sun?* That was one of these camps."

"Right. I did see that movie. So, these Sephardi families here weren't rounded up because they were Jews, but because they held British passports, right?"

"Exactly. The Japanese weren't inclined to emulate their German allies as far as Jews were concerned. Some say they were enduringly grateful to Jacob Schiff and his banker friends in New York for loaning them money to fight the Russians in 1904. Which no doubt propelled the czar to unleash yet another vicious pogrom. Which sent Russian Jews to China, as well as the US. And the world goes round."

"Simon, you're digressing."

"Sorry. Back to Shanghai after Pearl Harbor. Someone like your Uncle Erich remained free as a recently arrived European Jew, while his employers and their friends—even bigwigs like some of the Sassoons, by the way—went into the camps. In fact, Erich was entrusted with the business and told to stay in their house, where the Torah was. But that didn't last long. A year or so later the Japanese did bow to pressure from Germany. They forced the Jews who'd come from Europe since 1937 to move to a tenement area called Hongkou. It became like a ghetto there. Still not a concentration camp but very crowded and squalid. That's when Ruth's mother's family first got the Torah."

I was having a hard time taking all this in. Europe was my background and education, its history central to my life, my studies, and, frankly, my interests. When Arthur and I were in China in the early 1980s, we'd been wined and dined by government officials intent on picking his brain—and those of the other economists in our group. We toured a bit, seeing the prominent handpicked sights—the Great Wall, the Forbidden City, the Summer Palace, and Mao in eternal waxed repose in Tiananmen Square. We were flown to Xian to see the "parade" of Terra Cotta Warriors. Our guides steeped us in Mao lore. And kept us on a tight leash. We assumed our rooms at government guesthouses were bugged.

I remembered thinking about Uncle Erich on that trip. I wondered if somewhere in a sea of Chinese faces I'd spy a lone western one, a seventy-five-year-old male version of what his twin, my mother, would look like, if I could imagine her having survived to that age. I didn't know then that he had already been dead for twenty years. And I certainly didn't know and could never have imagined that ten years later I'd be back in China, retracing his life with a daughter of his I'd known nothing about until a year ago.

"And everyone thought Shanghai was safe for Jews," I said. "That's why he came here. I remember the night he came home from the Chinese consulate in Vienna with his visa to tell us he was leaving. It seemed to be the last place in the world Jews could get into and be safe. But no, as it turned out, Jews weren't safe anywhere back then."

"At least it wasn't wholesale slaughter in Hongkou. Certainly, there was plenty of disease and a lack of food or medicine. Ruth thinks this is when Erich's health began to deteriorate. But, for the most part, the people in Hongkou were way better off than the Jews who stayed in Europe. Plus, the

Russian Jews who'd been here for years were free and could provide some help."

"Right. The Russian Jews. Why were they left untouched, not herded into either the camps or the ghetto?"

"They were stateless—they had no passports or identity documents from anywhere. So, they were lucky enough not to qualify for either the prisoner-of-war camps or the Hongkou ghetto. Mostly, they lived around here—in the French Concession—but they had unrestricted access to all parts of the city and helped bring food and other support for the ghetto and the camps that were nearby."

"But Erich left his employers' Torah with a Chinese family. Why not with some Russian Jews?"

His eyelids had begun to droop, and the hand on my neck had fallen onto the bed. He visibly started when I said his name and propped himself up on an elbow, trying to look alert.

"Okay. Bear with me," he said. "The family Erich worked for and Ruth's mother's family were friends. Ruth's Chinese grandfather was a prominent scholar and professor. He and Erich and Erich's boss used to get together to talk history and philosophy. When Erich found out he was going to have to move to Hongkou, he decided the Torah would be safer with this upstanding Chinese gentleman. After the war the employers and Erich returned. But Erich was entrusted with the Torah again when the employers left for good—to Hong Kong—in 1947, before the Communists took over. He was left in charge of their whole raft of belongings, which he was supposed to bring when he followed them. But he never did because of his wife's difficult pregnancy with Ruth, and that's why he stayed in China."

"And kept the Torah?"

"And kept the Torah."

"So how did the aunt and uncle get it?"

"Erich died when Ruth was what—about twelve? You know her mother was shipped out during the Cultural Revolution. Apparently, this uncle of Ruth's—her mother's sister's husband—was enough of a big shot that he didn't need the so-called re-education. He and the aunt weren't touched during the Cultural Revolution. They stayed in Shanghai, which made them the new custodians of the Torah. And, of course, Ruth's mother never came back, so it stayed at their house ever since."

"And the theft? What do they know?"

Simon was clearing running out of steam and his head dropped off his arm and onto a pillow. "Can we leave something for later, Lily? I'm exhausted."

"Okay," I said. "I suppose you're entitled to a little nap. I just don't want us to fall asleep and miss Ruth—or not sleep the night because of jet lag."

He turned on his side and pulled me down for a passionate kiss. "If we get a little exercise first, we can sleep an hour and feel refreshed," he said.

"Now, there's a novel theory on beating jet lag," I replied while edging myself close enough to know that there was one part of his anatomy decidedly not fatigued. This revelation and our weeks apart led to a frenzied bout of mutual disrobing and uncommonly hurried coupling that left us both truly spent just a scant ten minutes later when the phone rang. Ruth said she would come for us in two hours, at 5:30.

"Better set the alarm," I said, grabbing my travel clock, "or we won't be ready."

No answer, but a satisfied looking face breathing with an audible sigh. I snuggled in and closed my eyes, too.

At 5:10 we made our way down to the Jin Jiang lobby trying to think of something appropriate to take to the aunt and uncle. I hadn't considered hostess gifts during my hasty preparations to leave New York. A quick consultation with my new friend, Christina the concierge, led her to take us, almost by the hand, to a tiny subterranean floral shop we never would have found—on the next block the opposite direction from where I'd eaten. By the time Christina finished bargaining with the proprietor, we made it back to the hotel just as Ruth emerged from a taxi. She smiled as she appraised the sight of Simon clutching a large, if somewhat bedraggled, bouquet of reddish pink plum blossoms in a glass vase, all wrapped in gold foil and tied with a red satin ribbon.

"For my aunt and uncle? They'll be thrilled. Plum blossom is the special flower of winter, the sign of spring coming soon. Confucius says it's a symbol of virtue. Now, Communists see them as a positive sign of revolution, survival, because they're most vibrant at this time of year. For this reason my uncle, especially, will be very pleased." She pointed up the stairway to the lounge. "Let's have a cup of tea before we go."

"Why aren't we going over there right away?" Simon asked, setting down the flowers to shuck off his overcoat.

"They need more time to prepare for dinner. And I need to fill you in, because we can't discuss the Torah tonight. Too shameful for my aunt and uncle. They're so upset. And because of another guest who's coming, the boyfriend of my cousin."

"Boyfriend?" I was surprised again. "Your cousin? Your aunt and uncle's daughter? She lives with them? How old is she? Doesn't she have a son? How old are your aunt and uncle?"

"Helena—the English name she uses, a new fad for young Chinese—she's twenty-four. Auntie was about thirty-five when she was born, so she's sixty or so. Auntie was ten years younger than my mother. Uncle is maybe sixty-five now. The little boy is three."

"Doesn't Helena have a husband?" Simon got that one asked before I had a chance.

"He died. At Tiananmen."

"Oh," Simon and I said simultaneously.

"Obviously, not discussed in the house," Ruth continued. "With Uncle's background in the government, it's a wonder they let her and her son back to live with them."

"Ruth, Simon gave me a general idea of how your aunt and uncle got the Torah. It surprises me that they still had it after all these years."

Ruth stayed mum until after a waitress had set down three tiny cups of steaming tea and retreated.

"This was the Torah's home. The Torah has—or had—its own special cabinet, like an Ark, very fancy Ark, Louis XV. This house was my childhood home, too. Didn't Simon tell you that my aunt and uncle live in the same house where my parents lived, where my father's employers, the Joseph family, lived? Not far from here, in the French Concession."

"You probably did mention that, Ruth, but sorry, I don't remember," said Simon. "At this point I barely remember my name, not to mention what country I'm in."

Even Ruth, tense as a wire coil, managed a giggle before going on.

"Soon after the Josephs left for Hong Kong, my mother was pregnant with me, so she couldn't go. They left my father in charge of everything. The Torah, the house, the business here—what remained of it—and Mr. Joseph was setting up in Hong Kong. There were many beautiful things, paintings.

The Torah—it's very old, was brought from Baghdad in a beautiful round silver Sephardic Torah case, twelve precious stones representing the Twelve Tribes, three diamonds, three emeralds, three rubies, three sapphires, oblong stones lined up vertically, six along each side of the opening. Stones the diameter of a US quarter, about twenty-four millimeters each."

Simon whistled the knowing whistle of a gem dealer.

I'd seen some round Sephardic Torah cases, of wood or metal, so much more substantial than the fabric covers that commonly concealed the fragile parchment scrolls in Ashkenazic synagogues. Although the Seder plate I'd lost as a child and found again was an Italian antique fashioned of silver, Murano Venetian glass, sapphires, and pearls, I'd never contemplated a Torah covering so elaborate or valuable.

"Of course, the house was much larger when the Josephs left," Ruth continued. "The Communists thought those houses were too big for just one family. So, they subdivided it. My father and mother and grandparents and aunt—she was young then—were all shoved into an area less than half the size of the original house. I remember the Torah cabinet was the biggest piece of furniture we still had. The old house had many bedrooms, but in the small version I shared one with my aunt before her marriage, and my parents and grandparents shared one large room that had been the parlor, with a blanket between their two beds. My grandparents died when I was very little—Grandfather was disparaged by the Communists for being a famous scholar from a rich family, and both he and Grandmother became depressed and old and sick very quickly. Then Auntie married Uncle, already an officer in Red Guards. They got the whole bedroom, and my parents slept with me."

"So, with the house divided up that way, it must not look anything like it did when Uncle Erich got here and the Josephs lived in it, right?"

"No, Lily, it's completely opened up again. My uncle is very important."

"But not important enough to have kept your mother from being sent away during the Cultural Revolution," Simon muttered.

Ruth didn't answer, just looked away from us for a moment.

"I still don't understand why they had the Torah all these years," I said. "And why did someone steal it after so long?"

"Someone must know," said Ruth.

"Know what?" Simon and I answered in unison.

"That the Torah and its case are so valuable and next year it's to be presented by China to Israel. There's a plan, you see . . . "

"Yes, of course, 1992" Simon interjected. "China and Israel are to begin diplomatic relations next year."

"How do you know?" I couldn't imagine this was public knowledge.

"Guess," he said.

"Right. Of course."

Most of the time I forget about Simon's sideline beyond his business and communal involvements, beyond his family, beyond me. As a part-time Mossad agent, he calls himself a consultant. "Guess" is his little code to clue me in whenever we meet someone or hear something he can't otherwise explain.

Mention of Israel reminded me to ask Ruth if she'd spoken to Boaz since she had arrived in China.

"No. Long-distance telephone is expensive if I use my aunt and uncle's phone. I tried and offered to pay for the time, but they refused to consider that. A 'Catch 22.'"

"I'm sure they're okay," said Simon. "But why don't you try on my mobile phone right now?"

"Can I? Oh, Simon, thank you." He handed her the phone, and we took a little walk into the hotel's so-called gift shop.

Five minutes later a visibly relieved Ruth came round to find us examining cheesy painted fans.

"Everything's fine," she said. "Well, not exactly fine. They're still spending the night in a shelter."

"Still at Mossad headquarters?" I asked.

"No," said Ruth, "At Weizmann. They've outfitted several more safe rooms in the past few days. Boaz and the kids can go to the building next to his lab and office. With me gone, it's just more convenient—less driving— for them to stay in Rehovot."

Boaz works as a scientist at the Weizmann Institute in the city of Rehovot. He and Ruth and their twins, Eli and Talia, live there. It's almost midway between Tel Aviv, where Ruth used to work at the now-defunct Mosaica Gallery, and Jerusalem, where she works now at our art registry and foundation located on Hebrew University's Mount Scopus campus. Mossad headquarters is in Tel Aviv.

"But it was so wonderful of you, Simon, to make sure we were taken care of right away," she said, "and Boaz said to tell you that he and the kids give Mossad's place five stars. All the TVs and the sound system. The gadgets. The food. Now they have to bring their own."

"Yes," said Simon, "leave it to the Mossad to operate the Ritz of bomb shelters."

Chapter 4

When the cab pulled up in front of the grey (what else?) stucco façade on a street off a busy thoroughfare the driver had just darted across, I tried hard not to laugh. My canny cousin noticed.

"What's funny?"

"This house, Ruth," I said. "It looks like an English Tudor airlifted from the Cotswalds and plunked down in China. It's just . . . I don't know . . . incongruous."

Simon continued his history lesson. "Shanghai was more a foreign city than a Chinese one from the time the British won the Opium War. This was the home of the Josephs, remember? Your Uncle Erich's employers. They were British citizens, so many of their homes emulated the architecture in England. They lived a colonial life. In this case an Orthodox Jewish British colonial life in China."

A narrow slanted five-inch gap in the paint on the right doorpost of the front entrance was evidence that a mezuzah once graced that spot.

"You'd think they would have painted it over by now," Simon said.

"Chinese are not so conscious of home maintenance," Ruth said. "I am happy it stays there as a reminder of Jews who lived here. It's a reminder of my father."

The fact that I was walking into the last residence of my Uncle Erich was just sinking in as the door swung open before we'd knocked or rung.

Two elderly Chinese people, both sallow-faced and roughly the same height—five feet three at the most—stood framed in the doorway holding out their hands in greeting. At first glance they looked androgynous in grey wool pants and brown turtleneck sweaters. The man, stockier with squared-off shoulders, was the one not wearing little silver earrings.

"Lily and Simon, these are my uncle Chen An and aunt Chen Yingfan. But I just call them 'Uncle' and 'Auntie.' You can, too."

When she switched to Chinese, all I caught were "Lily" and "Simon."

A younger woman, slightly taller, peeked out from behind the door she was holding. "Hello," she said, "I'm Helena. Chen Hu. And this is Joey, Chen Junjie." She pushed the elfin child hiding behind her toward us.

"*Nihao*, Joey," I said, leaning down to shake his hand. He broke into a large grin before taking off to scoot up the staircase that rose just behind the welcoming party.

Simon and I and the older couple nodded repeatedly as we stepped into the foyer. Its mottled and chipped green marble floor bespoke faded grandeur. Ruth took off her coat and motioned us to follow suit. Auntie charged between us and grabbed them one by one, though the bundle nearly concealed her head until she slid them onto a threadbare tufted green velvet bench under a small telephone niche in the wall. The uncle put his arm around Simon's shoulder to lead him toward the large room to the left, pointing out the two small steps that led down into it. Ruth and I walked in ahead of her aunt. When the Chens had pointed us to the sofa and then seated themselves, Simon and I remained standing for the grand gesture of presenting the plum blossom. They looked pleased and nodded thanks, but Uncle set it down on a table without removing the gold foil.

The furniture in the parlor testified to past glory. The maroon brocade upholstery on the sofa looked washed out, and a black wool throw arranged on one side didn't quite cover the gouge on one of the carved wooden arms. Auntie and Uncle occupied two dark blue velvet French provincial chairs opposite the sofa, and a lounge chair bearing typically British pale blue chintz sat incongruously along a wall. Underneath was a mostly burgundy Oriental rug that probably harked back to the Joseph family's Baghdad roots. Worn and partially threadbare, the carpet sprawled over a scuffed dark wood floor. On the walls were two large, tacky Mao-era oil landscapes and a lithograph with Chinese calligraphy.

Helena, a studious looking young woman with wire rim spectacles wearing a hunter green cable knit sweater over brown pants, resembled Ruth, our mutual cousin, minus the blue eyes, of course. She remained in the archway above the steps for a moment, then withdrew from the group and returned to the foyer, peering out through one of the two glass panels on either side of the front door.

"She's waiting for her boyfriend," Ruth said, after listening to her aunt's scolding tone. "They don't like him much, think he's bad influence on Helena, detrimental to her studies."

"What's she studying?" Simon asked.

"Biology. She wants to be doctor. Or, at least, Auntie and Uncle think she should be doctor."

"Just like Jewish parents," I said. Auntie laughed immediately and translated for Uncle, who then followed suit.

"You speak English?" I asked Auntie.

"Oh, yes, but not so well anymore, as I don't get much practice," she said. "My parents were very well educated, both had degrees from the States, and they insisted that Suling and I learn English as girls."

"Suling was your mother?"

Ruth nodded.

Auntie and Uncle were our contemporaries—Simon's and mine—but life in China had exacted its toll. Despite the privileges his government position had afforded them, such as sole occupancy and the reunification of this formerly subdivided mansion, their chipped brown teeth betrayed both years of substandard dental care and a lifetime of smoking. They resumed the latter activity as soon as the introductory pleasantries ended and we'd arranged ourselves on our respective seats. As Auntie lit up a new cigarette, I noticed the ashtrays overflowing with wizened butts on a side table pocked with burn marks. Possibly one explanation for the holes in the carpet, too. Also for the pungent aroma I'd tried to ignore since walking into the house.

"No, thanks, no, *xie xie*."

I tried to smile while shaking my head and uttering one of the two Chinese phrases I'd mastered in refusing the cigarette poking out of the package in Uncle's outstretched hand. When he bowed and moved on, I watched carefully and saw only a slight hesitancy before Simon shook his head, too. Smoking was an issue when we met, but now he'd been smoke-free for several months. I was relieved to see that his two weeks in Israel—a smoker's paradise even without

Scuds raining down—hadn't lured him back to the habit. Ruth's overt fanning of the haze with her arms didn't deter her aunt and uncle.

General smiling and nodding constituted social interaction as an ancient woman in black-and-white checked polyester pants and a spotted beige turtleneck slowly entered through a swinging paneled door carrying a tray of filled tea cups and small bowls of peanuts for each of us.

"This is Ayi," Ruth said, reaching up to pat the woman's slightly quivering arm as it managed to set a cup down without spilling the steamy brew. "Ayi means housekeeper or nursemaid. It's embarrassing, but everyone calls their *ayi* 'Ayi.' I know it doesn't seem right. I don't even know her given name."

At this point Uncle asked what we were talking about, and Ruth waited until the older woman had retreated back behind the door before translating. For some reason the old Party man found the *ayi* tale funny. His bared stained teeth and his equally brown fingertips flicking an ash as he laughed heartily gave me the creeps.

The aunt looked down at the floor and whispered, "Her name is Feng Nien. We used to call her Nina."

Uncle ignored her and launched into a monologue. From his grandiose hand motions we sensed this was a major pronouncement.

"He's talking about Chinese reverence for Jews," Ruth said, when he paused for her to fill us in and at the same time apparently instructed his wife to go get something in another room.

Auntie returned a moment later carrying a book covered in dark blue. She handed it to Uncle, who immediately flipped it open to a page of photos. One showed a Caucasian family carrying suitcases off a ship docked below the Bund, Shanghai's riverfront port area. Another showed a group of similar-looking people gathered around a diminutive Asian man with thick spectacles who stood only a bit higher then them, despite his position on a small platform. A third photo was a street scene with a sign that said, "H. Klein, Shoemaker" next to Chinese lettering.

"These are the refugees from Europe, like my father," Ruth explained. "Uncle is talking about how they came to China, and were welcomed. The little Japanese man is Ghoya, the commander of the Hongkou ghetto, where my father and the rest had to move. They say he was sinister, and you never knew what kind of mood he'd be in. Some of the Jews had work permits to leave the ghetto, but many times he wouldn't allow them out. My father tried to go to the Joseph company office but was rarely permitted. Then sometimes Ghoya would laugh and joke and say he was 'the king of the Jews.'"

The uncle interjected. "Ghoya was no good," Ruth translated. "A 'Japanese dog,' he says. But the Jews were tough, and the Chinese made sure it was okay for them here. Uncle is very proud of this."

Then Auntie spoke up, looking at me, with tears formed in her eyes

"Did you know Erich? He was the only refugee that I knew, though I was just little girl then, many years younger than Suling."

"I did know my Uncle Erich," I said, "I, too, was a little girl. He left Vienna when I was only eight years old, but I remember how sweetly he treated me. Sometimes, he even took me along when he had a date. Now, it's hard for me to believe this really happened; it was only in the daytime, often skating in the winter and out for hot chocolate afterward. I wonder what the young ladies thought, a guy who showed up with his young niece. Either he was testing if they liked him enough to be nice to me or I was a line of defense, if he didn't care much for them."

I was surprised at how heartily Auntie laughed at this before responding.

"He was just waiting for my sister, nice Chinese wife. I remember he was very handsome. And my father loved it when Mr. Reuben Joseph brought him over. They had such good discussions—philosophy, history, comparing Jews and Chinese. Father was very learned, had a PhD from University of Michigan. Chinese from good families had opportunities, you know. 1919, he got his degree. My mother, too, went to the States, Oberlin College. Do you know Oberlin?

"The Josephs were wonderful people," Auntie went on. "They even invited us for Passover Seder and took us in when the Japanese wanted our house for their officers. We stayed there all during the war when the Josephs went to the camp and Erich had to live in the ghetto. How our family got the Torah."

It startled me then to hear her bring up the taboo subject of the Torah. Ruth looked surprised, too, as she translated to Chinese for Uncle.

"We had to move out of our own house a few blocks away, also in the French Concession. Such a beautiful home. Russian Jews lived in the neighborhood. The Russians were the only Jews who didn't get sent anywhere else during the war. Nice people, many ran wonderful stores along Houihai Road.

Mrs. Rabinovich owned a children's store—she sold my mother the party dresses Suling and I wore. My mother had a fur coat from Russian furrier."

Uncle look exasperated. Apparently, he wasn't used to his wife taking center-stage and he put his finger to his lips when she talked about the Torah. He broke into the conversation, pointing to us.

"He wants you to know," Ruth said, "that Jews and Chinese have much in common. Both peoples are smart, they think education is very important. They are very family-oriented. And now, even Communists are going into business, he says, and are good in business. Like the Jews."

"To them that's the highest compliment." Simon whispered to me.

Uncle continued to expound, and Ruth continued to translate, repeating the same themes about Jews and Chinese. Auntie would pipe up in one language or the other now and then to add something about the past. Simon and I both just nodded and interjected an occasional *xie xie*. I soon felt myself tuning out the monologue and struggling to keep my eyes open in the stuffy room after the long plane trip. I jerked to attention, though, when Ruth translated Auntie's seemingly stream-of-consciousness musing about the Torah and pointed to an ornate French cabinet across the foyer in the dining room where it had been kept.

"That really is Louis XV," whispered Simon. "Quite an Ark."

"Erich, he kept it safe. Now we are dishonoring his memory. It's gone."

She started to cry when a door chime that sounded like Big Ben striking two put an instant end to this outburst. Even Uncle clammed up as Helena ran to the door and then ushered into the room a young man with slicked back hair wearing black pants and a black shirt.

"Li Dawei," she said, holding her left hand on his back as if to sweep him right in our direction. Behind him young Joey came bounding down the stairs and ran around the newcomer, who stopped and picked the boy up with a hug. Obviously, someone in the family approved.

"Please, call me David," he said in English with a nod in our direction followed by a more pronounced and deferential bow directed toward Helena's parents. Before he could sit down Uncle stood up and gestured toward the dining room, where a stained red table cloth covered a round table topped by a lazy Susan. The surrounding cane-backed chairs were upholstered in red velvet. Simon and I were shown to seats of honor between the aunt and uncle. Joey sat between his mother and David.

Instantly Ayi came in with bowls of cold pickled vegetables and fish. She muttered as she placed them on the lazy Susan.

Ruth laughed.

"Ayi says it's good to cook for Jews again. It was a sad day when pork first came into this house after the Josephs left. They would have been so shocked. No kosher meat tonight, can't get it, but no pork or prawns either."

The old woman beamed as we smiled and nodded our thanks. Not that we wouldn't have eaten the verboten foods, but it was yet another paradox in this setting. I still found it hard to visualize a Shanghai with a kosher-keeping Jewish community that employed Chinese cooks who tended to the dietary laws.

David laughed more vigorously than we did.

"Kosher meat in Shanghai. That's a good one! There's Chinese food in New York, why not kosher here?"

"You've been to New York?" Simon asked.

"Yes, yes, with my father. Business meetings with old friends of his."

"Please, tell me about your business."

"Trading. We do trading"

"Trading. And what do you trade?"

"Many things. Many Chinese do trading."

"Yes, yes, I've heard that. But certainly you must have some sort of specialty. Tea? Food? Antiques?"

"Antiques. Porcelains. Paintings. And furniture. Chinese things are getting popular in the US."

"Really? I hadn't heard that. Tell me about the people you do business with in New York. Maybe I know them." I'm the journalist, but here was Simon probing David. The Mossad training.

Perhaps sensing he was being interrogated beyond social pleasantries, David abruptly changed his mode of response from garrulous to laconic.

"Doubtful. But here is my name card, if you are interested in some antiques." He stood up, pulled a white card from his pocket, and thrust it, two-handed, over the food toward Simon. The elder Chens looked mortified.

Helena surprisingly filled the vacuum. Thrusting her forearm toward the center of the table, she said, "Look what David brought me from New York. A silver bracelet from Tiffany's. You know Tiffany's?"

"Of course," Ruth said, "Lily and Simon live in New York, and Simon is in the jewelry business."

"Your store is like Tiffany's?" David jumped back in.

"Smaller," said Simon.

"Tiffany's the best. Such a big store in New York and so many stores in the States. See, I got a Rolex, too," David went on. "Rolex is also the best." Another arm lunged over the lazy Susan.

Even I could tell this was a fake, but both Simon and I smiled and nodded in admiration. What was the point of doing otherwise?

"Your business," David redirected to Simon, "tell me about it. Only in New York?"

"My only retail store is in New York, but I have an office in Israel, too. There's a diamond trading market there, and in Europe, and that's a significant part of my business."

"Jews trade diamonds in Israel? I didn't know that."

"Only a little in Israel, and there's a diamond cutting industry there, too. But there's considerable diamond trading in New York. There's one area, just one long block really, on 47th Street, where hundreds of dealers trade. Most of them are Jewish, many very devout, with beards and long black coats. And other jewelry, watches. Too bad you didn't see it when you were in New York. It's a very active and profitable business district there."

A somewhat cowed David had nothing more to say. Auntie and Uncle, smiled to convey pleasure in seeing him apparently one-upped. Joey angled for David's attention, while Helena seemed pleased that he got it, especially when David encouraged the boy to eat his dinner.

"You know, I might be Jewish, too." David glanced around the table as if to ascertain the impact of this out-of-the-blue statement before continuing. "My family could be Kaifeng Jews. Have you heard of them?"

"Kaifeng Jews have become extinct," Ruth said. "A few have come to Israel and can't prove their lineage. If they want to stay, they need to go through formal conversion."

"Not necessary to convert, if they stay in China," David said.

"That's true," Ruth said, "but they don't know Judaism or practice it anymore here in China. Even in Kaifeng. Do you even know anything about being Jewish?"

"Matzo ball soup! I ate it in New York."

I tried to add some levity. "See, even in China there are gastronomic Jews."

Simon laughed, but Ruth muttered under her breath, "And phonies everywhere," only audible to Simon and me.

Ayi bustled in and out until a total of seven courses, two or three dishes each, had been served over a period of about an hour. Auntie and Uncle kept up their cigarette consumption during brief lulls. Between the smoke, the food, toasts drunk with the noxious liquor *baijo,* and the apparent discomfort generated by David's conversation, I suddenly felt a need to escape. It was like a three-ring circus in there, way too much to sort out. I wanted a breath of fresh air.

"Excuse me," I said, a moment after Ayi had just ladled green tapioca beads into a small bowl and placed it before me. "I am very tired from the trip. I hope you will all understand if we leave in a few minutes." I took a bite of the green goo and smiled while Ruth translated.

"I'll walk out to help you find a taxi to take you back to the hotel," she said to us.

The renewed nodding and gesturing signaled that even Uncle understood. Exaggerating a yawn, I stood up, as did Simon, and we both *xie xied* our way toward the door, with Ruth and her aunt and uncle following us. Auntie embraced me and put her hands against an ear to express lying on a pillow.

"Good sleep," she said. I nodded, and we both laughed.

Just a first quick breath of the cool air outside began to clear my head, if not the malaise of true fatigue compounded by confusion. This I tried to conceal from Ruth, whom I surely didn't want to offend.

"Get some rest, Lily. I won't call you until about ten in the morning. Maybe you'll be able to sleep late."

"Thanks, Ruth," I said. "I hope your aunt and uncle aren't insulted, but I simply didn't think I could keep my eyes open much longer."

"Not to worry," she said, as she opened a cab door for us and leaned in to give the driver our hotel name. "Sleep well. We have much to do."

Settled onto the seat, Simon's arm around me, I said, "Yes. Too much to do. How are we ever going to find that Torah? This is ridiculous. We have nothing to go on. It's like looking for the proverbial needle in a haystack."

"Don't be so sure. That David alone gives us clues."

"Well, you, even with your Mossad-style interrogation, you didn't get very far. David's just puffing, trying to impress Helena. And the little boy, where it seems he's succeeded."

"He's trying to impress us. But let's not dismiss him so quickly."

That was the last thing I heard before falling asleep on his shoulder until the cab pulled up to the Jin Jiang. Simon gently dragged me into the lobby and up to our room, where I fell on the bed in a stupor that lasted nine hours.

Chapter 5

The next morning, with Simon still sleeping, I crept out of the room and made my way across the street to the pool at the Garden Hotel. While my swim might have fulfilled its mission of loosening the kinks in my body, it didn't do its usual job of smoothing me out emotionally or clarifying my thinking.

Did I dream the previous evening? The Chinese aunt and uncle living in the former home of a Jewish family. The *ayi* bemoaning the lack of kosher meat. Sleazy David trying to impress us and, by extension, his girlfriend, her son, and her parents. Lap after lap, with all this reverberating in my head, I could almost even smell the smoke as I replayed the scene over and over.

Ah, swimming—a rote activity providing time to ruminate. Today there were more questions than answers. If the exercise and the trip itself were going to be of any benefit, I needed to forge ahead and simply enjoy the pool, which I had all to myself after a lone Chinese man in his twenties got out and lit a cigarette before putting on a robe and heading toward the men's locker room. I've swum all over the world, and this competed well among other indoor pools. A full twenty-five meters in length, the temperature was warm enough for me to get used to it after several laps but cool enough to keep me invigorated for forty minutes worth. Its lining and surrounding deck looked newly tiled, and the lounge chairs bore spotless tan cushions that a female attendant was repositioning after overnight storage in a cabinet next to a sauna door. Light pouring through a solarium glass roof brightened the space as I swam. The prospect of a sunny day helped to dissipate my angst.

After showering and getting dressed, I set out to go back to the Jin Jiang. Crossing the street at the intersection with a traffic light seemed a wiser choice than the more direct jaywalking route, even though the bicycle traffic was less dense at this spot. The walk to the corner gave me a chance to survey the food stands that had opened up while I was swimming. All down this block was a row of griddles and steaming vats, and at the corner I could see more vendors down the cross street in the opposite direction. Locals walking by were nibbling on buns and what appeared to be omelets or pancakes wrapped in paper. Swimming is guaranteed to pique hunger, and mine was further roused by the scent of hot oil, garlic, onion, and a potpourri of miscellaneous spices that wafted through the chilly air.

I saw five teen-aged girls wearing matching brown jumpers and a rainbow of colored quilted nylon jackets sitting under a tree surrounded by backpacks and chattering between bites. Next to them three boys dressed in what must have been the male brown trouser version of the same school uniform huddled together and exchanged furtive glances with the girls. A woman in a long green cotton coat hurried by holding her squirming little boy's hand while wiping off his face with a pink cloth. Behind the food stands was a small grassy area where a dozen elderly people gently moved through their *tai chi* routine.

My sense of adventure kicked in, and I made up my mind that this trip could be fun. If only for the food and the people-watching. By the time I returned to the room, Simon was up and dressed, waiting for me with a big hug.

"You were out cold last night," he said. "I'm amazed you got up and out so early."

"It was nine hours of sleep. Come on, get your coat. We're going out for breakfast."

We toured past all of the stands to make an initial assessment of the outdoor buffet. Almost everything looked delectable, which only made it harder to pick and choose and avoid stuffing ourselves. While the deep-fried dough looked a little greasy and difficult to digest at this hour, we couldn't resist the round bread dotted with scallions and sesame seeds. Simon pointed and held up two fingers to order from the lady seller bundled up in brown puffy coat with her wool scarf wrapped twice around her head.

"*Shao bing,*" she said, smiling, as she handed them to us.

Another *bing,* according to the shouted come-on of the frozen looking "chef" in denim jacket, was an omelet spiced with cilantro and wrapped in a crepe, resulting in what looked like a Chinese burrito. As we ate these, I noticed a little girl laughing and pointing to Simon, who had egg dribbling down his chin. I fumbled in my purse for a tissue. Napkins were in short supply at this open-air restaurant row.

"Let's get a cup of tea to wash this down," I said, eying a nearby vendor artfully pouring from a long-spouted pot into tiny cups.

Fortunately, what I didn't see until after we each drank two servings, was the bucket, full of murky water, where the used cups were dunked for washing. I pointed it out to Simon.

"When in Shanghai, . . . " he said.

After grabbing "just one more thing," an order of steamed chive dumplings, we waddled back to the hotel. Ruth was pacing the lobby looking frantic.

"Lily, Simon, I was so worried."

"Why? We're not late. We didn't expect you for another ten minutes," I said.

"I came early. I walked over to get some fresh air. And the sun's out. When I called your room and you didn't answer, I went to the dining room to see if you were having breakfast. Where were you?

Simon put his arm around her. "We *were* having breakfast—on the street, like all good Shanghainese. Lily went swimming early and discovered the outdoor food stands. It was great."

Ruth made a face that looked like she'd just stepped on a skunk. "Yuk! I'd never eat that stuff on the street. It's so dirty here. I hope you don't get sick."

"The only place I've ever gotten sick in Asia," I said, "was after eating at a fancy hotel dining room in Bangkok. A western hotel chain, by the way. We'll be fine. Don't you eat falafel on the street in Israel?"

"Sometimes, with the kids. But that's Israel. This is China," said my Chinese-Jewish cousin. "Are you ready to figure out our next move in finding that Torah?"

"Ruth, I was thinking we should go to an antiques market or gallery and see what kind of place might buy such a valuable object," I said, "without asking questions about where it came from, of course."

"My plan exactly. But, first, you and Simon go up to your room to use the bathroom. They're not exactly western-style, or clean, where we're going."

Ruth had a point. It was one thing to try street food. But, as I remembered from my previous trip to Beijing, a woman needed strong knees and vital capacity to hold her breath for a while in order to withstand the stench while doing her business in a public restroom in China.

Back out on the street, we agreed that the half-hour walk to the market would be great on this sunny day. Our route took us out of the French Concession to Nanjing Road, where we turned right and walked toward the center of the city.

"How are your aunt and uncle doing this morning, Ruth?"

"Muttering to each other all through breakfast. Uncle grunts and shakes his head. I think he's genuinely worried that the government will arrest him and take him away if the theft of the Torah is discovered. He thinks he'll be blamed. Auntie cries. Helena tried to talk about David, and that only upset them more. Joey jabbers 'David, David,' all the time. He's how Helena met David in the first place."

"What do you mean?" I asked.

"David volunteers in a program for kids without fathers. Helena signed Joey up, and David was assigned to him. They've developed a great relationship, it seems, but I can't tell if David's attention to Joey is the main attraction for Helena, or if it's David himself. I don't think she's had any other boyfriends since her husband's death. The whole thing was pretty traumatizing."

"We can certainly understand that," Simon said. "But, back to the Torah, why would your uncle be blamed? He'd hardly be accused of engineering a theft from his own house."

"This is China."

That seemed to be her universal answer.

After a brisk fifteen-minute stroll, we approached the antiques market, a group of "stores," some no more than open-air displays out of wooden or metal garage-like structures interspersed with a few freestanding shops in small wooden shacks. Unlike the sidewalks to get there, the marketplace was almost deserted. Only a few non-Asians strolled around. Chinese faces, other than the merchants, were even scarcer.

"Let's go in here," Ruth said, gesturing toward one of the shacks. "The sign says it's been in business since 1910."

The old man behind a counter-topped glass display case looked like he could have been working there when the business was founded. Wielding a blackened cloth, he was intently polishing a brass gong that hung in the middle of a two-foot wooden stand elaborately carved and decorated with mother-of-pearl leaves. The sight of three potential customers entering his deserted business was sufficient motivation to lay down the cloth and come out from behind the counter to greet us, very softly, in Chinese, which Ruth translated.

"Welcome. I am Mr. Xu. How can I help you?"

"*Ni hau*, Mr. Xu," Simon bowed as he spoke. "We are honored to be in your store. I hope your business is going well."

"Ah, English." Now the old man looked around, as if worried someone threatening was listening and whispered with a distinctly British accent, "I'm honored to have you . . . "

"That's a beautiful piece you're polishing," Simon said.

"Thank you, yes, of course. Please excuse my manners, but we should speak softly. English is always a signal for suspicion these days. Certainly not like the old days, when my father started out or when I came in after university. When Shanghai was rich and fun-loving. Ah, life back then . . . But I'm re-educated, one of the lucky ones. I came back from my little 'Mao vacation' in the countryside. Another sort of university education. I get by. Lucky to be alive."

"Yes, you are a lucky one," Ruth said with uncharacteristic iciness. The old man could only shrug at her comment. She glared at him in silence for a few moments. She rarely spoke about her mother, but I could tell for Ruth the Cultural Revolution was a treacherous topic. Especially when she encountered someone who had survived it.

If this was a cue to break the awkwardness, I plunged in. "Your English is so good. You must have learned it young," I said.

"To do business in the old Shanghai it was necessary. And to be a gentleman. My father sent me to Oxford."

Ruth regained her focus. First in English, and then, we assumed, repeating herself in Chinese, she asked Mr. Xu to show us his special items. She shot a sidelong glance to Simon and me presumably to let us know it was crucial to inform Mr. Xu he wasn't dealing just with naïve foreigners unschooled in doing business here.

"Well, you see, I have this gong from about 1880. A beautiful piece." He returned to his station behind the counter, picked it up off the stand, and held it out to at me. I had to agree—it was beautiful. Not exactly anything I needed or had room for, but impressive.

"Look around, please," gesturing with open arms down at the glass case and around the room. The inventory included some furniture—a few small chairs and several tables, ranging from a carved teak round for dining to lower rosewood side tables. Price tags hung from all of the tables, which also functioned as display stands for ceramic vases and teapots and the odd jade bowl or incense burner. Under the five-foot-long counter, the glass case offered a random display of jade bracelets, one sumptuous bib-sized gold and pearl necklace, silver-tipped ivory chopsticks, a couple of pewter chargers, and spoons.

"Oh, my God!" I cried.

My outcry sent Ruth and Simon, who had converged around the carved tabletop, instantly flying to my side. Bending down, I pointed to a singular item crammed between a black jade bangle and an ivory Buddha pendant on the lowest shelf in the case.

"Look at that."

It was a silver-filigreed mezuzah case, about four inches high with the Hebrew letter ש (pronounced "*shin*") etched in gold. This traditionally signifies "*Shaddai*," one of the names for God. On a mezuzah, which is posted in the doorways of Jewish homes, it's an acronym for "*Shomer Daltot Yisrael*," Guardian of the Doors of Israel. Unlike the gong and other metal pieces, the case was tarnished. Obviously, Mr. Xu didn't expect anyone to ask for it.

When I stood up, I saw him shuffling papers at a desk tucked between two waist-high replicas of Terra Cotta warriors.

"Mr. Xu, can you take this out?"

As he unlocked the case and withdrew the mezuzah, Simon asked, "You know what this is?"

Mr. Xu nodded. "For the houses of *Yuteren*. Jews. None are here anymore. You Jewish, right?" He looked at Simon and me. Of course, he didn't suspect Ruth.

"We're all Jewish." Ruth's comment enhanced the effect. Mr. Xu did a double take but didn't comment. "Do you know many Jews?"

"Oh no, not any more," he smiled. "But they were best in business, and some were very, very nice. Mr. Hardoon a good friend of Dr. Sun Yat-sen. You know that big white house they call Children's Palace now? That was the Kadoorie house. Marble Hall. Sir Elly, a knight. Another good man, he was my customer, his cousins and friends, too. Sassoons, too, all rich people but very nice. Jews who came from Germany later didn't have so much money, but some brought me things to sell for them. Small things—coins, silverware—they hid from Nazis when they left."

"Is that when you got this? That long ago? You've had it for fifty years?" Ruth's look was incredulous.

"Can't remember exactly. No, it could have been just forty years, since the Communists came and the Jews left. By 1950 or 1951 all the Jews were gone. Most even earlier, 1947, 1948."

"Where was this and all your inventory while you were away?" It was obvious Ruth didn't exactly trust Mr. Xu's memory, or just plain didn't trust Mr. Xu. It was like she wanted him to have survivor's guilt without even knowing about her mother. It was a side of my normally gentle cousin I hadn't experienced before.

"Here and there," said the old man.

Switching gears, Ruth pulled out of her bag a black-and-white photo that I recognized as Uncle Erich standing alongside an attractive couple. Curiously, though both men were wearing *kippot* and prayer shawls, the woman was the person holding the Torah case. She was thin with curly hair, and wore a dark suit with a pleated skirt and a small pillbox hat from which descended a web of netted veiling that grazed her forehead.

The old dealer reacted instantly, which Ruth clearly didn't expect.

"Yes, yes, Mr. and Mrs. Joseph. Wonderful people. I knew them. Mr. Joseph was a very good businessman. Mrs. Joseph. Good lady. No children, but she helped poor Chinese women and their children. That man with them their very good friend. He came from Germany before the war started. He was a lawyer, good lawyer. After the war he helped me get some pieces back that Japanese took without paying."

"He was my father," said Ruth quietly and with a bit more warmth. "But he came from Vienna, not Germany."

Mr. Xu studied her. "He your father? But you're Chinese. You live here?"

"Yes, he was my father, Erich Heilbrun. My mother was Chinese. I was born here but I live in Israel now. My name now is Ruth Sofer. And this is my cousin, Mrs. Lily Kovner, and our friend, Mr. Simon Rieger, both from New York. You said my father helped you get back antiques the Japanese took? That's such a coincidence, because that's what we do—my cousin and I.

We trace art stolen by the Nazis and help their owners or their families get them back."

Who would have suspected that Uncle Erich pioneered this family occupation? After this piece of information sunk in, I directed Mr. Xu's attention back to the photographs.

"Do you know what this is, this case?"

"Yes, Jewish Torahs are kept inside there."

"Have you ever seen this or anything like it?"

"Sure. I was in synagogue a few times, the big one on Shaanxi Lu, called Seymour Road back then. Built by Mr. Sassoon in memory of his mother. All closed up now. It was so beautiful. Too bad."

"The name of the synagogue was Ohel Rachael," Ruth whispered to me. "It's in the government's Ministry of Education compound now."

Simon meandered over to a glass-fronted bookcase against the wall behind the counter. He craned his neck sidewise to look at a partially unrolled Chinese scroll.

"This is very impressive. The real thing. From when, Mr. Xu? Ming Dynasty?"

Mr. Xu looked impressed. "Of course the real thing. No fakes ever in the Xu family business. From my father's time all the way today. I studied the history of Chinese art and I can detect fakes when I see them. Do you, Mr. Rieger, know Chinese manuscripts?"

"I study and collect Jewish manuscripts mostly from Europe and from the same time as the Ming Dynasty—the medieval and Renaissance periods. Mostly they're written in Hebrew, some in German or Yiddish. I don't know Chinese but I can usually tell the age from the paper or parchment. Do you ever see any Hebrew ones, Mr. Xu? Like the scroll and the case in that picture? We're actually looking for that one here in Shanghai. We want to take it back to Mr. Joseph's old house but we don't know where it is."

"Oh my. That's terrible. No way it could still be in Shanghai. No one would be using it here any more. There's no religion now. And Jews all gone. Such good customers. Such a pity—all that's happened. But you can't seriously think such a valuable Torah would be anywhere near here. Why you need to take it back to Joseph house?"

Ruth said something in Chinese that must have indicated to Mr. Xu the significance of our quest. Maybe she offered him a fee. Or maybe she told him that Simon was a world famous expert. In any case Mr. Xu reached out one hand to Simon and grabbed him by the shoulder with another. From Ruth's shocked look I figured this was a rare display of affection. The two men came apart when Mr. Xu reached into his pocket and withdrew a wrinkled ivory business card that he presented two-handed to Simon. Simon accepted the card, read it with deliberate concentration, and offered his, also with both hands, to Mr. Xu, who repeated the acceptance and reading ritual. Then he turned to Ruth and took both of her hands.

"Madame, I will try to help you find the case in the picture. Josephs were my friends. Your father, too."

We had no way of knowing if Mr. Xu really knew the Josephs and Uncle Erich, but how could he have invented the story about Erich helping retrieve some goods after the war? It didn't matter. The discussion warmed me to the old dealer, and I asked him how much he wanted for the mezuzah.

Incredibly, he took it out, put it in my hand, and said, "No charge."

"No, no, I can't do that."

Ruth intervened.

"*Xie, xie*," led to a five-minute conversation in Chinese, the upshot of which was her telling me to give him 20 RMB, the equivalent then of about three dollars. Business concluded, she suggested to Simon and me that we give Mr. Xu *our* local contact information, since calls to the Chen household could send Auntie and Uncle into either terror or rage. So, Simon had written our names on a Jin Jiang card's backside, and I offered it to Mr. Xu in the local two-handed fashion.

"We're staying at the Jin Jiang. See? Our names are on the back. You can call us, too."

"Yes," said Ruth. "better than at my number in Shanghai. My aunt and uncle are very upset. But here is my professional card, too."

Mr. Xu looked especially impressed. "Israel," he said. "PhD."

"Okay, this I will do," Mr. Xu said. "Call the hotel and leave message if I hear or see anything. Happy to meet you, Missy Lily, Missy Ruth, and Mr. Simon."

After that, it seemed anti-climactic to check out the other dealers. They stood around in groups smoking and laughing with their neighboring shopkeepers. Most were younger than Mr. Xu, probably less knowledgeable about the marketplace, and certainly less experienced in business. Clearly a generation unacquainted with the Shanghai that Mr. Xu remembered so fondly and the clientele he had served. Still, we walked around showing the photo everywhere. The proprietors all shook their heads and went back to their conversations. This was certainly the antithesis of the new hardworking entrepreneurism reportedly rising in China.

Only one chubby, crewcut guy showed some sign of ambition and salesmanship as he gestured us toward his display case of rusty old medals and lacquer boxes. The rest looked oblivious to the presence of potential customers in their midst. Whether or not we even took a look at their wares was apparently of no concern.

Back on the sidewalk, Simon shook his head and said, "Is the Iron Rice Bowl alive and well in the antiques markets? These dealers can't really be getting a guaranteed wage from the government, can they, Ruth? They're not exactly hustling business."

"Old habits are hard to break. Not everyone is cut out to be an entrepreneur. Rent here is cheap, and they don't need to make a lot of money to get by."

"But wouldn't western visitors be natural targets?" I asked. "When Arthur and I were in Beijing eight years ago, we couldn't walk two feet without guys grabbing us to check out what they were selling," I said. "Actually pulling us, until our government minders shooed them off . . . "

"Eight years from now, or less, it will be entirely different."

Simon pointed to two large empty lots across the street, where the detritus of a building lay scattered and locals were picking through small piles of wood that they bundled in cloth bags. In the middle of the vacant space stood a narrow brown brick structure with a storefront on the ground floor and windows hung with laundry above. A few Chinese letters on the store's sign were painted over English that one could still make out: "A. Goldstein, tobacco."

"A Jewish business in the old days," said Ruth. She sighed and kept walking, her head down.

"Come on, Ruth," said Simon, "We're almost at the Bund. Let's show Lily the Jewish sights in Shanghai. I've been here before, but you're the native. The Peace Hotel can't be far. That's a highlight."

Simon's suggestion buoyed my cousin who seemed so depressed, no doubt torn between the mystery of the Torah and her faraway family facing Scuds nightly. "Well, okay, but that won't get us anywhere in looking for the Torah. We shouldn't take time off to play."

Simon put his arm around her shoulder. "Nonsense. Getting familiar with the territory might lead to something. The history could give us some clues."

"And we need to talk about David," I said. "Whether Helena and Joey love him or not, something tells me he's got something to do with this. That whole bit about being Jewish . . . "

"I know. Creepy and weird," Ruth said.

Within about twenty minutes, we'd walked all the way to the Bund, Shanghai's wide boulevard overlooking the Huangpo River. Coming from a German speaking background, I would have pronounced this famous thoroughfare "Boond," but I'd read it rhymed with "fund" and was Persian meaning quay or embankment. On one side there were several blocks of massive stone European-style buildings in shades of dirty grey or brown and in varying states of disrepair or decay. Still, it was the one roadway I'd seen in Shanghai so far where automobiles actually predominated over bikes. We crossed over to the riverfront side, where a wide promenade was dotted with trees and people, some dangling fishing rods into the murky water.

"This plaza is new, maybe five years old," Ruth said. "Turn around and look at the row of buildings." She pointed her finger and panned the view from right to left.

"There's the Russian consulate, the one with the red tile roof. Across the street the Astor Hotel. Then, past the Garden Bridge over Suzhou Creek, that grassy enclave was the British Consulate. That building was the Bank of China. That was the Shanghai Club. The Peace Hotel is the one on the corner with the green tile roof. The Communists took them all over for use as government offices. But now they want the big banks to come back. They're trying to make the Bund a center for business and tourists again. Especially before they retake Hong Kong in 1997. They want Shanghai to be established as the financial center of China, to surpass Hong Kong. This side of the river is called Puxi, which means west bank. It is the main area of Shanghai. But see that grassy land across the river? That area is called Pudong, or east bank. Soon that empty space will be all built up with skyscrapers. The government announced last year that Pudong will be developed for business. And that bridge being built over there? Supposed to open later this year. There will eventually be a giant new airport there, too, probably before the year 2000. I don't know when you were here last, Simon, but isn't it already starting to look different? It does to me, even in just the two years since I came with Boaz and the kids . . . "

"Yes, I'd say there are differences since I was here about three years ago. Besides the land cleared of old buildings, the people look busier and happier. I see more smiles and hear more laughter."

"Why were you here? Business?" I'd met Simon nearly a year before, and we had never discussed his previous trip to China.

"One of my Hong Kong colleagues brought me here to meet with some up-and-coming diamond dealers. Or I should say potential investors in the diamond trade. None of them knew anything concrete about the business, but cash is starting to flow in and out of here, and they figure there will be a market for jewelry and other luxury goods. We've already seen the Japanese exhibit a tremendous appetite for status name labels. The Chinese business people I met led me to believe the newly affluent Chinese will also crave Gucci and Prada, as well as glittery jewelry. No doubt, Tiffany and Cartier will open retail stores here eventually. You heard David. He already knows about Tiffany. And Rolex, though he can't tell the difference between the real and the faux."

"It's hard to imagine those names here and Chinese people buying their products," I said. "This really means capitalism is the new Communism."

"No one will put it that way, Lily," Ruth said, "but Deng Xioping paved the way for economic reforms that could transform these people's lives. My uncle is a hard core Mao man and he wanders around complaining that the ideals of the revolution are going the way of evil Chiang Kai-shek. 'Money, privilege, corruption' . . . he's launched into this diatribe three or four times since I've arrived. It's the only conversation that distracts him from the fear of what will happen if his pals in the government find out the Torah's gone."

I couldn't help but comment on the irony. "Your uncle protests, while he lives in a huge house that was subdivided during the revolution for several families but is now reconnected just for him and his wife and daughter and grandson. And, oh, yes, his servant."

Ruth laughed. "I never said Chinese couldn't be hypocrites, Lily. Do you think Mao and Chou En-lai lived like peasants? Extending a better life to the more educated urban classes at large—this is what's new. Allowing them to own businesses again. Opening up to the rest of the world. Simon meeting with guys who want to invest in the diamond trade. Who would have believed this possible? Yet, still such a paradox, I agree."

"Ruth, don't you think on some level this new wave is an acknowledgment that the Communist experiment of the last forty years hasn't worked?"

"Of course, but no one will admit that either or frame the changes that way. Just a progression. I'm worried there will be a huge shift back to a double standard of the very rich and the very poor. China is such a big country and still so many poor people. Not just in the countryside, but the cities, too. If you look down the smaller streets off the main streets, you see it. People live in hovels without running water or electricity. These reforms won't touch them or change their lives. And their homes will probably be destroyed to make way for new construction. Then what will happen to them?"

After a while we crossed back and entered the hulking building with the green tile roof. The dark and drab lobby of the Peace Hotel, to me, made the shabby Jin Jiang look fresh and up-to-date.

"Simon, what's so special about the Peace Hotel? This is pretty depressing."

"It's a property built originally by Sir Victor Sassoon. In the twenties and thirties it was the premier hotel and watering hole in Shanghai for what would today be called the international jet set that traveled here. Movie and theatre people, politicians—this was one of the top spots. Noel Coward wrote 'Private Lives' here. It was called the Cathay Hotel back then."

"When I was very young, after the Communists took over, it was used as a municipal government building," Ruth said. "It came back as a hotel sometime in the 1950s. Certainly, you're right, Lily, it's dark and could stand to be redone, but look around. This white marble floor—even with its cracks, you can tell how elegant this lobby once was. And those sconces on the wall are Lalique. I think we can go up to the top floor, where Sir Victor had his private suite. There's a grand view from a balcony up there."

The lumbering elevator dragged us up twelve stories. At least the sunny day afforded us a different vista up and down the Bund, the riverside promenade, and the open space across the river in Pudong that would supposedly be a bustling business hub in the future.

Soon the chill breeze made me shudder, suspending my tolerance for standing outside on the hotel balcony.

"Come on, let's go down. I'm getting cold. I'm sure Sir Victor and his guests didn't stand here freezing, unless they were drunk."

"Which they probably were, at least the guests." Simon put his arms around both Ruth and me and hustled us back inside. "Let's check out the ballroom, where the best Shanghai parties took place. It's on the eighth floor."

Tables and chairs were stacked up against the walls, and the carpet looked like it hadn't been replaced since 1929. The ballroom was as dark and desolate as it was cavernous, despite the long French door windows that overlooked the river. I tried to visualize elegant Chinese and European couples dining and dancing. Ruth had the benefit of her parents' memories to make the room almost come alive for us. Almost.

"The Josephs had a party for my parents' marriage here. It was a tea dance. My mother used to show me the pictures. She had a flowered dress that she wore with a big hat that had a veil. Mrs. Joseph bought the hat before the war and gave it to her. There were two tables of Chinese and Jews, sitting together, my grandfather right next to Mr. Joseph. It was 1947. A terrible time in Shanghai. All craziness. The war with the Japanese had ended, but the revolution was coming. China's long civil war. Inflation. Money was worthless. Mr. Joseph must have paid for the party in gold. Everyone's smiling, but the Jews were getting ready to leave. My parents would have left, but, of course, Mother got pregnant with me . . . "

Ruth wasn't crying, just couldn't continue talking. I looked at Simon and inclined my head toward the elevator.

Back downstairs he asked if we wanted to have lunch in the bar-coffee shop adjacent to the lobby. Though I still felt satisfied by our Shanghai street food breakfast, I didn't protest, and we walked into the dark space.

A few tables were occupied. Caucasian men drinking beer and eating skinny, limp sandwiches on white bread regaled one another with apparently hilarious tales. I heard some German and some English.

"Australians," said Simon. I don't know how he knew that, but whoever these men were, they were so noisy and rowdy that I wanted to escape.

"I'm really not hungry," I said. "Unless either of you can't live without one of those stale-looking sandwiches, let's go. I'd rather eat Chinese than bad western food, anyway."

"Are you up for going to Hongkou, where my father lived during the war?"

Ruth's look made me think she doubted I'd go. But how could I not?

"Sure."

She hailed a taxi that made a U-turn and drove along the northern end of the Bund after crossing over Suzhou Creek on the Garden Bridge. Ten minutes of breakneck weaving around bicyclists and peddler carts landed us on a street reminiscent of vintage photos of New York's lower East Side in about 1910. Except the signs were written in Chinese, not Yiddish, and more than a few were painted over English. People of all ages pushed their way along. Some dragged oversized plastic shopping bags. Others hawked wares either while walking or squatting along the edge of the sidewalk. It looked like you could buy anything: pots and pans, knives, tiny hummingbirds in metal cages. The bargaining between buyers and sellers was vociferous. Elsewhere, groups of men hovered over live foul engaged in cock fighting in the middle of the sidewalk. The men's cigarettes stayed fixed between their lips even as they catcalled and slapped one another on the back.

We walked past a green and grassy clearing, like a New York City "pocket park," but way more astonishing in this teeming district. More bizarre still was a metal plaque mounted on a rock and engraved in Chinese, English, and Hebrew. It read, "20,000 Jewish refugees survived in Shanghai during the Second World War. To all the survivors and friendly Chinese people we dedicated this plaque."

"Who put this here?" I said.

"About five years ago a group of Shanghai Jewish survivors presented this in gratitude to the city government," Ruth said. "A couple I know in Israel told me about the project. I donated to it."

Walking down another street Ruth suddenly stopped in front of a brown brick building. Through a half-open metal gate, we could see a rickety stairway with a dust-covered wooden bannister. Next to it, on ground level, was a filthy and uneven linoleum narrow passageway lined with two folding chairs, a red lacquer chest padlocked on the bottom and red-plastic-covered on the top, a broom, two bicycles, a space heater, and what appeared to be a dehumidifier topped by two pails, a large covered tea mug, and a pile of white rags.

Ruth pushed the gate and crept in, Simon and I following her. I gave Simon a 'what's this' look, but he put his finger up in a gesture of wait and see, just follow now, and find out later. We edged past all this "equipment" toward an apparent dead end blocked by a refrigerator wedged in at an angle. But it only partly obstructed the passageway to another hallway with four doors opening onto it. When my cousin came to the last one on the right, she knocked. A boy about ten years old came to the door. After Ruth spoke a few words in Chinese to him, he nodded and let us in, calling out "Ma" at the same time.

We entered a cubicle with a window that couldn't have been larger than fifteen inches square. The room's furnishings were a single cot and a small table with two shallow drawers topped by a boom box. Posters of tennis star Michael Chang and a Chinese gymnast adorned the walls. When "Ma," a woman no more than four-and-a-half feet tall, wearing a blue-and-white polka dot blouse and a stained pink apron over light green pants, emerged from another door behind us, she trapped us inside her son's room, despite the smiling and bowing.

"This is the place," Ruth said softly.

"What place, Ruth?" I said.

"Where my father lived during the war. He used to bring me here when I was little, just to show me. Then my mother would bring me after he died. I've always kept the address. I come here every time I'm in Shanghai. Last time Boaz and the kids were with me."

I put my hand on her arm. I understood the significance of a place where one felt a special connection to a lost parent. I'd returned to Vienna. Once. Our old apartment building no longer exists, though I can visualize it as vividly as I saw it the night the Nazi criminal Bucholz and his men broke in and made off with our precious Seder plate—and my father. Ruth as a child had lived with her parents in a house that still exists, where her aunt and uncle now lived. Yet, I could easily understand that she also chose to return over and over again to this hovel, on this perpetually dilapidated side of the city, where her father had been forcibly moved when the Japanese acquiesced to the will of their German ally and created a ghetto for the European Jews who had escaped Hitler by going to Shanghai.

"You still come here every time you come back to Shanghai?" Simon's life experience was different—he was born and raised in New York.

"Yes, like Lily goes to Yad Vashem whenever she's in Jerusalem," Ruth said. "But it's different for me in one way. Lily, you knew you were Jewish your whole life and you personally experienced persecution. For me—well, it all happened before I was born. And here in China I didn't have any taste of normal Jewish life to identify with. By the time I was born, no religion was practiced. My father told me stories about holidays, maybe even about the beautiful Seder plate, but this was the only place he could show me that was connected to his being Jewish. So it connected me."

The mother and son who lived there now stood in the doorway obviously moved by Ruth's tears. The little boy whispered to his mother, who nodded and spoke in Chinese, pointing toward the room directly across the hall. Ruth nodded, smiled, and replied.

"He wants to know if I'm all right," she told us. "Very sweet. The mom says she knows Jews lived here during wartime. Her father's family lived in that room next door, six of them in just that space. She wasn't born yet. Now she and her husband have all four rooms, just with one son and her husband's parents. That's a rare luxury in this district. I've met the parents before, but never her and the boy."

She took one more sweeping glance around the space. "There were two small beds squeezed in here before. Can you imagine? I've seen pictures. My father roomed with an old man who snored and wheezed, probably had TB or something. It was either freezing cold or stifling hot. My father hardly got any sleep. Living here started the decline in his health."

"I've read the Japanese sometimes gave passes for the day for people to go to work," said Simon.

"It was very sporadic, as Uncle mentioned last night. My father also told me that Ghoya, the Japanese official who ran the ghetto, swung from being generous and benevolent to cruel and vengeful. Mostly the latter. That bridge we crossed on the Bund, the Garden Bridge over Suzhou Creek—that was border of this district. There were guards and a guardhouse that became notorious. Jews were occasionally detained there and released in much worse shape than when they went in. Papa said he rarely got out of Hongkou. The Joseph office, like other businesses owned by the Sephardic families, was in the central business district on the other side of the bridge. Their employees tried to keep them open as best possible while their owners were in prisoner-of-war camps because of their British passports. Of course, hotels, clubs, and restaurants stayed open for the pleasure of the Japanese. When Sir Victor Sassoon came back after the war, his companies paid every employee all the back wages they would have earned throughout the war—four years' worth—whether they'd been able to actually get to their jobs or not."

75

Ever the businessman, Simon asked if the Josephs had done the same.

"My father never told me. The Josephs were well off, but they weren't the Sassoons. Money was nearly worthless by that time, and they were preparing to leave, so I doubt it. But they still treated my father like a son, did what they could for him, and expected him to join them in Hong Kong, where their fortunes would probably rise again. Because of me, my parents never made it to Hong Kong."

I put my arm around her shoulder and said, "Ruth, you can hardly blame yourself for your mother's pregnancy. That's ridiculous. You were certainly a joint and joyous undertaking for both of them. And, if she had complications that kept her from traveling, that happens. Certainly, you brought them great happiness afterward, even if they were trapped in China."

Nodding silently, she wiped her eyes. We said our formal goodbye to the mother and son, with more bowing and nodding of heads, and walked back down the alley and onto the bustling street. The sun had evaporated, and the wind blew a few sprinkles onto our heads.

"Unless there's something else you want to do in this neighborhood, Ruth, let's get out of here," said Simon. "It looks like a cabby convention on that corner. Let's grab one."

What we didn't see until we approached the conclave of five drivers, forming a human circle in front of their vehicles parked at all angles over half of a two-lane street, was that their boisterous gestures and yelling focused on two other men, who squatted on the sidewalk to place bets and cheer on their respective battling crickets. It was hard to get a driver's attention, but Simon managed. I didn't see it, but he probably flashed some paper money he was holding. We made a beeline for the cab door.

"Don't we need two cabs—one for Ruth and one for us?" I asked.

"No, Lily," she said. "You can drop me—like in New York. Auntie's house is on the way. Then I can give the driver your hotel address."

"I have another hotel card with its address in Chinese, in case there's a problem," said Simon.

"Shouldn't be. Since Nixon everyone knows Jin Jiang. Very popular place for foreigners to stay."

Indeed it was. We dropped Ruth off and quickly found ourselves out of the cab and walking into the Jin Jiang lobby.

Suddenly, someone said, "Mrs. Kovner? Over here! Wait . . . "

I spun around and saw a familiar square face atop a conservative navy blue skirt suit. Without the cap and gun it took me a moment to recognize her.

"It's Jennifer. Detective Wong from the San Francisco Police Department."

I ignored the stunned look on Simon's face as I held out my hand and tried to greet her with equal graciousness, if not equal exuberance.

"Hello, Detective. So nice to see you again. What are you doing here?"

I hoped my quiet tone and a slight negative shake of my head while I aimed my eyes toward Simon would tip her off to say nothing about how we'd met. I hadn't told Simon or Ruth about the threatening incident in San Francisco. In fact, I'd almost forgotten about it. I'd have to tell him now but wanted to be able to pick the right time.

Thankfully, Wong caught the hint.

"Just investigating a smuggling case," she said in normal voice. Then "We have to talk," she added in a whisper, almost under her breath.

"Detective Wong, this is Simon Rieger."

"Nice to meet you, Detective. Smuggling what?"

"Antiques," Wong said. "Chinese antiques that are being illegally moved out of the country and sold without provenance in the US."

I could tell this response didn't completely satisfy Simon.

"You're a San Francisco police detective? Why are you involved in this? Wouldn't this be federal jurisdiction?"

"There's a San Francisco connection—suspects in and out of town, and one just arrived in Shanghai. SFPD has been collaborating with the FBI on this, and agreed someone should come over. I have relatives here, I speak Chinese, so here I am. Mrs. Kovner told me where she was staying, and my boss is thrilled with the low cost of this hotel. It's cool, so historic. And a lot more comfortable than staying with my cousins."

"How did you and Lily meet?"

"Let's sit down and have something to drink," I said, playing for time before I had to tell Simon the truth.

"A cup of tea would be great," Wong said. Once up the marble stairway, we occupied three of the lobby's rattan backed chairs surrounding a small round table.

"Good idea. It's so damn chilly," said Simon.

"I will have a short brandy," I said, disregarding his shocked expression—it was only three in the afternoon. I needed to steel myself for the conversation I could no longer evade."

"A little early, isn't it?"

"I'm cold beyond what tea can do for me right now. Simon, I met Detective Wong in San Francisco when she came to my hotel to investigate a threat I received there. A threat about this search for the lost Torah."

Simon's eyes widened, and he started rubbing his left arm, the bad arm, the one shattered in a tank in the Negev in 1949. This was the first time I'd seen him do that in months. Maybe it was the chill. More likely, using his right hand for this purpose prevented it from slamming onto the table.

"And this threat was what, Lily? A letter? Phone calls? Like last year?" He spoke much more softly than usual, another tactic used for self-control.

Our order arrived in record-breaking time. I quickly gulped a swig of brandy to fortify myself against the cold, both that outside and the indoor version—Simon's icy glare. Jennifer Wong picked up her teacup and started sipping. Simon barely noticed his cup on the table in front of him.

"Just a piece of notebook paper with a note in crayon that said 'Lily Kovner, don't go to China.' And a Chinese character."

"What did the character mean?"

"Death," I said.

Finally, Simon let go of his left arm and picked up his tea with both hands.

Jennifer Wong revived the conversation. "I couldn't find any evidence of who sent the note, Mr. Rieger. Nothing's happened since you've arrived, has it? No further threats?"

"Everything's fine," I said.

"You mentioned last year. I don't understand." She looked to Simon to explain.

"Last year Lily searched for a an antique Jewish ritual object that was looted from her childhood home by the Nazis. She first saw it, after more than fifty years, at an auction in New York. That's where we met, as a matter of fact. It turned into quite an escapade, and not only was she threatened, but someone she wanted to interview was murdered, and she came damn close to being killed herself."

"I see," Wong said. "Well, I certainly haven't forgotten about what happened in San Francisco. My jurisdiction is not exactly the same here, but the

Chinese are fully cooperative with the case I'm working on, so I should be able to ensure a measure of protection. You should keep me informed, if anything else crops up."

"Now tell us about the suspect you're after." I was desperate to change the subject.

"His name is F.W. Tang, but his pals call him Freddy," Wong said, "especially his old KMT contacts."

"KMT? You mean the Nationalists, Chiang Kai-shek's party both here on the mainland and later in Taiwan?"

Simon perked up. "You're telling us there's still someone active from Chiang's crowd here in Shanghai?"

"He's in his late seventies, but very spry. His connections flow from his father, who was a real big shot, a businessman, one of Chiang's most loyal backroom advisers—and a most generous financial backer. The Tang family left for Taiwan when Chiang did, a couple of years before the Communists really took over. They also established themselves in business and real estate in the States through some of Chiang's contacts."

"Probably through the 'usual suspects,' Chiang's China lobby in the fifties and sixties—Henry Luce of *Time*, Colonel McCormack from Chicago. A charming group that egged on the vilification of the 'old China hands' in the State Department and ruined so many lives," Simon snorted.

"Yes, I'm glad to see you know exactly what I'm talking about," Wong said. "Well, Freddy has come to Shanghai, and I've just found out he's staying at the Hilton Hotel. Not far from here."

"Yes," said Simon, "Close geographically but a million miles up in comfort and amenities. Of course, he would hardly be impressed by the Jewish and Mao-Nixon history of this dump . . . "

Wong dug for something in her bag.

"Okay, Simon," I said, raising an eyebrow. "Enough already."

Wong showed me a small black-and-white photo of a white-haired Chinese man in a three-piece suit with a small squared-off mustache.

"Maybe you've seen him? He was staying at your hotel in San Francisco," Wong said.

"I don't know. He looks familiar. Perhaps I saw him at the pool. There was a big Chinese family swimming that morning—it looked like three generations. I didn't really pay too much attention to them. I was just trying to avoid the kids as I swam laps and I didn't have time to sit around there afterward. Was he on my plane?"

"No, he flew to Taipei first, then through Hong Kong to come here."

"How can someone with his background even get into China?"

"You'd be surprised," Wong said. "Where there's money to be made, old Chinese ties run deep."

"Yes," said Simon, "I've heard that the level of animosity with Taiwan is declining sharply as the mainland is trying to rise economically. Business deals with the Taiwanese are on the increase. Money talks louder now than politics and history. Ultimately, there will be political rapprochement, too, probably direct flights someday."

Wong put a few coins on the table and stood up. "I've got to be going. It was nice to meet you, Mr. Rieger, and, both of you, please keep in touch. I've got one of those new cell phones, but it doesn't seem to work here. Only the Japanese businessmen I've seen around seem to be able to use them."

Simon picked up the coins and pressed them back into Wong's hand. "Please, we invited you—it was only tea. I've got a phone, too, from Israel, and it's worked once, at least. Please call me Simon, by the way."

"And I'm Lily," I said.

"Jennifer, of course," the detective answered. "Do keep me posted on your Torah search. If you have any problems with anyone, any more threats, I'm in room 516."

Simon sat down again. The waitress came over poised to pour him some more tea. He shook his head and motioned for the bill. I sipped the last of my brandy. Neither of us spoke for about two minutes while he rubbed his left arm again. The check appeared. He stopped his massage long enough to sign it and then broke the silence.

"When were you going to tell me about the threatening note?"

"I almost forgot about it, to be honest."

"Did you tell Jacob before you left San Francisco?"

"Are you kidding? He'd nagged me enough the night before about this trip. And about . . . "

"And about what?"

I hesitated. "About you. Our relationship. But we straightened it all out and left on a very upbeat note. Come on, let's go upstairs. Don't you feel like a nap?" Our private code.

"No, not really. Not right now."

I gave him a pretty dirty look.

"Okay," he said, "We can go upstairs. But we need to sort this out, Lily, before we do anything else."

I sulked into the elevator and all the way to our room. I took my time taking off my coat and boots and using the bathroom. When I came out, Simon was sitting on the small over-stuffed sofa and patting the place next to him as where I should sit. I chose to lie down on the bed. All the walking and the brandy had made me drowsy, and the forthcoming discussion was not what I'd had in mind after the day's excursion with Ruth. I felt deflated and headachy. Despite this, I took an aggressive stance.

"I don't know why the men in my life think it's their duty to protect me and judge me and track my every waking moment."

This time Simon did slam his good hand on the table in front of him. "Damn it, Lily, you act like I don't value your independence and self-reliance, all that. Do I treat you like some fragile damsel in distress? Or like some brainless nincompoop? I know you can take care of yourself and you do so very well. Don't you understand that I just don't want you to be hurt—or worse? I just can't believe that you wouldn't have shared this piece of information with me. After all we've . . . after all you've been through . . . "

"I'm sorry, Simon, really. I told you I'd sort of forgotten about the note. I figured now we're together, you're with me, Ruth's uncle has government connections, if we get into real trouble . . . "

"And what about Jacob? What was on his big scientific mind? Does he think I'm just some lecher debauching his virginal mother, angling for her money, just biding my time before I drop you?"

I couldn't help but laugh. "Well, that was the general idea but not in those terms. He'd prefer to see us married."

"And whose doing is it that we're not?"

"I told him it's mine. But that we're in a very committed relationship, you're none of the above, and it's none of his business. He isn't too crazy about this round-the-world sleuthing either."

"Well, considering what I just found out about San Francisco, I might be close to agreeing with him on that. Was your daughter-in-law in on this conversation?"

"Amy was most supportive on both counts. She likes you very much and thinks I'm cool for doing all this. She virtually accused Jacob of being an old fuddy-duddy."

"Listen, Lilly, I'm the one who called you from Israel and said we should help Ruth. But now I think we should call it off. Tell her enough is enough, you've been threatened. It's *déjà vu.* China is not Israel. We have no obligation to do this, and, frankly, I can't imagine we will have any luck, unless that birdbrain David, the Chinese Jew, has the Torah under his bed. Which Helena should be able to find out on her own. I'm calling Ruth right now and then I'm making plane reservations for us to go back to New York. And out of this rathole historic hotel."

"Are you crazy? What's gotten into you? If you want to go home, go home. But I'm staying. Right here. This hotel is fine with me. I spent months of my childhood in the Tube sleeping next to half of London. You're welcome to leave any time. Either the hotel or Shanghai."

"Wow. I'm trying to protect you, and this is what I get? Lily, I'm sorry. I just love you so much that I don't want to see you in danger. Now, how about that nap?" Taking off his shirt, he approached the bed.

"No," I said. "That isn't going to work right now. You think sex will fix this? I appreciate your concern and your desire to 'protect' me, but I do pretty well on that front, thank you very much, and I can't believe you're willing to pull the plug on helping Ruth. You are welcome to leave any time, or I will ask the hotel for another room. Don't forget, I have my personal police detective here."

"Don't bother to call her," Simon said. "I'm packing up."

Chapter 6

Remarkably, I had a good night's sleep, which I felt guilty about in the morning. I went out swimming first thing and came back to the room to drop off my bag before breakfast. Just as I walked back into the room, the phone was ringing. Maybe it was Simon. No, it was Ruth. I decided not to mention my altercation with Simon on the phone.

"It's still tense here," she said. "No news about the Torah. But David wants you and Simon and me to have dinner with him and his father. Six o'clock, a restaurant in the area. And I don't know what you're doing today, but would you like to go with me to see this Chinese Jewish studies professor who wants to meet me?"

"A Chinese Jewish studies professor? You're kidding."

"No, really," she said. "I know that sounds ridiculous to you, but there are a few of them. How scholarly their scholarship is—that's another question."

"Do his Jewish studies focus on the Jewish history in China or on the Bible? Hebrew?"

"I don't think he knows Hebrew or Torah. Probably more on the Jews in China."

"I'm still learning about the extent to which there was a Jewish community here. I did some reading before I left home about the Kaifeng Jews that David talked about but I couldn't find much else. In my experience China meant a safe harbor for the Jews escaping Hitler, but a very strange and foreign place. I remember my grandmother—our grandmother—practically sitting *shivah* when your father left. She kept yelling 'China, China, who goes to China? Marco Polo.' If only we'd all gone with him. If only, a lot of things . . . "

Obviously, Ruth didn't have the patience for my historical commentary or my morose walk down our family's memory lane.

"I've got to go, Lily. I'll pick you up at 1:45. It's walking distance from your hotel to the institute."

I decided it was time for breakfast on the street and a little tour of the French Concession. Strangely, while I missed Simon, I felt Shanghai had become much more manageable and I was determined to see more of it.

Despite the sun peaking through the clouds, it was still chilly for *al fresco* eating. But partaking of the outdoor buffet for the second day in a row made me feel like a local. Moreover, the vendors smiled as if they remembered me, which was entirely possible, because there were no other non-Asians in sight. The toothless lady selling the sesame and scallion buns held her hands out with two ready for us when I got to her stand, and she looked around expecting my companion to take one of them. Oh, well. The omelet guy at first didn't see me but came over and pulled on my sleeve to lead me back to his skillet while I munched a mushroom-filled bun a few stands down. Reasoning that I'd evaded an attack of Mao's Revenge the day before, I downed two more steaming servings of tea to neutralize the invisible fragments of chili pepper that made their fiery presence known when I bit into a dumpling.

A walk was definitely in order by the time I finished breakfast. Armed with an off-scale tourist map in Chinese and English that Concierge Christina had marked for me, I navigated my way down a side street off the nearby main drag, Huaihai Road, until I reached a large house with crumbling white paint set back from the road behind a gravel driveway and surrounded by stiff brown grass. It looked familiar, and I realized I'd seen its photo in Marty's Aunt Teddy's scrapbook. The sign in front said it was the Shanghai Conservatory of Music. The former Jewish Club! It was hard to envision Jews floating in and out of here for their communal meetings, musical and cultural programs, cards, and mah jongg.

I took a few steps onto the grounds and seconds later I saw a Chinese boy, who looked no older than seven or eight, backing out the front door, holding on to one end of a cello case and followed by a thin woman lifting the other end as she walked out facing forward. Their outerwear—the boy's thin windbreaker jacket and the woman's rain poncho—offered scant protection from the biting wind. But they did have a cello. Somehow, this seemed both very

Chinese and very familiar. No doubt, there were some young music prodigies in the Russian-Jewish community, too, and parents who sacrificed warm coats in favor of an instrument.

I knew the Baghdadis—like the Sassoons and the Josephs—had arrived in Shanghai before the Russians. With their business and social success, I suspected at least some of them considered themselves the established aristocracy compared to the more come-lately Russians. Like German Jews looking down on "greenhorns"—also mostly from Russia—in America. But, while trading opium didn't seem like a high-class business, what country's aristocrats didn't engage in less than noble practices? Slavery?

Baghdad. Babylonia. Iraq.

The first destination of the Jewish diaspora after the Temple in Jerusalem was destroyed, when vicious Nebuchadnezzar forced Jews into Babylonian exile. Eventually, Jews flourished there; Judaism, too, with the conception of the Talmud, academies boasting learned scholars, literature, and music—a true cradle of a large chunk of Jewish civilization and history. There were times when Jews held government positions and lived in harmony with their Muslim neighbors. Long ago. I knew some Iraqi Jews in London and New York who had escaped in 1948, when Israel's birth ended any possibility of open Jewish life in their homeland. They recalled happy times and treasured their Sephardic heritage. Some, like many who came to Shanghai, had waylaid in India before the States; a few still had relatives there.

Did these prosperous and well-connected Jews in Shanghai deal with the notorious local crime syndicates and their leaders? Certainly, Chiang Kai-shek and his cohorts harbored no compunction about their countrymen addicted to opium, if a profit was involved.

And how did the Josephs figure into this equation? Apparently, they descended from the Baghdadi line. But they had taken in Uncle Erich, had been friends with Ruth's grandparents, had introduced Erich to Ruth's mother. Mr. Xu had spoken of Mrs. Joseph as being kind to poor Chinese women. I wondered if Ruth's Jewish Studies professor could, or would, answer some of these darker questions. Given the sensitivity of the missing Torah, I didn't think I would ask.

I returned to Huaihai Road and, following the map, turned to the right down another street, passing a peaceful park toward a leafy neighborhood that could have easily been mistaken for Paris, save for the Chinese—and

English—street signs. I approached a greenish grey stucco house with red paint trimming the windows to match its red tile roof.

This was the home of the sole president of the short-lived Chinese republic, Sun Yat-sen. It had only recently opened to the public as a museum. I wondered if there would be reference to Mr. Hardoon, whom the antiques dealer Xu had mentioned as a Sun Yat-sen supporter.

I paid the small fee and went in. Of course, there were the requisite photos of Sun and his revolutionary colleagues, but the furnishings were supposedly left just as they were during his life here with his much younger wife, Soong Ching-ling. She was Madame Chiang Kai-shek's sister, one of the three famous Soong sisters, the one who rejected her family's wealthy and greedy ways and chose the Communists over Chiang early—immediately after Dr. Sun's death in 1925. His widow remained in the house until 1937, when the Japanese takeover of Shanghai persuaded her to live in Beijing. Later, when the Chiangs and the Soongs escaped the Communist takeover by fleeing to Taiwan, Madame Sun remained on the mainland, and would stay for the rest of her life, an iconic supporter of Mao.

This house had been donated to the Suns by overseas Chinese allies in Canada. While far from grand, it's a substantial residence for a revolutionary. Sun's spectacles sitting on his desk made it look like he'd just gone out and would return soon to sit there again. There he'd be surrounded by thousands of books and a collection of hanging maps, one he allegedly hand-painted himself. A small covered porch with black-and-white checkerboard floor and green bamboo furniture looked like the only place for Sun and Soong Ching-ling to relax under cover from the harsh Shanghai summer sun. Otherwise, the home exuded hard work and history. The couple looked diligent and serious in all their photos. No reference to Mr. Hardoon.

My Chinese history was both rusty and minimal, but I remembered why Sun continues to be venerated by the Communists, considering he founded the Kuomintang, ultimately the Communists' arch foe, and died in 1926, more than twenty years before they came to power. Sun is seen as a unifying figure. He not only helped take down the Qing Dynasty and its emperor but continued to fight against the feudal warlords who clung to their fiefdoms throughout the country during the Republic. Mao, of course, agreed with Sun that these relics of the old China and imperial rule had to go. But Sun's death and Chiang's ascendancy to power obliterated any possibility of a long-term alliance between the KMT and the Communists. The two-decades-long civil war that ensued usurped the strength of China's participation in fighting the Japanese during World War II.

I realized it was almost time to meet Ruth at the hotel. My hours of walking around the French Concession had been so interesting and pleasant that I'd almost ignored the bicycle traffic every time I crossed a street. I was getting used to weaving and darting through the ubiquitous congestion. So, I wasn't paying attention as I strolled up Huaihai toward its busy intersection with Maoming Road, a block from the hotel. Suddenly, a double lane thick with about a dozen bikes converged in a tight pack, heading toward the next corner and veering en masse to the right.

"Ruth!"

The familiar voice came from the opposite corner. Simon dashed into the street and zigzagged through the moving obstacle course like an Olympic steeplechaser.

Craning my neck to follow the action, I saw him grab Ruth, who stood paralyzed in the face of the onslaught, and pull her out of harm's way to the nearest curb. By the time I negotiated my way across, the attackers had passed, though a few stopped and peered backward, gesturing to one another in apparent frustration. Simon panted heavily and mopped his forehead with his handkerchief. The usually composed Ruth held his shoulders and babbled nonstop.

"Simon, Simon, you okay? Thank you so much. I don't know how to thank you. I froze, just watched them. That bunch of bikes looked like they were coming straight at me. To run me down. Lily, don't you think so?"

"Yes. I suppose it could have been deliberate. But I couldn't see you until I saw Simon grab you. Did you sense that anyone was following you? On foot or bike?"

"No one specific," she said catching her breath. "I don't think like that. Anyway, in these crowds how could I tell?"

"Maybe it's the same people who sent me the threat in San Francisco."

"What threat?"

I'd forgotten that Ruth didn't know.

"Lily . . . got a crude note . . . with a Chinese death character," Simon said, still a little breathless and grasping Ruth's right arm. "I just found out yesterday. She met a detective who investigated. The . . . detective is actually here in Shanghai now. Staying at our hotel."

Our hotel?

Ruth whirled around, still clutching Simon. "What? A death threat? A detective from San Francisco is here investigating it?" She sank down into a squat on the sidewalk and held her head in her hands. "It's all my fault. I feel so guilty dragging you and Simon into this. In addition to leaving Boaz and the kids during a war . . . "

I leaned down and stroked her hair. "You were just nearly run over by a mob on bikes. That's sufficient reason for you to be shaken and upset. But about us, Ruth, forget about feeling guilty. We're in this together. And the detective from San Francisco is here working on an antiques smuggling case, not the threat to me. It's only a coincidence that she's here."

"But still," now Ruth was crying, "If this attack by the bikes was another threat, it's another sign this trip is a huge mistake."

"Listen, Ruth," I said. "We may be in this together, but if you are having second thoughts related to your own safety, that's another story. You call the shots here. If you want to go home, it's your decision, and we will go along with it. Meanwhile, right now, are you sure you want to carry on with this appointment with the professor? Wouldn't you rather go back to our hotel or to your aunt's house to recover?"

Standing up again, she said, "No, we'll go. I'm fine. I'm just so worried about everything at home—and here—and now someone's trying to stop us, like the problems you had with Bucholz . . . "

In the commotion I'd almost forgotten about Simon. He was hunched over, still breathing heavily, holding onto Ruth's arm when she got up—but not talking. His foray into the street had obviously been a physical challenge for a sixty-six-year-old man, never mind a magnificent demonstration of courage and caring.

"Are you okay? What you did was . . . " I took him into my arms and kissed his sweaty face.

Taking a deep breath, Simon straightened up, released Ruth's arm, but was obviously still winded when he started to speak again.

"We'll . . . try to call Israel again today . . . see how everyone is doing. Whew! For now, Ruth, if you still want to go, tell us . . . about this professor and what you want to accomplish in this meeting."

At that moment the estrangement between us seemed altogether frivolous. My love and admiration for this man revived as if we'd never had a cross word, never mind spent the previous night apart. For me the war was over. Now, of course, was not the time to discuss it.

"Professor Pang Tian, yes. Really, it's only a formality. I need to bolster my *guanxi* in China as a Jewish antiquities expert for the foundation. He knows we specialize in art looted by the Nazis. He's made something of a reputation by collecting, and probably copying without permission, photos and memorabilia of Shanghai Jewish history. His focus has been mainly the refugees from the Holocaust, and he knows my father was one of them. But don't say anything about the missing Ezra Torah, please. Professor Pang is considered the government's Jewish expert. Could be dangerous for my uncle if word got out that the Torah that's supposed to go to Israel was stolen. The Torah that was in Uncle's safekeeping."

The Shanghai Jewish Studies Institute consisted of a suite of offices and classrooms along a dingy hallway within an international studies center. Along the walls of the hallway were historic black-and-white photos of distinctly non-Chinese people.

A slight man in his forties wearing a shiny light grey suit, Professor Pang Tian spoke excellent English, and he followed the vogue of sporting a non-Chinese moniker: "Call me Tim." But his manner was so unctuous that I had the feeling the pores on my fingers would ooze oil after shaking his hand. He showed us into a conference room, where he sat the three of us opposite him, Simon between Ruth and me, in the middle of a long table. Soon a young woman appeared with teacups and brew. After she'd poured and crept out, Tim gushed over Ruth as a cherished academic colleague.

"Ah, Professor Sofer, such a pleasure. Hebrew University, a fine institution. I hope to go there someday, maybe do an exchange with our center. I know of the reputation of your colleague, Professor Shaul Rotan, an expert in Jewish ritual objects. How is his health? He has retired now, right? Getting old?"

The mention of a key player in the previous year's search for my family's Seder plate turned my stomach. Rotan played a despicable role in the diabolical conspiracy. Only his ultimate confession that led to the capture of the notorious and long-pursued Nazi war criminal, Rudolf Bucholz, saved Rotan from public disgrace and even prosecution. He'd been able to retire quietly from the university, his reputation intact.

"He does just fine, still active. I don't see or talk to him often," said Ruth. In fact, her former mentor had so disappointed her she hadn't spoken to him since the revelation of his involvement in the Bucholz treachery. Once almost a father figure to her and a surrogate grandfather to her children, Rotan was no longer welcome in Ruth and Boaz's home.

She quickly moved the conversation elsewhere.

"Like Professor Rotan and myself, Mr. Rieger here is interested in old Jewish books and manuscripts. He collects them."

"This is your business?" You could almost see dollar signs in the professor's eyes.

"No, I own a jewelry business and I trade diamonds on the Tel Aviv exchange. The rare books and manuscripts are a hobby, a leisure activity."

"Yes, I know what a hobby is," Tim said. "Are you trading diamonds in China? Or looking for rare Jewish manuscripts?" He chuckled, the only one who found this funny.

"Neither, of course," Simon said. "But I have been in contact with potential trading partners for the future."

"So, you're not here in Shanghai on business? Why then?"

"Ruth—Professor Sofer—was coming to visit her aunt and uncle . . . "

"Yes, the Chens, of course . . . "

Simon resumed, "So we decided she'd be a good tour guide."

"Interesting," Tim said, "typically not a popular time of the year for tourists."

"It's a time I was able to get away," Ruth said. "Though with this war on . . . the Scuds . . . "

Simon touched her hand. "We'll call soon. I promise."

"Professor, how did you get interested in Judaism and Jewish Studies?" I asked.

"When I was very young, my family lived next door to a Jewish family, the Haddads," he said. "It was a sad little family group: an old grandmother, a young widowed father, and his son, my age. The grandfather and the boy's mother had both died in the prisoner-of-war camp, where the boy, Sammy, was born. By the time I knew them, most of the Jews had already left Shanghai—Jews with enough money—but this family couldn't leave until 1951. Some relatives in London finally scraped up enough to send them tickets. By then there were no more Jewish schools, and the synagogues were closed. Sammy's father took care of the buildings; he was called 'the *shamash*.' The grandfather had been the *shamash* before him. It wasn't common that Jewish and Chinese children mixed before this, but Sammy had no one else his age. I used to love going over there to taste whatever the grandmother had cooked for the Shabbat and holidays. She would tell us stories about the days of glory, how the rich Jews entertained, their fine houses. Some even kept their own Torahs at home . . . "

"Their own Torahs? Really?" Simon sounded appropriately shocked and intrigued. "What happened to them? Did they take them to Hong Kong and the other places they went?"

"I assume so," Tim said. "Ah, you're interested, Mr. Rieger, because of your hobby. I've heard one family had a very old and famous Torah scroll. The Ezra Torah. Someone told me it could be traced back to Baghdad, possibly even to Ezra the Scribe."

"*Ezra Ha Sofer*," said Ruth. "Our last name. My husband's family was originally from Egypt. Tim, that's unbelievable. Going back to Ezra would be about 2500 years. He left Babylonia—Iraq now—and led Jews back to Jerusalem. Simon, is there any way a scroll could have survived that long?"

"Possibly, with loving care and proper travel and storage conditions. And if no one ever really used it."

"I wouldn't want to be quoted," Tim said, leaning toward us lowering his voice to a whisper, "but I heard it's still in Shanghai." His manner implied a state secret. Which, of course, it was.

"Really?" Although genuinely surprised to hear this coming from him, I played along. After all, that's what Miss Marple would do.

The professor rummaged in his top desk drawer, mumbling to himself in Chinese, which only Ruth could understand.

"He's asking himself 'where is it?' Where is what, Tim?"

"A name card. Ah, here it is," he said, withdrawing his hand and holding up the small white card with a distinctive black, red, and gold logo. He read us the name:

"F.W. Tang, antiques dealer. From New York."

I hoped my involuntary eye widening didn't betray how startled I was to hear this name. I avoided glancing at Simon as the professor continued talking.

"He came to visit me perhaps two months ago. He'd heard about this Torah, came to me to ask if I knew where it was. I'd heard of it, but not its whereabouts. He told me he thought it's still in Shanghai. But that's so hard to imagine, don't you agree?"

"Yes, it certainly is, Professor, with all the Jews gone. Did he say why he was interested in a Torah, of all things?" Ruth, too, acted fascinated.

"Not really. Just general talk about Jews in China, the old days. I told him about the Haddads, too. He said to contact him if I ever came across this Torah or any information about it. Not likely, I told him. If such a thing existed, the Jews leaving Shanghai would have taken it with them long ago."

"True, true," said Simon, turning to me with an infinitesimal nod toward the door to signal "let's get out of here." I wasn't quite ready, because I suspected Tim knew more.

"Did you know Mr. Tang before this?"

"No, but people tend to find me in matters related to Jews."

To my slight annoyance, Simon rose fully then and announced that we should be going. The professor insisted on showing us the photos in the corridor, explaining them one by one. Most were scenes of the European Holocaust refugees living in Hongkou, with a few token shots of the earlier Jewish settlers in Shanghai.

"You see," he said pointing to a large family gathered around a cabinet, "their own Ark for the Torah. I don't think this was the family with the Ezra Torah, but it was common in the Sephardic households. Such interesting history. Wouldn't it be wonderful if someday there would be a museum of the Jewish history of Shanghai? The trick is finding the money. Perhaps your foundation?"

"Our mission is to help find looted art," Ruth said.

"Well, perhaps, Mrs. Kovner and Mr. Rieger, you know American Jews who would help with this worthy cause. Or yourselves?"

"Perhaps, but we must be going," Simon said.

Once we were out of the building and back on the street. Simon and I turned to each other.

"Tang!" We exclaimed at the same time. Ruth looked at us confused.

"Who's Tang? You know this name? I never heard of him."

"Ruth, the policewoman from San Francisco is here to investigate the possible criminal activity of one F.W. Tang. He's the guy she suspects to be at the center of the illegal antiques trade."

"Ah. I see." Suddenly, she inched toward a sign pole and leaned against it. "I guess."

"Ruth, you need to rest. Let's get you a cab," I said. "We can walk back to the Jin Jiang. What are the plans for tonight?"

"Dinner with Helena's boyfriend."

Ruth started scribbling on a small piece of paper, which she handed to me.

"Here's the Chinese address of the restaurant. If you could take a taxi tonight, I'd appreciate it. My aunt and uncle have a government banquet that they're very nervous about because the Torah is missing. I'll come with Helena. It will be more convenient than picking you up at the hotel."

"No problem, Ruth. And try to get some rest before dinner," said Simon, as he opened the passenger door of the little red cab that had just stopped in front of us, and we waved Ruth off and set off for the Jin Jiang.

"Lily," he started, "we need . . . "

"To talk?"

"Yes. And I need to apologize, I suppose . . . "

"That reeks with sincerity," I said, and instantly regretted it.

"I am sincere about not wanting to threaten your independence, your self-reliance, and about making such an issue about it. That said, call me old-fashioned, if you must, but I won't apologize for being concerned about your safety and for wanting to keep you safe and, dare I say it, protected. At the very least, I don't want you to keep me in the dark about threats like you got in San Francisco. We're in this together—don't forget that. I can see not telling Ruth, though after today, that's not a good idea either."

The reference to Ruth's near miss brought back the sight of Simon rushing in to wrest her from what could have been an unthinkable fate.

"Seriously, Simon," I said, "even if I wanted to, after today I will never accuse you of overprotectiveness again. When I saw you dash into the street and grab Ruth out of the path of those bikes, all I could think of was how much I love you. I probably made too big a deal out of yesterday, but being self-reliant and independent is a sensitive issue for me . . . "

"No kidding," he said.

"I promise to tell you about anything or anybody suspicious. Okay? And let you be my knight in shining armor, most of the time, because you are really good at it."

By this time we passed through the brick fence surrounding the Jin Jiang and approached the main entrance.

"So, why are you still here? I thought you would have hightailed it for the Hilton. Or gone home."

"No, you can't get rid of me that fast. I got another room here, which makes ours look like the presidential suite at the Pierre. Coming back to our room will be a return to paradise. For more reasons than one. If you will have me back."

We stopped at the desk, and I asked the clerk to leave a message for Jennifer Wong to call "our" room and took Simon by the arm as we approached the elevator.

"You can pick up your stuff in the other room later."

The phone was ringing as we walked in.

"That was quick," I said, picking it up.

"Mrs. Lily, you didn't pay attention to our message in San Francisco."

"What?" It wasn't Detective Wong, but a voice I didn't recognize, speaking English with a Chinese accent. "Who is this?" I asked.

"And today in the street with your friends and the bicycles. Don't look anymore for that Torah. Worse things will happen."

Hearing no further conversation on my end, Simon whirled around from the closet where he was hanging up his coat and gestured inquiringly with his hands. I must have looked stunned, since he came over and grabbed the receiver.

"Who is this?" After a few seconds he hung up.

"Did he say anything when you got on?"

"Just 'you and the ladies will be sorry.' Who was that guy? What did he say to you?"

"Oh, just that . . . uh . . . I didn't pay attention in San Francisco and today in the street, stop looking for the Torah, just routine threat garbage. I've heard worse."

"'Routine threat garbage?' Here we go again. I still can't believe you're so cavalier and nonchalant about it, Lily. It's serious. You know, maybe we should stop and go home. Enough already."

I shook my head. "No way. You of all people want to stop? My knight in shining armor? My protector? My personal Mossad agent?"

"The Mossad is not in China—yet," he said.

"But you're here."

End of conversation, as I reached out for him.

When we arrived at the restaurant, Ruth and Helena were already sitting with David and his father, Li Wei, so there was no opportunity to privately tell them about the threatening phone call. David was playing host in a grandiose way.

"No shellfish or pork," he announced in English to the waiter whose English proficiency had only been revealed through the word "sit."

He and Li Wei made the point, loudly, that they were hosting this party of their "new Jewish friends." From the half-empty bottle on the table, it looked like they'd gotten a head start on Shanghai happy hour.

The father was compact, bespectacled, and scholarly looking, wearing a charcoal wool turtleneck under a corduroy jacket. Even drinking, he was also soft spoken, humble, and self-effacing, especially compared to the braggart son. And he used no English name, though he did speak our language.

"That's for young people. To be, what do you say, 'cool'? I'm just a regular Chinese guy. Maybe even Jewish, like you. Li is one of the seven original names Jews were given."

"And one of the most common Chinese names in general," Ruth said under her breath.

I smiled though I wasn't exactly in the mood for a deep "roots" conversation. In truth I probably wasn't in the mood for any of the fake niceties we had to observe with these people. It was at that moment, sitting next to Ruth and listening to the Lis prattle on, that I thought about the phone threat juxtaposed with her near miss on the street and suddenly had to admit to myself that both had made me more uneasy than I'd let on to Simon. Yet, this crazy day had yielded a tiny bit of progress in the search for the Torah. Hearing that F.W. Tang was also looking for it was a breakthrough, the first solid lead. But David had been our first suspect, so I couldn't discount the possibilities of this dinner; the façade of cordiality with our hosts had to be maintained. Somehow, I managed to channel my annoyance with the table discussion toward a strategy of maneuvering it to find out if the Lis knew Tang.

"Yes," Simon said. "David has mentioned that you might be descended from the Kaifeng Jews. But many generations away from practicing, aren't you?"

"Kaifeng Jewish community certainly has hard times," said David, "but coming back. You know about Kaifeng Jews? Long history, since the Silk Road traders. Kaifeng had synagogues for hundreds of years. Now the last one is gone, a hospital is there, and a cistern for a well." He dropped his voice. "Only a few relics remain to be seen. Like a stele with Hebrew on it. From 1663. Hard to find, but my father has one to sell."

I'd read about the inscribed Hebrew stelae, stone tablets much like gravestones, that remained in Kaifeng. It shocked me that the average antique dealer could be legitimately offering one for sale.

"Wouldn't something like that be in the municipal museum there?"

"Not all of them," said Li Wei. "If you're interested . . . "

"Not at the moment," said Simon. "But, tell me, are there any Jews living in Kaifeng today?"

"Man named Moshe Zhang claims to be, but I don't think so. Very sad," said Li Wei.

"Did your family actually come from Kaifeng?" Ruth asked.

"Yes, for sure, on my father's side," he said. "He was born in Shanghai, but his older brothers were born in Kaifeng."

"When did they move to Shanghai?"

"Early 1900s. My grandmother was born here, and she hated living in Henan Province. Too backward and far from a nice city. My grandfather came to Shanghai and worked for her father's business. Eventually took it over. It was a very profitable business, back in the day, as one says."

"And what business was that?" Simon was picking up on my thinking.

At that moment four waiters arrived bearing two platters each that they plunked down on the built-in lazy Susan in front of us. Most were vegetarian. Next to us another waiter ceremoniously fileted a whole deep-fried fish and handed each of us a portion. Once tea and bottles of beer and premium Maotai brand *baijo* appeared, toasts were offered, and the conversation resumed on a different thread, as Helena piped up for the first time.

"David, this is the best restaurant. Thank you."

"Nothing but the best for our Jewish guests from America." He was shouting and already reeked of the gasoline-like liquor.

"And Israel," Helena said, taking her cousin Ruth's hand.

"How is it to be a Chinese Jew in Israel? In case we ever want to go there and be Jewish again," Li Wei said.

Ruth said, "For me it's good, but I get many stares from strangers. And I get stopped longer at airports than my husband or children. But I'm used to it. It's my country. Though under siege right now. And I'm not there..."

Simon plucked his mobile phone from his pocket. "After dinner, Ruth, we'll call. It will still be early enough there."

Ruth smiled at him and continued. "I love Israel, I love being Jewish, and I love being Chinese. By the way, Helena's right. This food is excellent. One thing we don't have in Israel is Chinese food as good as Shanghai's."

We all nodded, mouths full and chopsticks in hand. Simon swung the lazy Susan around for another helping of noodles with bok choy, then restarted the talk.

"So, Li Wei," he said, "you've lived here all your life. Did you or your family associate with any of the Shanghai Jews, maybe do business with them? Do you remember?"

"My grandfather and his father worked occasionally with Jews from the time the Jews first came. They traded . . . "

"Opium?" I asked

"Whatever there was to be traded," Li Wei said. "Later, when Jews built buildings, our family helped them find Chinese contractors and laborers and made sure the work got done. We had the Chinese *guanxi* connections around the city."

"With the government?"

"The government, sure. And the other powerful people here."

"So, the family supported Chiang Kai-shek?" Simon asked.

Li Wei bowed his head and said nothing.

"My father broke with the family and their associates," David said. "As a young man. He became a good Party man, just like Helena's father."

"Weren't your relatives punished by the Communists, or at least deprived of their homes and businesses, even though you were in the Party?"

"No," said Li Wei. "My grandfather was dead by that time. My parents went to Taipei. A group of my father's business associates had bought property there before the war. My father wasn't that wealthy, so he had a job helping them manage the workers. My parents had a good life there, I think, but I never saw them again."

"It must have been unusual for someone from your background to turn to the Communists," I said.

"Not so unusual as you think. I saw things I knew were wrong in the family's business dealings, the way some people treated others. Chiang was a snake. And his wife. The whole Soong family, except for Ching-ling, Madame Sun. She introduced me to Yu Yun, David's mother, at a meeting for teenagers enthusiastic for Mao. Yu Yun was like me, a renegade from her family. Her father was Shanghai's number one dealer in Chinese cabinets and chests. But Yu Yun thought art and fancy things were useless."

"But now you've taken up that same business again," I said. "Did she approve?"

"She died when I was only twelve," David said. "She didn't get to see this new China." He stared down at the plate in front of him and tapped his chopsticks on it.

"Oh, David, I'm so sorry," I said. I'm not sure why but I figured this was the moment to slip in the question.

"By the way, I meant to ask you. Have you ever heard of an antiques dealer in the States called F.W. Tang?"

He tapped again, still looking mournful, and shook his head, mumbling, "No, sorry." Was it wishful thinking, or did his face really redden?

His father started talking again. "My wife, I miss her so. Like you must miss your husband, Mrs. Kovner. It's hard to be alone, isn't it? Too bad Mr. Rieger met you before me."

His voice had dropped to a pathetic whine. He took yet another swig of *baijo* and reached for my hand.

At which point Simon stood up and squeezed my shoulder. "I want to thank you for a wonderful evening, David and Li Wei. We have had a long day, haven't we, Lily?"

As I got up, I saw Helena whisper to Ruth, who then stood and put on her coat.

"I need to take Lily and Simon back to their hotel. So, yes, *xie xie* for this wonderful evening and the delicious dinner."

"Thank God," Simon said as we got out of hearing distance from the table. "Ruth, you know we can get back on our own."

"Of course. But Helena whispered to me that, since David and his father came separately, she hopes he'll take her to the movies. Anyway, I needed to get out of there, too. I still don't like David at all. Or his father."

"Creepy," I said.

"Pretty deft way to drop F.W. Tang's name, Lily," Simon said. "Miss Marple would be proud. And the Mossad."

"I still think David knows more than he's saying."

Ruth stayed with us long enough to come up to our room to call Boaz.

"*La-azazeil!*" Damn, in Hebrew. "Voicemail!" She left a quick message and hung up. Grabbing the one-channel TV remote, she said, "Maybe there's news."

A talking head read from a script Ruth translated. "China supports the Coalition, Saddam should leave Kuwait. Nothing about Israel. I've got to get some sleep. See you tomorrow, you two."

We never got around to telling her about the phone threat. Which was just as well. She had enough on her mind.

Just after Ruth left, Jennifer Wong called. She suggested it would be better to talk in the lobby rather than on the phone. She came down dressed in a grey sweat suit and sneakers. When we told her F.W. Tang had visited Professor Pang and inquired about an old Torah a few months ago, she looked both relieved and puzzled at the same time.

"Tang's involvement in this doesn't surprise me at all. But what I can't figure out is how he pulled it off. He's been under surveillance in the States for months and he didn't even leave San Francisco until the day after you did, Mrs. Kovner."

"By then the Torah had been missing for at least two weeks," I said.

"Exactly. He must have accomplices here."

"In other developments today," Simon said, "Lily's cousin, Ruth, was nearly run down by a pack of bike-riders that looked like they were aiming right toward her. Which they were, according to a threatening phone call when we got back to the hotel late this afternoon."

Jennifer asked, "What exactly did the caller say? And was it a man or woman?"

"A man speaking English with a Chinese accent who told Lily that the note in San Francisco should have been enough, but now with today's near miss attack on her 'friend,' we should certainly stop searching for the Torah. Then I got on, asked who it was, and the voice said 'you and the ladies' should stop."

"Whoever is behind this sure has help here," Jennifer said. "To organize a pack of bikes aimed at your cousin. She must have been scared to death."

I asked Jennifer if the Chinese government authorities were involved in the investigation against F. W. Tang.

"If so," I said, "you need to be really careful about the Torah that's gone missing. It's highly sensitive and confidential, because Ruth's uncle, Mr. Chen, was entrusted to keep the Torah safe until the government plans to return it to Israel next year."

"Not to worry, Lily. The only information shared with the Chinese relates to our suspicions about Tang's antique smuggling. If there's any sign that he's taking anything out of the country, the Chinese customs people are alerted to pounce. Other than that, I'm on my own—with surveillance backup provided by the US consulate here in Shanghai. We're not exactly the Mossad, of course . . . "

She laughed, not knowing how ironic her little joke was.

"Tang's got to be too sharp to attempt to leave China with any contraband in his possession," said Simon.

"That's why we've got him on surveillance, to find out who he's working with here."

"Check out a David Li." He fished into his pocket and drew a business card out of a small notebook. Handing it to her, he said, "Li Dawei in Chinese. He sells Chinese furniture and so-called antiques, too. We think he's involved, although he denied knowing Tang. We just had dinner with him and his father, Li Wei. To me it sounded like the father's family business, in the heyday of Shanghai, was to grease the wheels for the mob here, maybe even the Green Gang, and that continued when a lot of them fled to Taipei. Doesn't Tang come from that kind of background?"

"Absolutely," Wong said, reaching for David's card. "You guys are good. I will get right on this with the American consulate."

100

Chapter 7

When we returned to the hotel after our *al fresco* breakfast the next morning, Concierge Christina hailed me over to the main desk.

"Oh, Mrs. Kovner, I just took a message for you and put it in your box. Here it is."

The message read, "Call Mr. Xu. Information about Tang." Back in the room we called the phone number on the message but got no answer.

"Let's just go over there," I said. "I want to do some shopping, anyway, and I think the Friendship Store is near his shop."

When we arrived at the antiques market a mere thirty minutes later, we saw police and emergency vehicles parked at skewed angles on the street and on the grounds of the market itself—alongside Mr. Xu's shop. There was a crowd gathered in front, and Simon led the way clearing a path for us to get to the entrance. However, we were stopped and blocked by a couple of skinny and dour policemen presiding over a makeshift barrier of sawhorses and rope. Their expressionless faces and avoidance of eye contact reminded me of the Queen's Guard in London. Of course, the resemblance ended there; the olive drab police uniforms just didn't compete with the snappy gold-buttoned red tunics and the fuzzy black hats.

The younger antique dealers, gulping some steamy liquid from large cups between drags on their cigarettes, surrounded us, gathered in unaccustomed silence and, like us, forbidden to enter the shop. Gesturing toward the shop door, Simon tried to ask one of them what happened. We didn't expect an answer in English. But the return gesture was unmistakable in any language.

"Xu," the man said, before pointing to his heart and acting out a fake fall to the ground.

"Dead?" I said. Rhetorically, I thought.

"Yes, dead," said a tall, bespectacled woman who had emerged from the shop and passed by as I'd spoken. She looked about forty and wore a uniform jacket similar to that of the policemen, but her pants were surgical scrubs.

"Doctor?" Simon asked. "You speak English, right? Can you tell us what happened?"

"Not authorized," she said. "Man dead. Old man. All I can say."

She moved on, toward to a car on the street, and we just stood there.

"Simon, do you think Mr. Xu just keeled over from natural causes, or maybe someone killed him?"

"He wasn't young. Are you thinking murder? Lily, perhaps you're letting your imagination run a bit wild, don't you think?"

"But his phone message said 'information about Tang.' After the threats, the bike attack on Ruth, and remember poor Helen Wolf . . . "

I'd consulted with Helen Wolf, an art historian and former Monuments (Wo)Man, during Afikomen. When I arrived at her flat in London for an appointment, I found her dead. Briefly, I was a bit of a suspect, until an autopsy pronounced her a victim of accidentally overdosing herself with morphine from a stent for cancer treatment. Later, the overdose was revealed to be murder and in fact related to my quest for the Seder plate. And, even dead, Helen turned out to be key to solving the mystery.

"I felt so guilty about Helen," I said. "It would be terrible if Mr. Xu died because of looking for the Torah. But at least in London I could speak with the authorities, and we eventually found out what happened. Thanks to the Mossad. We will probably never know about Mr. Xu."

"Nothing we can do now," said Simon. "Still want to shop for gifts?"

"No, I'm not in the mood now. Let's go back to the hotel. Maybe Jennifer Wong can contact the local police about this."

We rushed back to the Jin Jiang and called Jennifer's room to no avail. So I went downstairs and left a written message asking her to call us later in the evening. It was frustrating to feel so isolated from information and so disadvantaged at being able to get it. For Simon this was especially difficult. Back in the room we could only speculate about what Mr. Xu was going to tell us.

"I think Tang might have come to him and asked about the Torah," I said.

"But, if already Tang stole the Torah, or had it stolen, what would he want to ask about?"

"Good point. Maybe he wanted Mr. Xu to help him work on the Torah, especially the case. Mr. Xu did seem like a champion polisher, after all. That gong was like a mirror."

"That's a possibility. But a dead Mr. Xu won't be shining anything up again. You know, Lily, he might really have just had a massive heart attack very suddenly."

"I don't know. The timing is just too eerie for me to accept that. On the one hand, I hope you're right. On the other, either way Mr. Xu is dead, which is a shame for him and another dead end—ooh, sorry, I really didn't mean to say that—for us. His mention of Tang made me think we were getting somewhere."

When the phone rang, we figured it was either Jennifer Wong or another threat. This time it was Ruth telling us she was going with her aunt and uncle to a doctor's appointment at two-thirty, and we should come to the Chens' at five.

Before we could even touch the buzzer, Ruth opened the door.

"I'm so glad you're here. It's been a nightmare all day. My aunt and uncle are completely paranoid. Since that banquet they went to last night they've been consumed by the thought that everyone they know in the government who was there stared at them accusingly. I know they were up all night. I was, too. I could hear Auntie and Uncle alternating between crying and screaming, and the smell of smoke oozed out their bedroom door to the whole house, I swear. Helena got home late and slammed her door. Joey woke up and whimpered half the night. Today Auntie felt sick—that's why we went to the doctor—and it turns out her blood pressure was sky high."

"Where are they now?" From the overflowing ashtrays and rank odor I expected to find them just beyond the entry hall in the parlor, where Ruth was pointing us as she took our coats.

"Upstairs, trying to rest. It's finally quiet. Ayi has made dinner for all of us, but I told her to just feed Joey and to put the rest away for my aunt and uncle to eat later. I really need to get out of here for a while. With her here, I don't have to worry about leaving them."

"Just as well they're resting," said Simon. "We need to get something done without discussing it with your aunt and uncle. We didn't have such a good day either."

"Really? Why? What happened? I'm sorry—I'm so absorbed with things here . . . "

"Mr. Xu is dead," I said. "The antiques dealer. He left us a message this morning to call him for 'information about Tang.' We called, and when no one answered, we went over to the market. There was a crowd in front, police barriers. Someone gestured a heart attack. A police doctor walking by said Xu was dead, but she wasn't authorized to say more. I'm convinced he was murdered, or at least helped along on the road to death by Tang or his henchmen."

"Oh, Lily, I don't want to think that way, but you may be right. It sure sounds like Tang gets around," Ruth said. "It's almost as if he's tracking us. He must be involved in the Torah theft somehow. But it just doesn't add up, because the Lis said they don't know him, and I still can't help but think David and his father are mixed up in this, too."

"What about David and his father? What do you mean they're mixed in this?"

We hadn't even heard Helena come into the house so we didn't know how long she'd been standing under the arch that led from the foyer to this parlor. She had Joey by the hand but whirled him around and sent him scurrying upstairs with a pat on his backside.

"Why are you talking about them, Ruth?"

"Oh, Helena, we were talking about this man, Freddy Tang—F. W.— whom we think has something to do with the Torah's disappearance. He's an antiques dealer in the States. Maybe you don't remember, but we asked David and Li Wei if they knew him and they said they didn't . . . "

"And you don't trust David and his father, so you think they must be lying to you about knowing this Tang guy? And they all stole the Torah together? That's it, isn't it? You don't trust David and Li Wei." Turning on her heels and running up the stairs, she shot back, "That means you don't trust me either."

Ruth's gaze followed her younger cousin's upward flight, then turned back toward us. She shrugged and rolled her eyes.

"Aren't you going to go after her?" said Simon.

"Nah," Ruth said. "It's just temporary. Reminds me of me as teenager, even though Helena is older and a mother herself. Not that I had either the luxury of throwing a tantrum or an audience for it. I was pretty much on my own at a state school after my mother was sent away for 're-education' to a peasant's life in the south."

"She may not be a teenager, but Helena is acting like an adolescent," I said. "She reminds me of Elizabeth about age fifteen. Not a memory I'm fond of."

"You're right, but she's in love, and David not only accepts Joey, he does seem to truly care for the boy, which is really important to her, since my aunt and uncle disapproved so much of her husband and at the time gave her a terrible time about having a baby with 'that criminal,' as they called him. But David disappoints Helena sometimes as a boyfriend. Makes promises and breaks them. Last night, after we left the restaurant, he told her forget the movie, he had work to do. And Helena's a smart girl. Deep down she's probably worried herself there may be reason to suspect David. She'll be okay later."

"Ruth," Simon said, "If your aunt and uncle aren't going out, why don't you see if Helena wants to come with us for dinner?"

"Good idea," Ruth said as she rose to go upstairs. "I'll tell her we're going to the new restaurant on Rujin Lu. It's supposed to be very cool. Not that Helena is, but she's trying . . . "

An hour later we were sitting at a restaurant named, appropriately for its French Concession location, *Le Petit Garçon*, and located in what looked from the outside like a miniature version of a château. The dining rooms that flanked both sides of a large entry area with high ceilings and a marble floor were thoroughly Chinese, from their round tables of varying sizes and old Shanghai posters decorating the walls to the table settings replete with small teacups, chopsticks, and what we consider appetizer-size plates.

"David has mentioned this place many times," Helena said. "The food is supposed to be excellent. And it's so beautiful in this old house. They say it belonged to a French diplomat."

Such enthusiasm was rare for Helena. She'd not only recovered from her melodrama at the house but had done herself up as if she expected David or some other Prince Charming to appear any minute. The effect of newly washed and styled hair, makeup, and a red silk blouse with its scooped neckline accented by a string of pearls was a considerable improvement over the mousy, harried young mother we'd seen earlier. In fact, I was struck by how much she looked like Ruth, despite Ruth's mixed parentage.

We let Helena order dinner, and she was clearly flattered by this display of confidence in her and by Simon's attention, in particular. My swain was nothing if not charming. He raised his glass of beer, clinked hers, and proposed a toast just as the first course, Shanghai soup dumplings, arrived.

"To Helena, our special guest tonight. *Gombei* and *l'chaim*—that means 'to life' in Hebrew."

She blushed and nodded as we four clinked and took a sip. "We haven't had much chance to really get to know you, Helena," Simon continued. "We've been so busy with other things. It's nice to have this evening just with you. Last night was pleasant, too, with David and his father. They seem very nice. How long have you known David?"

"Three months, sir." The sheepishness was creeping back into her voice.

"No need to be so formal. Just call me Simon." He bit into a dumpling, and a drop of soup escaped his mouth. "Oops. This must be why they call them soup dumplings. Sorry." He laughed and wiped his lip and chin with a flimsy red paper napkin.

"Here's how you do it so no soup drips out," Helena said.

She proceeded to demonstrate the technique of coordinating the first nibble of dough resting on a small spoon held in the left hand by maneuvering chopsticks in the right to lift it toward the mouth without leaking soup, then to deposit a manageably smaller, but still stuffed, sac inside, where the tongue would deflate it and draw out soup—lips sealed. Our gentle bravos and light applause thrilled her enough to take a little bow with her head and upper body.

Pumped up by our obvious approval, it was Helena herself who restarted the conversation.

"I like that David is close to his father. And also maybe Jewish. Like you two. And Ruth." Her older cousin took her hand and squeezed it, then leaned over to kiss Helena, whose awe for Ruth was palpable.

"Your English is excellent, Helena," I said. "You must be a very good student. Ruth was, too, I imagine."

She held a finger up to signal she'd answer when she finished the final phase of devouring another dumpling. Then she opened her mouth to the broadest grin ever.

"Thank you so much. That's the highest compliment, to be like Ruth," she said. Now Ruth grinned and blushed.

"And you even look alike," said Simon. "Both beautiful."

Ruth studied Helena and said, "Thanks, Simon. I'm flattered, too. But she has twenty years to start getting these grey hairs . . . "

"What grey hairs? All two of them?" Hair color was something I noticed.

"Do you plan to study abroad, too, like Ruth did? Or maybe marry David and stay here?"

"Marry David? Why do you ask about this? Has he said anything to you?" Helena's blush now seemed to be combined with shock. "I want to be a scientist or a doctor. He's a businessman. This could be a good combination, but I don't know. He never talks of marriage but he's so good to Joey. It would be nice. No point in giving up my studies. Anyway, I think . . . I think he's only . . . "

All of a sudden she started to cry, but pitiably, not like the outburst in the house. Still, she was sobbing hard enough to attract the attention of diners at surrounding tables, who started to stare. Ruth reached over with to embrace and comfort her.

"Helena, Helena, tell me. What's wrong? You can tell me anything," she said glancing over at us with an expression that asked where did this come from.

Helena completely reverted to Chinese, which gushed out like a flood of soup from a giant dumpling. Ruth encouraged her to take a breath every ten words or so, then started translating. As the story poured forth, she became more and more agitated herself.

"She fears David stole the Torah. He's always talking to her about being Jewish, so she opened the cabinet and showed him the case. She asked him, 'you know what's in here?' He said, 'Of course, this is Torah, the holy writings of Jews. In Kaifeng, where my family is from, they had Torahs.' She even let him take it out of the case and unroll it a little before putting it back. She also says he whistled when he first saw the silver case with all the jewels and he asked if they were real. Joey was there. Her father had once taken it out to show him."

Now Helena took a deep breath. Ruth wiped her cousin's eyes with a tissue and waited for her to start talking again. Helena sighed and continued.

"She says her parents would kill her if they knew she did this. They know sometimes David comes over to take Joey to the park or to their play program. That's how they met—Helena registered Joey for a program for fatherless kids . . . "

"Big Brothers/Big Sisters of Shanghai," I said.

"Yes," Ruth continued, though I'm not sure she caught the reference, "Anyway, even Ayi was gone, shopping for food. Then, a few days later, David came over again when just Helena and Joey were there. He'd called and asked if they were alone. He said he really missed them and wanted to take them somewhere special."

Ruth, though dry-eyed, seemed to be getting so upset she couldn't keep up the nearly simultaneous translation.

"Helena," she said, "do you think you can switch to English, so that Lily and Simon can hear first-hand what you have to say? I'm getting out of breath trying to translate for them. You're speaking so fast."

"Okay. I will try. I don't know which will be worse for me, if David took the Torah or my parents find out he visited when they weren't home.

"That day, the second time, was about a week after I first showed him the Torah. It had been cold and it snowed the night before; Joey had never seen snow before. David said we should get Joey some ice skates and take him skating on the lake at Remnin Park. I said I had a lab report to type up for about a half hour or more, but we could go out after that. He said, 'no problem,' he'd come over and wait. First, I heard him playing with Joey downstairs, then it got quiet, and Joey came back up to get his jacket and hat and mittens. The next thing I heard, after David was there only fifteen minutes, he called up to tell me he forgot he was supposed to meet a friend and he'd call me later."

I said, "So that's when you think he took the Torah?"

Helena nodded and said, "I got upset. And you can imagine how upset Joey was. David didn't call again until late that night. Said he and his friend had been drinking and talking and he didn't realize how late it was. We did make a date for the next night, and he apologized for the day before and took Joey skating later that week. This was the time of regular New Year, early January, about three weeks ago. A few days later Father checked the cabinet and found the Torah gone. Oh, Ruth, what can I do? They'll never forgive me."

"Helena," I said, "when your father first discovered the Torah missing, did you think right away that it might have been David who took it?"

"No, not really. How could I? He's almost as good to Joey and me as . . .

She mumbled a name that must have been that of her late husband.

"I didn't want to think bad of him. But since last night that's all I've thought about. That's why I yelled and cried when I came home today. Just thinking how much he and his father talked about Jews and how nice they were being to you and Simon and Ruth. And I never heard David say anything before about his father's Party connections. That bothered me, when the father says he was a big shot like Father. Father's never heard of him."

"Which doesn't mean anything, does it?" said Ruth. "Millions of people are Party members."

"No, but Father had checked on the family when I first met David. Li Wei's just a member, not in any important position. So, I knew Li Wei was lying about that last night. Then I wondered what else he and David were lying about? All day I've been so worried, couldn't stop thinking about this . . . "

By this time we'd been served a refreshing mango pudding following (only) four courses. It had been delivered along with the bill, and Simon was counting and sorting yuan to pay it. Helena hadn't touched her dessert, which Ruth urged her to taste.

"It's very good, Helena, like the whole dinner that you ordered. Calm yourself down and at least eat a little of it before we go home. We will stand by you with your parents. Don't worry."

The younger woman ate a few spoonsful of the orange-colored fluff. A cab was waiting in front of the restaurant. The ride back to the Chens was silent, except for Helena's occasional sniffle and Ruth's whispered words of comfort.

"It will be okay. Don't worry." None of us were convinced, but we tried to keep cheerful faces as the taxi pulled up to the house.

"I'll handle this," Ruth said.

"Of course," said Simon. "Thank God," he muttered to me. I squeezed his gloved hand. After a couple of days of warmer and dryer weather, the evening wind was biting, and pellets of sleet had iced the walkway to the front door. One had to creep gingerly to avoid slipping.

"The weather fits perfectly," I said. "I'm chilled, even under this heavy coat. And now ice under foot."

The Chens were sitting on opposite ends of the sofa in the parlor so that each could commandeer a personal ashtray. The transition from the frosty wet air outside to the acrid cloud of smoke overpowering the room made me start to cough as soon as I walked in. Ayi deposited our coats on the bench in the foyer and we settled ourselves on chairs arrayed across from Auntie and Uncle.

Simon, the born-again nonsmoker of less than a year, blinked his eyes several times in the haze. Helena, whom I'd never seen smoking herself, seemed as oblivious as her parents to the adverse effects of their nicotine habits. Ruth sniffled and cleared her throat before diving into the sea of issues she'd promised Helena she'd confront. Helena reciprocated by translating for us.

"Auntie and Uncle, you should have gone with us to the restaurant. Helena ordered us a wonderful dinner." Here our translator smiled and blushed. "I hope you are feeling better than this afternoon. Did you eat something?"

Auntie nodded yes, while taking a drag. Uncle had just tapped out a butt and was lighting up again—he neither said nor gestured anything. Simon and I glanced at each other. This wasn't going to be fun.

"Auntie," Ruth continued, "Helena told us something that it's important for you to know . . . "

Both the Chens abruptly switched their attention to their daughter, who stopped translating for us and said something in Chinese to Ruth. From my cousin's hands held up, she was telling Helena she'd handle it.

"Anyway," Ruth went on in English, "her friend David was talking so much about being Jewish that one day she showed him the Torah when he was over here visiting. And another time after that she thinks he might have had an opportunity to take it when no one was around."

The aunt and uncle looked at each other and then at Ruth and then at Helena, first moaning as if in pain and then screaming words no one translated for us. Uncle got up, cigarette in his right hand, and swatted Helena on the cheek with his left. Ruth rose and pushed herself between him and his daughter. With a look of disgust, she wagged her finger and said, "*Fei*, no!" The old man backed off, sank again onto the sofa. Both he and his wife were still talking nonstop to Helena, who interjected occasionally either verbally or by nodding her head.

Ruth looked at us and explained.

"They're berating her for being alone, with Joey here, with David and about the Torah. Auntie says she doesn't know which is worse. Uncle says the Torah. What will happen to him when the government finds out? And the family's honor? So much loss of face. Helena's honor. To be in the house alone with this man, any man, and her own child. A slut! Who does she think she is? A movie star?"

We were relieved when Uncle stopped talking long enough to cough, which gave Simon an opportunity to steer the conversation toward another suspect.

"Do either of you know the name F.W. Tang, Freddy Tang? We think this man is also connected to the theft of the Torah."

After Ruth had translated, Uncle shook his head and sputtered something we took to be "never heard of him." But Auntie Chen opened up in English.

"Old Shanghai money, but dirty money. Chiang Kai-shek friends. Green Gang, too. Father very bad man. Hurt women. Nina's mother. Son tried to date Suling before she met Erich. Your grandfather wouldn't hear of her going with someone from such a low-class family."

A European Jewish refugee like my uncle was a more desirable match for a young Chinese woman in postwar Shanghai? That certainly constituted quite an indictment of Tang and his family.

"Auntie," I asked, "do you think Tang would have any connection to David and his father? Maybe from the old days? Even though Li Wei isn't the very important Party guy he claims to be, he did admit that his family background was KMT, supporters of Chiang."

Auntie shook her head while shrugging her arms. "Who knows? Probably some connections remain. That crowd no good, ever. It's possible, but I didn't know Li Wei then. Just the Tangs."

Mr. Chen spoke up with animated hand gestures of his own, coupled with gruff shouting. Ruth translated when he rested.

"He says, 'those old KMT guys are back now, even from Taiwan.' Money is all that counts now, it's the new source of *guanxi*—connections—business is all the government cares about now. No matter whose money it is."

The aunt waved her hand and put her finger to her lips as Ayi rolled out a scratched rosewood cart bearing a tarnished silver tea service monogrammed

MEJ

Ruth noticed me studying the initials.

"Miriam Ezra Joseph," she said. "The original mistress of this house. It was a wedding gift to her as a bride, and she gave it to my mother as a wedding gift. This coming from the Josephs' own possessions was treasured much more than a new one would have been."

"Of course."

"It's Georgian silver," said Simon. "Too bad it's so tarnished."

Perhaps not polishing the set was a way to uphold the Mao's principles and Uncle's Party face, even while using such a bourgeois household item from Shanghai's glittering past. Like the big house.

After all the hubbub of the past half hour, tea—served in the customary tiny porcelain cups, despite the elegant presentation—brought temporary silence to the group. Even Helena looked more relaxed, her brow smooth and her mouth almost smiling a little, the calm after the storm.

But we all knew that her revelation had to be pursued. Ruth put down her cup and quietly asked her cousin, in English, if she knew where David lived. Maybe, if he did take the Torah, it would be at his house? Did he live with his father?

"Yes," Helena said. "In a very big flat."

"Have you been there?'

"Yes, it's on Fuxing Lu, near the Sun Yat-sen house. A renovated flat. David says some Jewish family named Schutkin that owned theatres lived in that building on the whole top floor."

That her parents remained quiet when Helena revealed she'd been to David's flat was a testament to her father's complete ignorance of English and to her mother's lack of energy or will to further reproach her daughter. At least it saved us from yet another explosion. At this point both Chens did seem blessedly distracted while Helena lamented about David just using her and Joey to get the Torah. He hadn't even called her since dinner last night. When Ruth asked if she had any upcoming plans to get together with him, her cousin shook her head dejectedly.

Simon had an idea. "Why don't we just go over there right now?"

"I don't think that's a good idea without some pretext," I said. "Plus, we should go back to the hotel and try to find Detective Wong first. Ruth and Helena, why don't you come with us? Maybe we will still be able to pay David and Li Wei a visit tonight."

In the cab we discussed how we'd gain entrée to the Li residence on a friendly basis.

"Remember what Li Wei told us about the stele from Kaifeng?" I said. "Maybe we could call and say we're interested in it."

Luckily, Jennifer was at the desk cashing travelers cheques when our entourage charged into the lobby. I told her we needed to talk, and she joined the rest of us upstairs in our room for a quick update.

"We have a plan," I said, "to call the Lis and say we're interested in buying the antique stele from Kaifeng."

"He wants to sell you a stele from Kaifeng?" Her eyes widened at the prospect of another smuggling suspect.

"It's got to be a fake," Simon said. "But it's a way to get into his house."

"Absolutely. Make the call."

Helena provided the number, and Simon picked up the phone. After opening pleasantries, he cut to the chase quickly.

"When you said it was authentic, from 1663, I figured this was the one that's been missing for years. So, I thought it over and decided it's too special to pass up. Can we come over to see it tonight? . . . Oh, I understand. . . . Tomorrow. Seven o'clock. Yes. Thank you."

Simon hung up and faced a frustrated group of women. "He says tonight's not good. He has to go out. Tomorrow's better. Nothing we can do but wait."

Deflated, we all sat down. Someone had to break the spell of disappointment.

"I did some reading on Kaifeng before I left New York," I said, "but I didn't get this much background. I'm not surprised, but how did you learn about the stele?"

"Before I left Israel I went over to Beit Hatfutsot and spent some time with my friend, Rifkah Barlev, who's a curator there. I wanted some information on Jews in China."

Beit Hatfutsot is the Museum of the Diaspora. It opened on the campus of Tel Aviv University in the 1970s. Its exhibits trace the path of Jewish wanderings and settlement throughout the world.

"I haven't been to that museum in years. Does it have artifacts from Kaifeng?"

"The museum itself isn't exactly a treasure trove of authentic pieces or documents, but the history it depicts is sound. Rivka showed me a replica of one of the Kaifeng synagogues and told me about four stelae—that's the plural of stele . . . "

"What's a stele?" said Helena.

"It's an inscription on stone tablets that look like gravestones," Simon answered. "There were four in particular known to have been erected during the heyday of the Kaifeng Jewish community. They commemorated the opening of different synagogue structures and recorded family names in the community and the Jewish practices they observed. Three of the four are in a museum the city of Kaifeng opened a few years ago. One, made in 1663, was lost."

"But you don't think Li Wei really has it, do you?"

"Of course not."

Chapter 8

Walking in from my swim the next morning, I found Simon on the phone, this time speaking Hebrew. Mine is not fluent enough to catch his rapid-fire conversation. It must have been a business call with his Tel Aviv office, though it was the middle of the night in Israel.

"What's happening?" I asked him when he hung up

"If you mean in Israel, the Scuds are still flying in on a nightly basis," he said.

"Who in Israel is on the phone at this hour?"

He didn't answer that but said, "Poor Ruth. I don't know how she can stand to be away. She must be very conflicted. She looks so worn down. Let's hope we get to the bottom of this soon, so she can go home to Boaz and the kids. Come on, let's go down to meet Jennifer. We're late."

We'd made a plan to have breakfast at the hotel with Jennifer Wong, forfeiting for the cause the delicious greasy repast on the streets of Shanghai. The Jin Jiang's buffet featured everything from rubbery dumplings and congee—thick Chinese rice porridge—to made-to-order omelets and a huge display of the noodles, miso soup, dried fish, and pickles that catered to the palates of the Japanese businessmen dominating the dining room.

Detective Wong was already there, drinking coffee when we approached the table. After visiting the buffet, we discussed the forthcoming visit to David's house. We all sensed it could be key to unraveling the disappearance of the Torah, as well as to Wong's investigation into smuggling. It could also be very dangerous.

"I suppose involving the Chinese authorities isn't a good idea," Simon said. "The Chens are so sensitive to any word leaking out about the missing Torah."

"I *am* a cop, you know," Jennifer said, the slightest bit of peeve evident in her voice. "And I do have some reciprocal authority from the Chinese government."

Simon looked contrite to make amends with Jennifer, but without revealing the Mossad portion of his resumé. "Can you use a gun here, Jennifer?"

"Yes. The Chinese know I'm here looking for Freddy. They consider him evil, and very threatening, so they've granted me permission to use a weapon, if necessary, at least for self-defense. 'However you define that' are the precise words my Shanghai police contact used when he gave me the official permit letter. I had to take my gun over to the department office to be inspected."

All this talk about guns made me squirm, and I nearly choked on the ultra-sweet faux orange juice I was drinking. "Do you think it will come to that—gunfire?"

"I certainly hope not," Jennifer said.

"One can never be too cautious in a situation like this," said Simon with an air of professional authority that might have baffled Detective Wong, though she didn't question it. Perhaps she divined the diamond trade to be as dangerous as "a situation like this."

"Speaking of which, how could I have forgotten?" I said. "Mr. Xu, the antiques dealer we met, is dead. He left us a message yesterday saying he had something wanted to tell us, something about Tang, but when we got to his shop, he'd apparently just died of a heart attack. Do you think your Shanghai police connections can give us any information about his death?"

"Lily thinks he was murdered. By Tang or his people," said Simon.

"Could be," said Jennifer. "There are a million Mr. Xus in Shanghai, at least. I'm sure you have a card you can give me with his name and the address of the shop."

"Of course," I said, fishing it out of my bag and handing it to her.

"Let me see if I can find anything out. I rather doubt it. If it looked like a heart attack and your Mr. Xu wasn't young, I can't imagine that the local police would take the time to probe too much into his sudden death. But I will call my contact among Shanghai's finest."

It was a nerve-wracking day, and the weather didn't help. A steady drizzle chilled us so much that it seemed to penetrate right through our coats. Simon and I took a taxi to meet Ruth and Helena on Nanjing Lu, the main shopping street in downtown Shanghai.

Ruth looked like she hadn't slept in a week. Her normally bright blue eyes were puffy, and baggy pouches hung under them. Helena's attention was focused on a window display of cheesy-looking stiletto pumps.

The main shopping area of Nanjing Lu was a messy complex of honky-tonk stores strung along several blocks broken up by pedestrian overpasses. It was hardly Fifth Avenue. Chinese New Year was approaching, and light posts along the thoroughfare were draped in red and gold. Shop windows displayed curly white sheep—the stuffed variety—and posters picturing them.

"What's with all the sheep?" Simon wanted to know.

"This New Year will be the year of the sheep," Helena said.

Of course.

Given the ostensible business reason for our forthcoming call at the Li residence, we thought taking gifts would be an appropriately misleading touch. Simon and I couldn't imagine what, and our initial glimpses at the shop windows didn't help. A stuffed sheep just didn't seem to fit the occasion. A sacrificial lamb—maybe.

Curiously, it was Helena, though also red-eyed as well as grim and sulky, who seemed to take on the management of this project, and she marched ahead of us like a general leading troops to battle. Her despair over David's deceitfulness and the possibility she was responsible for the theft of the Torah suddenly seemed to energize her. A woman scorned but on a mission. She darted into and out of stores for block after block, shaking her head no, before we'd even caught up. Finally, she found what she was looking for.

"Like a bamboo plant will change anything," Simon said as we waited for the oversized specimen she picked out and he paid for—the tallest and most expensive in the place—to be elaborately wrapped in red cellophane and gold ribbon.

"Why this?" I asked.

"Bamboo is synonymous with vitality and longevity," said Ruth. "It grows in a barren mountain region, stubborn and tough. It's a good gift for men. Helena's choice is very complimentary to our hosts. Should throw them off the track of what we're up to."

Helena looked pleased with herself. She even managed an uncharacteristic little joke.

"Yes, but too bad it's not poisonous."

Then she bade us good-bye and caught a bus for the university, promising to be home at five-thirty to prepare for the visit. That left the three of us on the crowded sidewalk encircling the cellophane-encased tree to protect it from the masses rushing by. Simon took care to keep the ungainly pot vertical. The bamboo may have been symbolically correct, but transporting it posed a major logistical challenge. It looked taller than the width of the standard Chinese cab. We saw bus after bus so crammed with passengers that they made sardine cans look roomy; not even this hardiest of specimens would emerge with stalks unbent, assuming we could board with it upright. We didn't dare try to maneuver it across an intersection full of bicyclists.

Ruth was apologetic. "I'm sorry. I know Helena's not the most practical girl. She insisted on picking the gift from the moment we left the house, and I didn't have the heart to say no when she wanted this big plant. But I didn't realize she was going to leave us to handle it. Oy, what a problem!"

"Oy?" Simon and I said in unison. We'd never heard Chinese-Jewish Ruth utter any Yiddish. We all laughed, which helped to lower the tension level.

"We'll manage," said Simon, but with no real conviction.

When we finally hailed a cab, Ruth and I climbed into the back seat, then Simon tilted the bamboo pot sideways, holding the top, and gently eased it diagonally across our laps before getting into the front seat next to the driver. We took it back to the hotel with us, as Ruth said she hadn't exactly told her aunt and uncle where she and Helena were going, just that they were meeting us later, so they knew nothing about the plan for the evening.

By the time we got back to the hotel, it was nearly three o'clock in the afternoon. Both fidgety, we tried making love, our proven activity for relieving tension in more ways than one. But the prospect of what lay ahead that evening dominated our psyches to the point that we had to settle for some tender but unproductive touching and kissing. Arousal evaded us both. Simon was more upset than I, of course.

"I must be really getting old."

"Nah. It happens. I'm not really into it, either. I can't get my mind off . . . "

"What?"

"The gun."

"Lily, I honestly don't expect anyone will be shooting. I can't imagine David having a gun himself or even getting particularly aggressive. He may be devious but he's pretty wimpy."

I wasn't convinced.

Chapter 9

I can't imagine what the locals scurrying along the sidewalk thought of the motley group gathered on a corner huddled around a big red-wrapped "tree" that misty night, but no one gawked or even seemed to glance. They just kept on their way, maneuvering around us.

At precisely 6:55, Jennifer, Ruth, Helena, Simon, and I had met on a corner opposite the building where David and his father lived. Helena pointed out the Li flat on the first level, slightly elevated above the ground. Our position and blazing lights inside afforded a perfect view of David talking on the phone, pacing back and forth, and gesturing with his hands as if engaged in a heated conversation. Suddenly Li Wei came into the room and raised his arms as if to ask what was going on.

We had agreed that Detective Wong would stay outside on the corner. When I saw Simon give her his mobile phone before we ventured across the street, I wondered why but didn't ask. Crossing the street was always daunting in Shanghai, but this passage proved to be especially challenging as we negotiated ourselves and the bamboo tree, evading the bicycles, most of which lacked lights, in the dark.

Li Wei opened the door after Helena rang the bell. From the small foyer we saw David quickly hang up the phone.

"Oh, it's seven o'clock, of course. Come in," said Li Wei. "David, our visitors."

David gave Helena a slight peck on the forehead. Li Wei took our coats and directed us into the parlor we'd seen from the street. Simon handed the bamboo plant to David, who plunked it down, still wrapped, on the floor in the middle of the room and muttered some thanks. He pointed us to a grouping of three chairs and a sofa, all looking new but tacky, with square lines and lime green wool upholstery that seemed comically out of place in a room with 1920s Art Deco fan-shaped sconces lit on its lavender walls, white painted molding, and a black-and-white checkerboard floor like at the Sun Yat-sen home I had toured nearby.

A red plastic tray holding a teapot and small blue cups, a bowl of peanuts, and a bottle of *baijo* and small shot glasses sat on a faux Danish modern teak table with metal legs in front of the sofa. But the jumpy demeanor of both David and his father told us our invitation had been issued at a better time than this appointed hour of arrival. They hovered over us as we sat down.

"It's very gracious of you to invite us over," said Simon, "and we hope you will join us for dinner in a little while, so we can reciprocate your hospitality. We would like to take you to Jade Garden Restaurant."

Li Wei spoke as he leaned down to pour the diesel fuel liquor into the shot glasses, "Oh, I'm afraid this is unfortunate timing. Since we spoke to you earlier, an important meeting came up for us later this evening. So sorry to only have time to drink a toast to you and wish you a safe return to America . . . "

"And Israel," David said bowing to Ruth. "*Gombei*," as he gulped the dreadful stuff.

"*Gombei, l'chiam*," said Li Wei, showing off.

Simon said, "I know you have to go, but I assume you remember we did plan to look at that stele from Kaifeng."

"Oh, that, yes, of course," David said.

It was hard to believe that a potential sale could have magically evaporated from his mind. He hastened over to the corner behind him, where a narrow and rectangular object covered by a scrubby looking brown blanket was leaning against the wall. He lifted it onto a table and whisked off the blanket to reveal what looked like a rough granite tombstone about three feet high and one foot wide. An inscription was carved in both Hebrew letters and Chinese characters. Devoid of any scratches or dents, it was in remarkably mint condition for something purported to be at least over three hundred years old in a country not known for high standards of upkeep. Simon took out his glasses to examine the plaque, posturing just so, to appear the connoisseur and scholar he is.

"Hmm, hmm, very interesting."

"If you're interested," Li Wei said, "We can make you a great deal. But tonight's not a good time. Tomorrow, maybe?" Both he and David were fidgeting, obviously anxious to leave.

I gulped down a mini-cup of tea and asked to use the restroom. David led me to a small hallway behind the main foyer, beyond which I could see the kitchen. Thankfully, this being a twentieth-century western-built property, no squatting was required. When I emerged, I faced a half-open door. Behind it was an old-fashioned pantry room, all shelves and wooden cabinets of varying sizes. A huge bag of rice was the only edible provision I saw. It was nearly impossible to walk into this room, as lined up along the floor were several cases of *baijo* and cartons containing kitschy looking tea and incense pots colored green but clearly not jade, laughing Buddhas, black cloisonné snuff boxes, and blue porcelain plates. And another three "Kaifeng stelae."

Quite the antique business David and his father ran. There was a tall cabinet close to the entry accessible to my reach. As I started to open it, I felt a hand grabbing my shoulder, fingers digging into my skin.

"What are you doing?"

Li Wei stood behind me. Without waiting for an answer—not that one would have come to me off the top of my head—he pushed the cabinet door shut with his other hand, swung me around toward the hall, keeping his grip on my shoulder all the way back to the parlor, where he led me to my previous seat and pushed me down into it. Conversation I'd heard en route stopped. The so-called one-of-a-kind stele now leaned against the side of a dusty spinet piano.

"I asked you what you were doing opening a closet door in my house."

Before I could open my mouth, Helena stood up and pointed at David, who was sitting on the edge of a piano bench, one foot shaking nervously. "I know you stole the Jewish Torah from my house. That's what you cared about, not me or Joey." She stayed on her feet glaring down at him.

Flabbergasted by her sudden bravado, the rest of us stared at her but remained speechless.

David's first inclination was to stand up to face Helena and deny her charge. "Helena, how can you say such a thing? I care for you very much. Torah? No, you're wrong. I . . . "

"David, enough!" Li Wei interrupted his son. "Sit down."

The father took a deep breath and addressed us all. "Yes, David took the Torah. But it's ours. It belongs to the Kaifeng Jews. Our ancestors were the ones who brought it on the Silk Road from Baghdad, not the Josephs or the Sassoons or the Hardoons or any of those rich Jews who came to Shanghai to make money by getting Chinese hooked on opium. These Jews stole the Torah from Kaifeng Jews who brought it to show Shanghai Jews they were true to Torah teachings. They brought it in 1902 when Kaifeng Jews visited Shanghai to ask for help to rebuild the Kaifeng synagogue. My father told me about this meeting. His grandfather was one of the Kaifeng elders who came. One son, my great-uncle, let himself be circumcised in Shanghai—fifteen years old this boy was—to prove their loyalty to the faith. Shanghai Jews didn't care. It wasn't enough. These stupid Chinese couldn't be Jewish. Okay to give them little jobs in Jewish companies, but not to treat them as brothers."

"Li Wei," Simon said, "how can you say this Torah was brought to Shanghai by Kaifeng Jews when all the original Kaifeng Torahs were lost in the flood of 1642 and the Kaifeng Jews sold off most they had later?"

Simon stood face-to-face with the man.

"You're wrong, Li Wei," Simon went on. "This Torah came from Baghdad Jews. The Josephs never took it to Hong Kong with them, because they left in a hurry. Ruth's father and mother, who was Mrs. Chen's sister, were supposed to take it, but they couldn't leave, because her mother was pregnant with Ruth and not able to travel. That's how the Chens happened to have it in that house, which was the Josephs' house before. But it's very important that you understand. The Chens were keeping it only a little longer. The government—the Chinese government—needs it for a very special purpose. Soon. This is very, very serious. They must get the Torah back."

"What purpose?" David smirked. "The government is godless. Jews are not important to them. No religion is important to the government. You are just lying to us. You want the Torah for your collection of rare Jewish books."

"David," Helena spoke up again. "Mr. Rieger is telling you the truth. My parents have promised the Torah to the government. It will be bad for them if there's no Torah."

"What purpose could the government possibly have?" Li Wei asked,

"I can't tell you. It's a diplomatic secret," Ruth said, "but it will make you proud to be Jewish and Chinese."

Li Wei didn't respond to this. But his diatribe continued. Now directed toward me.

"And now you insult us, Mrs. Lily, by rummaging through my house. Again, the Chinese are stupid, you think. Stupid enough to keep the precious Torah here. Especially in that fancy decorated case with the precious stones?

A friend, a very honored friend who lives in the US, has it in a safe place, keeping it for us until we can take it back to Kaifeng and place it in a new synagogue he will help us build.

"Your friend Freddy Tang," I said. "Do you think Freddy will help you bring the Kaifeng Jewish community back to life? I can't imagine that. He's a smuggler, a crook. From a long line of criminals. Your family heritage is the honor of the Kaifeng Jews. His—the Green Gang."

"That was long ago. Freddy's father and grandfather, not him."

"I thought you didn't even know this Tang," Helena said.

"No. We do know him," said David. "But our business with him had nothing to do with you."

"Oh, but it does," I said. "Tang's been trying to stop us from finding the Torah every step of the way. He had me followed me since before I left the US to come to China. He threatened me in San Francisco. He's threatened us all here in Shanghai. He went so far as to dispatch a pack of bicycle riders to run down Ruth in the street. He might even have murdered an old antiques dealer we met. Tang's a crook. He's wanted in the States for illegal trafficking of Chinese antiquities. Stealing genuine treasures from China. Like Chiang Kai-shek did when he left for Taiwan. I wouldn't count on Mr. Tang, if I were you. You don't even know where he's keeping the Torah."

"He says it's safer for us if we don't know," David said.

"Sure," said Helena, rising and pointing her finger at him, "because the government is supposed to get the Torah. There's a lady detective here from San Francisco ready to arrest Mr. Tang and take him back to the States as a prisoner. What will happen to the Torah then? And to my parents? My father is to deliver the Torah to the government in a few days. If you are sincere about concern for the Torah and the Jews, you must help us get it back. I know already that you're not sincere, David, about your feelings for me, but that is not what's important right now."

"Helena, I'm sorry . . . I . . . " David's lame attempt at a response was met by a disgusted brushoff gesture. Newly empowered, Helena nearly hit him on the chest.

A shocked David joined his father and sat down on an upholstered bench a few feet from the rest of us. Both looked frightened and defeated. David even put his head in his arms, as if he were to begin weeping. Li Wei comforted his son.

"It will be all right." To us he said, "We will help get the Torah back. We have a meeting with Tang tonight."

No wonder they were so anxious for us to leave.

"We're going with you," said Simon.

Li Wei put out his hand, as if to halt traffic. "No, not a good idea. Too risky for you to come with us. Freddy's a dangerous man. We must go alone to see him."

Simon grudgingly agreed, but from his sidelong glance I knew he intended to follow them. He went along with the masquerade and asked when the Lis would contact us about the Torah.

"Tonight," said Li Wei. "We will call you at your hotel. It might be late."

"Sure, sure, that's not a problem," I said. "We'll wait for your call."

We kept up the ruse all the way out the door. Simon signaled to Detective Wong stomping around on the opposite corner to beat the chill. Immediately, she hopped into a cab parked in front of her, signaling another small red one to pull up and wait for us before hers took off after David and Li Wei, who sped away on a motor scooter piloted by the son with the father riding behind him. Our cab miraculously negotiated its way through a small cluster of bikes, picked us up, and followed Jennifer's. Only when we arrived did we find out that our "taxis" were unmarked Shanghai police cars and our drivers local detectives working with Jennifer.

In less than ten minutes we turned into a driveway that wound through manicured grounds to a sumptuous white house that sat well beyond street view.

Ruth gasped. "This is a famous mansion. Part of the Soong family compound. You know, Madame Chiang's family. Bankers. Thieves, too. They raped the country financially, profited from many businesses, while their soldiers lacked food and supplies fighting the Japanese and the Communists."

Alighting from the cab, we noticed David's motor scooter parked next to the steps to the door. Lights blazed inside the house, but outside it was dark enough to stand undetected below a window that was cranked open a tad. We could hear loud voices—apparently Freddy and Li Wei arguing—but we had to find a way to get in there.

"Let's just go to the front door and ring the bell," I said.

"Why not?" said Jennifer.

Freddy's version of an *ayi* answering the door was a man well over six feet tall built with a squared-off Mongolian face. Genghis Khan meets Lurch, the

Addams Family butler. But built like a Sumo wrestler. He opened the door and spoke in Chinese to someone in the house. The round-spectacled face from Jennifer's dossier appeared above a chubby body encased like a sausage in a three-piece charcoal grey suit. A gold watch fob hung across the vest that barely covered a well-fed stomach. Yet, Freddy was surprisingly distinguished looking. And he looked familiar to me. I was trying to place where I'd seen him before. Katz's Deli when I had lunch with Marty? I wasn't sure. Was his interest in stealing a Torah inspired by a fondness for our food? Was Tang also possibly the patriarch of the family I'd seen at the Palace Hotel pool in San Francisco? Again, I couldn't swear to that either, although Detective Wong had said he was staying at my hotel and that could have afforded him the opportunity to send me the death character message.

Tang inclined his head, motioning us to come in. As a welcoming gesture, Lurch Khan stepped out, grabbed Simon by a coat lapel, and yanked him into the house before enveloping first Ruth and me, and then Helena and Jennifer, with his arms and pushing us in.

The enormous green marble foyer faced a massive winding stairway any bride would pine for. Tang stood with Li Wei and David in the archway of a room to the right. They didn't look very happy to see us as Lurch propelled us toward them and into an oak-paneled library, its shelves crammed with porcelain and jade figures but very few books. A giant Victorian desk dominated half the room. Two brown leather couches faced each other, separated by a carved teak table with ivory inset on the top.

At the far wall beyond the couches, open folding doors revealed a row of hanging glass-fronted cabinets containing shelves lined with cocktail and wine glasses and liquor bottles. Set into the marble counter was a sink. A wet bar. But right in front of it, perched on a tall cane-backed chair with a rust-colored velvet seat, was a four foot cylinder of silver sparkling with precious stones that gleamed even in the dimly lit room.

The Torah case.

Breathtaking as it was, there was no time to stop and admire it.

We were deposited on the couches opposite David and Li Wei. Lurch positioned himself next to the Torah. Freddy remained standing.

"Well, look who dropped in for a visit. The treasure hunters from America and Israel." It was the voice I'd heard on the phone. "And there's your treasure. Magnificent, isn't it? Mr. Li here was just asking me when he and his son can take the Torah to Kaifeng to begin rebuilding the synagogue and the Jewish community there." He laughed. "Funny, don't you think?

"The Chinese Jews of Kaifeng. Ha! They still believe they're Jewish. No one in Kaifeng now is Jewish. What a foolish man. That's what they'd call in the States an old wives' tale. You're not Jewish, Li Wei. You're about as Jewish as I am."

"But," David said, "you told us you believed we were Jewish and that you'd get back the Torah for Kaifeng and help us build a synagogue and return our community to honor, after the shame of losing it and being rejected by the Shanghai Jews. A return to practicing our Jewish faith."

David actually spoke with such conviction that Helena's eyes widened and she smiled, impressed to hear him standing up to Tang.

"In Communist China?" Freddy's tone was incredulous. "Do you realize what this Torah is? It's the Ezra Torah. Very old. This Torah was never in Kaifeng. It's from Babylonia, Iraq now. Might have been in India for a while before Shanghai, but never Kaifeng. The case alone is worth a fortune. Madame wants it. I'm taking it to her."

"Madame?" Li Wei was astounded at the mention of this name, but no more so than our team huddled on the couch. "Madame Chiang Kai-shek? You mean that old whore Soong Mei-ling? You're taking the Ezra Torah to Taipei? What for?"

Simon mouthed "Oh, my God."

"Not Taipei. New York," Jennifer muttered, her investigation validated.

"Yes, Madame lives in New York full-time now." Freddy heard her and nodded.

Li Wei recovered sufficiently to ask, "What would she want with a Torah in New York?"

"Probably she'll sell it to a museum, maybe the Jewish Museum in New York. It would be a grand occasion and get lots of good publicity. Remind Jews of her friendship with them, that her Soong family did business with them here. Or she might sell it to some private Jews who would pay dearly for this Torah. It is so famous. And Madame could use the money."

"Madame Chiang Kai-shek selling a Torah to Jews?" I couldn't help blurting this out, albeit in a whisper. Simon and Ruth caught the humor, too, and we all tried to keep ourselves from laughing out loud. Helena, Li Wei, and David didn't get it.

"She needs money?" Li Wei said. "Didn't she manage to steal enough from China?"

"She's 94. She never thought she'd live so long. Her nephew Kung runs everything now since her sister and brother-in-law died. You remember Ai-Ling and H. H.? They were good with money. Especially for themselves. Anyway, nephew Kung thinks she doesn't need her big co-op apartment in New York, all her servants. Remember, the rich Jews in Shanghai were supporters of Chiang, didn't want the Communists to come and spoil their party. The Jews in New York will certainly understand her predicament and care for her."

"The Jews supported Dr. Sun," Li Wei corrected Tang. "Chiang was too crooked for them."

"How did Madame Chiang even know about the Torah?" I asked. "Did she know the Joseph family?"

"This was their Torah," Ruth said.

"Not theirs. Hers, Mrs. Joseph," said Tang. "This is the Ezra Torah."

"If you think a Torah written by Ezra the Scribe would have survived this long in China, you're crazy."

"Ezra the Scribe?" Freddy started to laugh. "Ezra the Scribe?"

"What's so funny? I said. "Do you even know who Ezra the Scribe was?"

"Yes, Mrs. Know-it-all American lady. Like Madame, I am a good Methodist. I know my Bible."

"Then what's so funny?" Now I was really confused.

"You all think this is called the Ezra Torah because of some foolish idea that it was written in the time of the Ezra the Scribe and Prophet? Before the time of Jesus Christ? That's a good one. This Torah is old, but not that old."

"Then why is it called the Ezra Torah?"

"Because, dear lady, it belonged to the Ezra family, Mrs. Miriam Ezra Joseph. Madame saw it when she was a young woman. She knew Miriam. They were friends, in fact. Good friends."

"M.E.J.," I said. "The monogram on the silver tea set. Miriam Ezra Joseph."

This revelation almost made us forget that we were Freddy Tang's hostages—along with the Torah. Until Li Wei jumped up.

"The Ezras were not righteous people. Mr. Edward Ezra—he was one of the Shanghai Jews who tricked the Kaifeng Jews into the meeting that came to nothing. When my great-uncle went through circumcision to prove he was Jewish. Worse, Edward Ezra was really a crook. So many good Chinese got hooked on opium from his business. He covered up the illegal side, got elected to Municipal council, built hotels. But he died young. Revenge for being a bad man and a bad Jew. Scum. If this is Edward Ezra's Torah, for sure it belongs in Kaifeng. Freddy, you've double-crossed me, just like Ezra did to my great-grandfather and the other elders of our ancestral city."

As Li Wei remonstrated, he edged away from the seating area toward Tang. Lurch Khan moved with remarkable speed to save his boss from assault and knocked Li Wei down to a spot on the parquet floor not covered by rug. For effect, because Li Wei wasn't going anywhere, the giant stuck a foot that looked like a bound edition of Webster's dictionary on the abdomen of the moaning victim. Another casualty was a life-size earthenware urn that had stood where he fell.

"Ming Dynasty," muttered Simon, surveying the bed of shards surrounding Li Wei.

As David rose to try to free his father, Lurch delivered a blow to his neck that sent him reeling down onto the floor in the opposite direction. This nearly knocked Freddy over. Disoriented and trying to maintain his footing, he reached for the counter of the bar counter with one hand and for the massive chair holding the Torah with the other. The giant's focus shifted toward his suddenly distressed boss, and he lunged to steady him.

All this movement vibrated against the Torah's perch, and the silver case, despite its heft, began to sway. I dodged over the crumpled Li father and son and behind Lurch to grab the Torah before it fell. It was heavy, so I cradled it like a baby as I barely steadied myself against the wall behind me.

I looked up and saw Jennifer pointing her gun at Tang and his strongman, who froze and stared at her for an instant. Then Tang pushed the giant toward Jennifer.

"No you don't," said Simon, as he jammed himself in-between them and delivered a knee to the giant's crotch. Groaning like a howling bear, Lurch collapsed onto a round ebony side table with spindly legs inlaid with mother-of-pearl, and the table buckled instantly.

"Five hundred years that Qing table might have survived, and in two seconds it's a pile of sticks," said Simon.

"F.W. Tang," Jennifer pronounced loudly, "You're under arrest for smuggling and trafficking in illegally acquired antiques, belonging to the People's Republic of China, to the United States."

I hadn't noticed the posse of Chinese policemen—at least half a dozen, including our bogus taxi drivers—that had swarmed in since the fracas began. One clasped handcuffs onto Freddy, and two more spun him around and pushed him toward the front door. An inglorious and likely final exit for Tang from his treasure-filled Shanghai mansion. Two other policemen reached under the shoulders of the still moaning giant to haul him onto his feet to be handcuffed by yet another of their colleagues. They pushed and kicked as their doubled-up charge stumbled on his way.

"Where did these guys come from?" I asked, as Simon and Ruth helped me ease back onto on the sofa with the Torah still clutched to my chest.

"Shanghai's finest," said Jennifer. "I'd arranged for them to follow us every step of the way tonight. I told you I had the full support and collaboration of the Chinese authorities in nailing Freddy. They're letting the US prosecute him in exchange for the return of the antiques he's already smuggled there. Because the goods are in the States, it's obviously more practical for us to retrieve and return them to China with Freddy's cooperation."

"Do you think he'll cooperate?" Ruth asked.

"Oh, he'll cooperate," Jennifer laughed, "because the possibility of prosecution in China will hang over his head. Believe me, after a few days as the temporary houseguest of the Shanghai jailers, he'll be relieved to fall into the open arms of the FBI in San Francisco for his trip back to New York. Even Rikers Island will look like a resort after the local jail."

"And the big guy?" Simon asked after his conquest.

"He's a local thug. The US government isn't going to waste any time and money on him," said Jennifer. "I don't know what they'll do with him here, maybe charge him with working for a smuggler."

"Or maybe recruit him," I said.

David and Li Wei, released from the giant's grip, came over to me and leaned down toward the Torah. Li Wei held his arms out ready for me to hand over this precious package. I was in no mood to debate the legitimacy of the Kaifeng Jewish community. Ruth and Helena crowded in next to me as buffers.

"Now the Torah can go back to its rightful home, Kaifeng," Li Wei said.

"No," Simon's imposing voice boomed. "The Torah isn't rightfully yours and it's going to be given to the State of Israel next year as a symbol of the good relationship between Israel and China."

"I don't understand," said David. "Israel and China? A relationship?"

"Diplomatic relations are to be established next year, and the Chinese government plans to present this Torah to Israel. That's why it was so critical that the Chens keep it in safekeeping. The government plans to get it ready for an official ceremony in 1992."

"And that's why no one can know about the theft," Helena said. "Can you imagine what would happen to my parents if the government found out?"

"You must agree to keep the secret and in return I will ensure that no charges will be pressed against the two of you, either for the theft or for selling fake goods as antiques," said Jennifer. "I'm leaving now to confirm travel arrangements for Tang with the Shanghai authorities and, if asked, I will tell them you are simply friends of the Chen family helping out."

"But," said Li Wei, "how are we to save the Kaifeng Jewish community and bring it back to life? The Chinese government doesn't care about this. Neither does Israel."

"I have an idea," said Simon "If you can prove you're descended from Kaifeng Jews, I'll recommend that the government invite you as honored guests to Israel when the Torah is given there. And I'll help you find another Torah for Kaifeng, which I'll donate. If you give me your word that you will remain silent about this whole matter. Then you're free to go."

The father and son looked at each other and, without a word, both nodded.

"Can I at least look inside the case and see the Torah? David told me he did at your house," Li Wei said to Helena.

"Not here," I said. "Let's take it back to the Chens' first. This house is tainted."

"I'm dying to see it myself. You're right, Lily," said Simon. "The conditions at the Chens' may not be perfect, but they deserve to know we've found the Torah. Let's go."

Chapter 10

Simon, Ruth, Helena, and I piled into a cab for the short trip back to the Chens' house, and David and his father followed on the motor scooter. The Torah sat on my lap between Simon and Ruth. Helena hadn't made a peep since we'd arrived at Tang's.

The Chens were so overjoyed when we walked into the house with the Torah they actually stubbed out freshly lit cigarettes and took turns hugging the case. They even welcomed the Lis with bows and handshakes before we all marched ceremoniously to the dining room table, which Ayi quickly covered with a clean embroidered cloth. Simon unclasped the silver Star of David latch that connected the rounded sides, which were hinged in back. Opening the sides of the case revealed a partially unrolled Torah scroll, and we realized that the two silver finials that rose above the case when it was closed were attached to the rollers. A hand-shaped silver pointer hung over it on a silver chain. In Hebrew this is called a *yad*, which means hand, and Jewish ritual dictates that it be used for reading the lines of Torah. Touching is strictly verboten.

"It looks so fragile," said Simon, "I'm not an expert on Babylonian Torahs, but from the condition of the parchment I'd be surprised if it were more than a couple of hundred years old. Ruth, what do you think?"

"Not my area of expertise at all."

"The script is elegant," I said.

"And relatively legible, considering," Simon said, "pointing to slightly smudged Hebrew letters that meant, "And God said unto Moses," a phrase that opens many portions.

Suddenly, little Joey appeared and, pointing to the Torah, said something that caused everyone to cry out in apparent shock.

"Ruth, what did he say?" I asked.

Ruth blanched as she translated this and Helena's reply.

"He said, 'Oh, David brought it back.' And Helena said, 'How did you know he took it? Why didn't you tell me?' Joey said, 'I was hiding in the closet over there. I was afraid you wouldn't let David come here anymore. Anyway, I knew he'd bring it back.'"

Joey ran over and hugged a sheepish looking David, who took the boy's hand when he and Li Wei bent over the scroll silently. But the expressions on their faces were joyful.

Finally, the father spoke, "*Liǎo buqǐ.*"

"Amazing," Ruth translated.

"We'll find out exactly how old it is, once it gets to Israel. Let's roll it back, so at least it won't suffer any more jostling before the government gets it."

Reluctantly, David and Li Wei nodded in agreement as each moved to one side of Simon while he began to manipulate the inside rollers to close the scroll, which also started to close the case. Suddenly, something fell from the back of the case. It was another round silver case, almost a duplicate of the other but in miniature, perhaps only four inches tall and no more than two in diameter. Simon handed it to me. I unhooked it and found an even tinier scroll, which I unfurled by twisting its skinny wooden rollers. Hebrew writing at the top of the first passage said, Megillat Esther, for Miriam Esther, Daughter of Nathan and Leah, born Purim 14 Adar II 5661, 14 March 1900.

"It's the Megillah," I said. "The Book of Esther. It belonged to Miriam. Look, there's a picture." I took out a yellowed black-and-white photograph that was curled around the tiny scroll.

There were three teen-aged girls—one with curly light hair dressed in a queen costume holding the miniature silver case. The other two were darker skinned and wore embroidered tunics over narrow pants. Apparently Indian. I turned the photo over. An inscription in small neat cursive read:

"To Miriam Ezra, Happy 18th Birthday to our Queen Esther from your friends Mena Johar and Maya Kocchar. The Three M's—friends forever! (Bombay, March 1918)."

We showed the photo to the Chens. Auntie grabbed it and went into the kitchen.

"Missy Miriam," we heard Ayi yell before she lapsed into a tirade in Chinese.

"What's she saying, Ruth?" I asked

"So beautiful when she was young. So good to me always."

Auntie returned to the dining room without the picture.

"Ayi was almost like an adopted daughter of the Josephs," she said. "She was beginning to learn English, and they sent her to a good school. But then the war started, Miriam and Reuben went to the prison camp, Erich went to the ghetto . . . "

"And everything changed," I said, putting my hand around her shoulders. "I know. For so many of us. I'm wondering, though, would it be possible for me to make a copy of that photograph? We could take it to the business center at the hotel and bring it back here in the morning."

Ruth and Simon looked puzzled. I'd tell them why later.

"I can make a copy right now," said Helena. "I've just bought a fax and copy machine for school work. Do you want copies of both sides, Lily? I'll take it upstairs and do it right now."

"Perfect, thanks so much, Helena."

"This tiny scroll is a wonder all by itself," said Simon. "I wonder if the Chinese will know what it is. We certainly need to leave it in there, but perhaps, Ruth, you should explain to your aunt and uncle. I think these miniatures are unique to Baghdadi Sephardim."

Gingerly he put the tiny scroll back into its case and reattached it to a thin silver bracket we found on the left side of the large case. Once the Torah case was closed, latched, and set into the cabinet, Uncle produced the key and locked it, patting the door for good measure. And smiling for the first time since we'd met him.

It was late, and we hadn't realized we were hungry until Ayi beckoned us back into the dining room, where the linen tablecloth remained, but the Torah had been replaced by a large platter of dumplings that occupied almost the entire circumference of the lazy Susan. A stir-fry of broccoli and bok choy and several small dishes of vinegar and hot sauces completed the wonderful spread. Plates, chopsticks, and glasses were quickly passed around before we sat down.

"Dumplings," Ruth said, "The special food of the New Year, which starts tomorrow. Let's sit down and eat. David and Li Wei, you too."

"Yes," said Auntie. "All of us."

Simon surveyed the table with delight.

"Kreplach!"

Kreplach, dumplings—whatever one called these meat-filled delicacies, just one more thing Jews and Chinese had in common.

"No pork in the filling," Auntie pronounced after Ayi whispered in her ear.

Once we sat down, Ruth lifted her glass—beer this time—and proposed a toast to Helena, who was sitting next to her.

"She's the real hero in finding the Torah. She was so smart to figure out that David had taken the Torah and so brave to tell us the truth. So concerned about the family honor."

Helena blushed, as Auntie made a statement in Chinese that gave Ruth pause before she translated to us.

"Auntie says, 'brave like her mother. Her real mother.' I don't know what she's talking about."

"Neither do I," said Helena.

As Ruth listened, her face blanched, even as Helena's turned redder. They looked at each other and started to cry. Auntie got up and put her arms around both of them, crying, too. Uncle grinned. We had no idea what was going on.

Finally, Ruth caught her breath enough to tell the story. "Helena's real mother was my mother. When she was sent for re-education in the south of China, she suffered such abuse. That I knew in general terms, but no details. She was raped, possibly by an officer. She found herself pregnant—over forty and living in squalor, horrible health conditions. No pre-natal care. She died in childbirth. This is quite a shock, obviously. All I'd heard was she died of an infection. Fortunately, one of Uncle's friends was assigned there, and he got word to them in Shanghai about the baby and my mother's death. They had been childless—Auntie had had three miscarriages by then—so they adopted this baby, Helena, as theirs. She's my half-sister. No, she's my sister."

She hugged Helena, who looked equally thunderstruck by this revelation. But finally she broke out in a huge grin and grabbed Ruth for a hug that lasted at least three minutes. It was quite a scene. Even Simon put down his chopsticks and took a break from dumpling consumption. David and Li Wei applauded.

"I thought you two looked alike," Simon said. "And some of the same mannerisms."

"I never thought I'd find the Torah, let alone a little sister," said Ruth. "How nice it would be to stay a little longer and spend time without all this stress. But I need to get back to Israel, see how everyone's doing with the war winding down. I don't feel too brave sitting it out in safe Shanghai."

"Ha," Simon said. "She's just gotten through an encounter with Chinese thugs and she says 'safe Shanghai.'"

"No scuds raining down on us here," I said.

As Ruth walked us to the street and hailed a cab, she remembered to ask, "Why did you want a copy of that photo of Miriam and her girlfriends?"

"There must be a story in it," I said, "and, let's face it, it would be the only story from this trip I can even try to tell. Everything else is way too sensitive—the lost Torah that was missing before the Chinese government was to prepare to present it to Israel. The role of Madame Chiang Kai-shek and her henchman, Freddy Tang. David and his father who want to revive Judaism in Kaifeng in a country that rejects religion. How can I write about any of this?"

"You can't, Lily, you're right," said Simon. "But digging into the story of Miriam and the two Indian girls from a picture taken in 1918?"

"That's why I'm such a good journalist."

"And our own Miss Marple," said Ruth, hugging me as Simon opened the taxi door. "Thank you so much for coming to Shanghai to help my family."

"*Our* family," I said.

Ruth left the next evening. Simon wanted to stay through the first couple of days of the lunar New Year. But he insisted we finally move from the Jin Jiang to the Garden Hotel across the street.

"You swim there, anyway. It will be more convenient, and it's more modern than this old pile. The location is equally desirable. I've had enough of Mao and Nixon."

At long last how could I deny him such a sensible request as moving to a more modern and luxurious hotel? After all, the lower floors of the Garden Hotel comprised the former French Club, built in the 1920s. After World War II the American military commandeered it as a headquarters. Enough tidbits to appease my history buff tourism. Our room in the newer tower could have been in any hotel anywhere in the world, but I had to admit the more comfortable bed and up-to-date bathroom were easy to get used to.

Our last day in Shanghai Simon and I finally got to that shopping trip we'd started on the day Mr. Xu died. We managed to navigate on foot to the Shanghai Friendship Store, the local branch of the government-owned chain of emporiums that sold all the stereotypical Chinese souvenirs one could find in any Chinatown in the world. Of course, buying in China felt more authentic. And I certainly wasn't going to go home without gifts for the grandchildren—traditional looking "silk" embroidered outfits for Jacob's twins, Gabriella and Joshua, and a really tiny one for their baby cousin, Charlotte, Elizabeth's daughter. Once I'd settled up in the children's department, Simon led me over to the jewelry counter, where he asked the clerk if she could open the case and take out some pearls. She did, after casting a look at a nearby man who nodded his approval.

Simon fingered a couple of narrow strands and pronounced them, "Shoddy. Let's move on. Walk a little."

We picked up a few pashmina shawls for our daughters and my daughter-in-law and emerged back onto the street. On the way back to the hotel we passed the antiques market and saw Mr. Xu's shop reopened. One of the younger dealers stood behind the main case. On the phone, smoking, and drinking from his big cup.

"We never did find out if Tang murdered Mr. Xu," I said. "Jennifer was right—the Shanghai police simply wouldn't touch the case."

"It doesn't really matter, does it? Mr. Xu was a nice old gentleman and he did his job, just by letting us know, however obliquely, that Tang was involved in what we were involved in."

That evening, our last in Shanghai, upstairs in the Garden Hotel's top floor bar thirty-three stories above the city lights, we clinked glasses and drank champagne from a bottle labeled in French. Pirated or ersatz, it was surprisingly good. Simon was ebullient.

"Another New Year's to celebrate within a few weeks. We should make this a tradition, celebrate the January first New Year and the Chinese New Year every year."

"And don't forget Rosh Hashanah," I said.

"Who could forget Rosh Hashanah?"

"We'll never top celebrating one New Year in Paris and the next one here in the former 'Paris of the Orient.'"

"We can always top something," Simon said, kissing me on the cheek and squeezing my knee under the table. "Especially this New Year! It's a second chance for you to change your answer on the question I asked in the real Paris."

"Oh. That."

"Yes. That."

Our controversy about whether to get married crept back and hung in the air between us like a cement bubble. For me saying yes would still be like having it cracked open. What I didn't want to smash was Simon's commitment. Our brief estrangement on this trip was our first major blow-up. It had passed quickly, repaired by Simon's heroic rescue of Ruth from the bike attack engineered by Freddy Tang. But it occurred to me how, despite my anger, I hadn't holed up in my room but had navigated around Shanghai on my own. I'd even had a good night's sleep the night I threw Simon out.

"Can't we just leave things as they are? You know I have my schtick about my own place, the TV remote, maintaining some space. Are you so unsatisfied with the closeness we have now?"

"No, I'm not. Even with our spat the other day—especially after that—I realized I love you so much that getting married would be the one thing that would top everything—even Paris and Shanghai for New Year's. If this is about the damn remote, okay, I'll share. You can have custody half the week. I'll take the other half. Wait—I'll even get you another one of your own. We can split our clicking time."

"Dueling remotes. Very funny."

Simon didn't laugh.

"I'm serious. I can't imagine life without you and I can't imagine a better way to have it than to make the ultimate commitment of marriage and completely sharing life."

I sighed. No wonder Simon was such a successful businessman. His negotiating skills were very persuasive. But I wasn't ready to have the deal closed.

"It's not about the remote. Well, not *all* about it, anyway. I went from my parents' home on the kindertransport to my aunt and uncle's home in London, then to my home with Arthur when we got married. This is the first time I've lived on my own, and it's only been two years since Arthur died.

We spend so much time together that my version of living on my own—my so-called independence—is an illusion—or my delusion, anyway. I'm just loving things the way they are now. Can you see that? I don't want to be with anyone else but for now I enjoy the little bit of space we give each other."

Reluctantly, he caved in. "Okay, but I'm not going to give up trying. Just wait until Rosh Hashanah!"

The next day we flew back to civilization. Not that Shanghai hadn't been civilized, but the news embargo in China was frustrating. Back at Tokyo's Narita Airport, CNN blared the fact that two Scud missiles had just been fired toward Israel, one to Haifa in the north and the other to the Negev desert in the south. No news had definitely been good news. As exasperating as the blackout had been, the respite had provided a certain delusionary bliss.

Iraq. Once upon a time Jews thrived there, the Talmud was created there, Torahs were written there.

PART III

Jerusalem
January 1992

Chapter 11

I had walked or driven by *Beit Ha' Nassi,* the official residence of the President of Israel, many times. It's a modern home in Jerusalem's Talbiya neighborhood, not far from my flat in Rehavia. But, until the weeklong celebration of China and Israel opening diplomatic relations, I'd never been invited in.

A year after the Ezra Torah had made its way back to the Chen home in Shanghai, it traveled to Israel on the private plane that brought Lin Zhen, China's first ambassador to Israel, to his new post. Months earlier, a delegation of Israeli experts had gone to China to verify the Torah's age and pedigree and to begin a restoration process. The scroll itself was determined to date from the middle of the nineteenth century. Its scribe was a disciple of the famous Baghdadi rabbi, Yosef Chaim, known as the "Ben Ish Chai," who blessed the Torah before Miriam's branch of the Ezra family moved to India. The ornate bejeweled silver case was crafted in India about 1900.

Though the Chinese embassy, like most others, would be physically located in Tel Aviv, Mr. Lin came to Jerusalem to present his credentials to President Chaim Herzog. This was an impressive ceremony and historic occasion on its own. But, when Mr. Lin handed the Torah to President Herzog, the Irish-born son of Israel's first Ashkenazic Chief Rabbi, the historical and emotional impact of the moment was palpable throughout the crowd. Even Prime Minister Yitzchak Shamir, a dour and anti-social man, appeared to soften his naturally taciturn demeanor as his eyes crinkled and lips curled up just slightly enough to express a modicum of pleasure for that brief moment.

Israel has come a long way from the casual open-shirted official dress code of David Ben-Gurion and his colleagues in the early days of statehood. Suits and ties were *de rigeur* for men, and the women attending all wore well-tailored suits or dresses. Waiters passed sparkling water and lemonade before the ceremony began, and I spied a familiar looking bottle of the strong Chinese liquor on a table behind the podium—next to one of sticky sweet Carmel Israeli wine. There were two toasts, the first with each official drinking the potion of the other and then changing pours to his own for the second. Both the ambassador and President Herzog looked grateful to return to the familiar. Could two drinks be less similar?

Afterward the hors d'oeuvres that circulated featured trays of large vegetarian dumplings that, in truth, resembled kreplach more than the traditional dish of Chinese New Year or the streets of Shanghai.

"No soup squirting out," Simon lamented.

"No pork either," I said. "Ayi would be pleased."

The mini-falafel balls were more popular, even with the Chen family. The newly expanded Chen family.

David and Helena were married the previous summer, an occurrence we'd once thought unlikely, considering Helena's sense that David used her to get to the Torah. But her suitor affirmed true love and even won over Auntie and Uncle. Ruth, Boaz, and their children had traveled back to China for the wedding, and Ruth had stood up for her younger sister. Eli and Talia, along with Joey, had fulfilled the Chinese version of ring bearer and flower girl roles. We'd seen the photos—this meant walking in front of the bride, Talia scattering petals and the boys looking sheepish, but all three adorable.

By virtue of Uncle's government career and his longstanding caretaker role for the Torah, David, Helena, and Joey had managed to be included in the official Chinese delegation, which gave them an opportunity to visit Ruth and her family on their home turf. Li Wei came, too. Although Israel didn't consider Kaifeng descendants to be full-fledged Jews, he and David had verified their lineage upward through several generations in that city's defunct Jewish community. That helped them get visas.

Ruth was translating furiously for all of them during the Hebrew speeches at the ceremony, obviously keeping up with Ambassador Lin's official interpreter, as they all smiled, laughed, and looked pensive simultaneously at just the right moments.

While the story of the Torah theft and its temporary disappearance never surfaced publicly either in China or Israel, one might have wondered why a certain female Chinese-American police detective from San Francisco was on the guest list. Or a tiny wizened old woman in a royal blue and gold brocade sari. This was Dr. Mena Johar, Miriam Ezra's ninety-two-year-old friend from Bombay. Simon's pal, Mossad Special Agent Avi Ben-Zeev, served as their translator—and sometimes mine—when the Hebrew went too fast.

In typically Israeli fashion, the Torah's future home had been the object of a controversy that, unlike in secretive China, had exploded in the press. The original plan was for it to be placed in *Beit Hatfutsoth*, the Museum of the Diaspora in Tel Aviv. The outcry that erupted when this was announced was three-pronged. First, the Ministry of Religious Affairs weighed in that a Torah was a living religious item, the holiest of sacred articles, and it should be placed in a synagogue for use. This led to a statement from the Mayor of Or Yehuda, a city with a population of predominantly Iraqi refugees. The Torah came from Iraq and belonged in a place where its Jews had settled. Never mind that the Jews of Or Yehuda bore no direct connection to the family that had commissioned, owned, and preserved the Ezra Torah on its journey from Baghdad to India to Shanghai and, through its Chinese surrogates, to Israel. Where the Torah would end up remained in dispute, but when the handover and reception at *Beit Ha-Nassi* ended, the magnificent case and the delicate scrolls—including Miriam's Megillah inside—departed in the hands of an official from the Department of Antiquities.

"Does this mean the Torah will be shut away?" I knew Simon could shed light on this.

"Not necessarily. But a Torah this old may not be exactly suitable to be unrolled and read every Shabbat, or even once a year."

"It could end up in a very carefully regulated display, like the Dead Sea Scrolls at the Israel Museum," said Ruth.

Even her family from Shanghai understood this would be a far different and more fitting home than the cabinet in their home. But their smiles and bowlike nodding up and down expressed their pride in having harbored such an important treasure of the Jewish people.

Ruth looked happy, but tired. Everyone was staying at her home, comfortable for four people and maybe an overnight guest or two, but cramped with six more. Simon and I had offered to take at least some of them off her hands either at my flat in Jerusalem or his house north of Tel Aviv. But separating this group wasn't an option.

"How's it going?" We had walked out onto the presidential terrace overlooking the Judean hills. Auntie and Uncle were outside, too, engaging in their favorite activity, alongside a like-minded Israeli, namely Avi.

Ruth sighed and nodded toward the trio. "Smoking is the only thing they do on their own," she said.

"Well, they're right at home smoking in Israel; it's a national pasttime," said Simon, who likely still harbored a slight tinge of longing to join them, a year-and-a-half after quitting.

"Are they smoking in the house?" I asked.

"No, I laid down the rules right away."

"Helena has really blossomed, don't you think?"

Ruth nodded. "Marriage becomes her."

"It's not marriage alone," I said, "It's your relationship. Look how great she and Joey get along with your kids."

"And Boaz told me David and his father are really nice guys—*menches*—and that David treats Helena and her mother like queens," Simon added. "After all that transpired before, it's truly amazing."

Ruth replied with characteristic modesty. "It's not me, it's my mother's genes. My mother was very special. But I have to admit I'm enjoying having a sister and a cute little nephew. Like I love having a cousin who's as close as a sister, Lily."

"Me, too," I said, as we hugged, with Simon snapping a photo at the precise moment tears landed on both of our cheeks.

"I'm only sorry," Ruth said, "that you couldn't get a hot story out of our search for the Torah."

"Never mind. That little photograph stuck into the tiny Megillah inside the Torah opened up whole new aspect that will make for a lovely magazine piece. I've mentioned that Mena Johar gave me a packet of letters she got from Miriam, beginning right after World War I. Believe me, Miriam was quite a woman. Her letters are like a history book. What she witnessed during her lifetime . . . "

"Auntie and Ayi have told me more about Miriam since we were in Shanghai. Isn't it wonderful Dr. Johar could come here? What a cute little woman she is! And a dynamo—so spry and energetic."

"Unbelievable," I said. "She went to a meeting at Hadassah Hospital all day yesterday and now she's off to visit a friend in Tel Aviv before her flight back to Bombay tomorrow."

"It's a wonder you were able to track her down. You never told me how you did," said Ruth.

"I didn't? I guess not—it's been such a hectic time since that trip to China. When I got back to New York from Shanghai with the photo, I called an Indian economist at the UN I'd met through Arthur who divides her time between India and the US. She told me, 'Everyone in India knows about Mena Johar.'"

"And, whoosh, Lily was off to Bombay in a flash," Simon said. "Dr. Johar is a legend in her time. She established two centers in Bombay, Maya House and Miriam House, which are havens for women and children who need shelter from abusive men. They have health clinics and educational and job training services. Apparently, she's considered a pioneer in championing women's rights in India. That's not exactly a popular cause there."

"And Miriam House is named after Miriam Ezra," I added. "Maya of Maya House was a friend of Miriam's and Mena's growing up—they all went to a fancy girls' school in Bombay. Maya was married in an arranged marriage right after graduation, and went to live at her in-laws' home. It didn't end well, which influenced both Mena and Miriam. Mena became a doctor, and separately Miriam opened a shelter, called Malka House in Shanghai, for women and girls."

"That I know something about. Ayi's mother was someone Miriam helped," Ruth said. "So, Miriam's Torah and her little Megillah have arrived in Israel with a legacy of a strong woman helping to strengthen other women. I like that."

"Speaking of strong women," said Simon, "I'm wondering, you two, if after this complicated mystery, your daily business of helping Holocaust survivors find their looted art is going to seem boring and routine. What are the Jewish Miss Marple and her team going to do next for adventure?"

"Boring and routine—that sounds fine to me," I said, kissing him.

"Maybe a wedding would spark things up," Simon said.

PART IV

Bombay, Shanghai, Hong Kong

1919–1949

Chapter 12

"Miriam's Megillah"

(A magazine article by Lily Weinberg Kovner)

The story of the Jewish festival of Purim is written in the biblical Book of Esther, known in Hebrew as Megillat Esther, Esther's Megillah. Colloquially, as *megillah* made its way from Hebrew through Yiddish to certain English-speaking circles, it's become a generic term for saga, as in "I had to listen to the whole megillah."

Purim celebrates the heroine Queen Esther, who legendarily saved her fellow Jews by taking the risk of informing her husband, the Persian king, that his trusted adviser was plotting to murder her people. In the Jewish calendar Purim is a joyous late winter festival celebrated with boisterous adult parties, children's carnivals, satirical skits, and the donning of costumes representing its key players—Esther, King Ahasuerus, the villain Haman, and Mordechai, Esther's cousin who discovers Haman's plot and urges her to take the Jews' case to her husband.

Miriam Esther Ezra was born in Bombay, India, on Purim in March 1900. Her father, Nathan Ezra, was a Sephardic Jew descended from a long line of Baghdadis, whose forebears were Jews exiled to Babylon, now Iraq, after the destruction of the First Temple in 70 A.D. Miriam's mother, Lena, was an Ashkenazic Jew born to Russians who escaped czarist pogroms by immigrating to London. Though both Jewish, Lena and Nathan were a "mixed marriage," particularly in the eyes of the Ezra family. Lena died when her daughter was a child. After Miriam's graduation from an elite girls secondary school in Bombay, she moved with her father to Shanghai, where other members of their clan were prominent in business. Miriam married a man named Reuben Joseph, also a product of a "mixed" Sephardic and Ashkenazic marriage. They stayed in mainland China until the advent of the Communists in the late 1940s, when they moved to Hong Kong.

I came across a photograph of Miriam and two Indian girlfriends in her former home in Shanghai, now occupied by a Chinese family prominent in government circles. It was curled up in a tiny Megillah scroll held in an elaborately jeweled silver case, Miriam's from birth, and enclosed within a larger, similarly ornate case holding a Torah scroll. Miniature religious objects, even petite Torahs, were common among Judaic ritual items owned by wealthy Baghdadi Jewish families. In fact, many of these families owned their own Torahs kept at home. On the back of the photo there was an inscription that noted the occasion was Miriam's eighteenth birthday party in Bombay in March 1918, and her friends were Mena and Maya, the "Three M's." Through a connection with an economist at the United Nations, Dr. Amitta Kaul, I was able to locate Mena, the sole living "M." She is Dr. Mena Johar, a physician who pioneered women's health and domestic abuse centers first in rural Indian villages and later in Bombay. At ninety-two, Dr. Johar remains active professionally in the operations of Maya House and Miriam House, two centers in slum neighborhoods of the city where she, Maya, and Miriam were born. When I asked Dr. Kaur if she knew of someone named Mena Johar, she replied, "Everyone in India knows about Dr. Mena Johar."

I visited Dr. Johar at her flat in the Nariman Point area near the Arabian Sea. Unlike Mother Theresa, she makes no pretense about needing to live in the tenement environment of her clinic patients and clients, and her home is filled with books and art, some inherited from her parents and some collected on her own travels. However, despite her age, she spends little time there. She still works at least six days a week at the centers and lectures at a local medical school. And then there is the constant fund raising.

When I called to seek an appointment to speak about her friend, Miriam Ezra, Dr. Johar choked up and started to cry, then giggled like the schoolgirl in the picture. She'd be delighted, she said, to meet me and give me—"on loan," she was very clear!—the letters she kept, letters dating back to Miriam's departure from Bombay in 1919 through her life in Shanghai and on to Hong Kong.

The letters are a treasure trove depicting a singular experience in the Jewish Diaspora, that of a contingent of Sephardic Jews whose roots are directly traced to the Babylonian Exile—a journey from the Middle East to the Asian subcontinent to China. Equally remarkable, it's the perspective of a woman born into an inbred community whose personal evolution moves with the historical and social dynamics of the times.

Where I've added explanations for terms, I've used [ ] to denote them.

Calcutta

2 January 1919

Dear Mena,

How very strange it is to have to write to you. I miss you and Maya already.

At least I could stay in Bombay for Maya's wedding. What an occasion! Anil looked so handsome in his tunic, though riding on the elephant didn't seem to be his cup of tea. He seems to be a fine man, even if he is her father's age. Maya's saris—all four of them—I liked the white one with gold best. And the emerald necklace from Anil's mother—very posh but so heavy it looked like a torture. Maya hardly has the chest to carry it off. A piece more fit for Queen Mary.

Can you imagine getting married? I can't, not for a long time. How lucky I am Father is so modern, not conjuring up a match for me, just because I've turned eighteen. Here in Calcutta, my younger girl cousins are already in the marketplace. Their life is totally different from mine. Their parents are very strict, and everything must be Jewish. Jewish school, Jewish parties, Jewish friends. No "normal" school for them, or Hindu or Muslim or Christian friends. My stories of my Indian friends and our school shock them. It's forbidden for them to go out to tea or to the shops without my aunt or the *ayah* [nanny]. Even for a walk to the Maidan [park]. Since I have been here, the only time we were allowed to go anywhere on our own was to a Chanukah party for poor Jewish children sponsored by the Jewish Women's League. Auntie stayed home, because the baby brother has a cough, and they are so fearful it is the influenza.

My uncle berates my father. How can you allow Miriam to even consider university? England? Alone? Unmarried? But Father simply laughs when the subject comes up at the dinner table. Then there are the discussions in Uncle's study they think I don't hear. I catch words. "Your Ashkenazi wife . . . no wonder . . . bad influence . . . traitor to our Baghdadi roots . . . immoral...be careful, no one will want her . . . " Then Father yells back, "Immoral? Who are you to talk about morality? The opium? That's moral? How you and the rest of this family have grown rich as the King and all the maharajahs together? Off the weaknesses of others. Now this scandal with the cousins in Shanghai part of it. The mess I'm sent to clean up. Redeem the family name? How dare you impugn the memory of my dear wife? My Lena was Ashkenazi, yes, and a fine Jewish woman. Not some whore."

Mena, you probably don't understand the conflict between the Sephardic and Ashkenazic Jews. I don't either, to be honest, because we're all Jews of the Diaspora, meaning we scattered to different places from the original land of Israel. Father's family is Sephardic and comes from lands around the Mediterranean. Ashkenzic Jews come from Russia, Poland, Germany, and other places in Eastern Europe. Perhaps because our family originally comes from Baghdad, which was Babylonia, where Jews were exiled after the destruction of the first temple, my uncle thinks we hold the first rank as the earliest Diaspora Jews. Or maybe it's the Babylonian Talmud they're always quoting from. The main differences I know from being a "half-breed," as my uncle surely thinks of me, are different music for prayers and food. Ashkenazic Jews don't think it's kosher to eat rice or beans during Passover. My mother was happy to give way to adopt that Sephardic custom. I wish you'd met her, Mena.

My mother's parents came from Russia to England, and she met Father when he was reading law at University College, London. Did you know he was a classmate of Gandhiji there? Grandmother Fannie and Grandfather Meyer, whom I'm named after, left Russia because of pogroms, which were terrible slaughters of Jews under the czar. The Ezra family left Baghdad for India because of persecution against Jews. So, it makes no sense that Jews divide amongst ourselves, when we have others who hate us. Why anyone hates Jews, of course, I cannot understand altogether.

Father is treated so badly here, considering he's agreed to accept this urgent family assignment, which forces him to suspend his law practice and us to leave Bombay. All for these cousins Edward and Judah in Shanghai—scoundrels, if you ask me. But no one asks me, even though I, too, am sacrificing—my life, my friends, and my university plans. Father does not relish going to Shanghai any more than I do, so it's my duty to at least make our home life comfortable for him. He is so proud of my school record and he has always allowed and inspired me to study and experience so much more than other Jewish daughters—even read Torah—that I can do this and postpone my university entry a bit. I will have to live it vicariously through you until I can go to England myself.

Now I can't wait until we sail for Shanghai in three days and say goodbye to dreary Calcutta. I'm glad the capital will move to "New" Delhi. Calcutta is a terrible place. This huge Victoria Memorial that's half-finished will be a landmark in this city that is losing its status. Another odd thing is the Magen David synagogue, the enormous one my grandfather built, has a cross on the top. Of course, that makes it tower above any of the buildings nearby, but with a cross it looks Christian, not Jewish. The only good thing about Calcutta is the delicious plum cake from Nahoum's confectionary. Nahoum's boy delivers some cake or bread here almost every day. I'm eating so much of it that my clothes feel tight, though I still hear my fat aunt whispering about "Nathan's Miriam—so pale and skinny."

Please write news. Have you seen Maya since the wedding? How is she managing life with her in-laws?

It has taken us so long to sail from India, because the P&O ships are still commandeered to transport soldiers home, so passenger space is scarce. Every day Father and Uncle go down to the docks and see men returning from the war. They say many look barely alive as they're carried off on stretchers. I suppose I will see some on our ship; I feel sorry for them but don't look relish the prospect. Except for finally getting on the ship.

I don't think I'll get any mail on the voyage but I'll try to write to you and post along the way. Father says the best address to give you is the Astor House Hotel, Shanghai. Cousin Edward is the owner.

I send my very best wishes for a Happy New Year! 1919! We shall turn nineteen years old. The horrible war is over, and we have our adult lives ahead. It is both thrilling and frightening.

> Very affectionately,
> Your Friend,
> Miriam Esther Ezra

Hong Kong
4 February 1919

Dear Mena,

What a voyage! The ship is still fitted out for soldiers, including a make-shift hospital. I've met a few healthy ones, have danced a bit, and walked on the deck with one named Reuben Joseph from Shanghai. He is among the few soldiers still aboard; most have already been delivered in Singapore and Hong Kong, where we've had stops of several days each. Reuben is 26. He read economics at Cambridge before the war, got his "first," worked for a while helping someone named John Maynard Keynes research a book on Indian currency. Father knows of the book and Mr. Keynes from the Royal Commission on Indian Currency and Finance. Reuben enlisted in London when the war began. Now his family wants him back in Shanghai to work in the family business. They deal in shares and property. No opium. Or so Reuben says.

Hong Kong is our introduction to China. The Chinese natives working menial jobs are treated like Indian untouchables. Here the English are the Brahmins—or simply the English, also as in India. Many of the Chinese men wear queues—long braids down their backs. They speak Cantonese, which I hear is a different dialect of Chinese from what is spoken in Shanghai. Like Hindi, Bengali in Calcutta, and how many different languages in India? Hundreds?

Naturally, we have Sassoon and Ezra relatives in Hong Kong. They are also related to Reuben Joseph's family and have close business connections. Reuben appeared at Great-Uncle Solomon's home for Sabbath dinner, and was seated across from me. We talked about university in England. I can't wait. Next year by this time...You're so lucky, Mena.

Reuben invited me to ride on the Victoria Peak tram. Father said yes, which scandalized the relatives who heard. Great-Uncle Solomon scolded him. "Nathan, you are too lenient with the girl. To go with a young man alone on the tram? It's not done. Next, I will find out that you also let her read from the Sefer Torah you carry with you." Little does he know. I will write more from Shanghai. I hope there will be letters from you, with news of Bombay and married lady, Maya.

With love from
Miriam Esther Ezra

Shanghai

22 February 1919

Dear Mena,

NO! NO! NO!

How wonderful it was to find three letters from you when we finally arrived in Shanghai. I was hoping for one; three is a bonanza. I read them chronologically by postmark. The third had the news about Maya. Why can't I be in Bombay so we could hold each other and weep together for her?

How she died haunts me. To become so desolate and hang herself from the length of her bridal sari. The cruelty she described to you in your last talk with her—it's unimaginable and inhuman. But bad enough to sacrifice her life?

It's shocking how the joy of the wedding festivities evaporated so quickly to utter slavery in the home of Anil's family. It is unthinkable that such terrible things could happen under that roof. I only visualize physical love as something tender and romantic. Perhaps I am naïve. I imagine that it hurts the first time but hope my husband would be gentle and considerate. To hear about Mena's husband tying her with leather straps while he cursed and beat her and forced himself on her. This can't be normal between a husband and wife. The bruises and cuts she showed you, the pain she described. His mother's indifference, being in the house when Maya screamed as she was beaten. And her own parents refusing to take her back home when she ran away? But how kind of your mother and father to welcome her into your home, if only for that one day before her parents and in-laws dragged her back to her marriage to "protect family honor." Father would have taken her in, too; we discussed it. He suspects your parents risked their reputation and business connections with Maya's and Anil's families in doing the right thing.

I support your pledge to change society so that young women like Maya can avoid her fate. As a doctor, you will be in a good position to take on that challenge. If I become a solicitor, perhaps I will be, too.

Mena, I am too crushed right now to write anything about Shanghai. My body might be here, but my heart is in Bombay, grieving for Maya alongside you.

With love, dear friend,
Miriam

Shanghai

24 March 1919

Dear Mena,

Thank you so much for the birthday and Purim wishes. Being born on Purim is why my middle name is Esther. It's always been special to me to have my own beautiful Megillah scroll. We've brought it here, of course, tucked into the bigger silver case of our Torah. My party this year was a poor version of the celebrations in Bombay, as obviously I have no friends yet. Father invited 20 of the relatives to Cousin Edward's hotel, and before dinner we took out the Megillah and he and I took turns reading it. Of course, the male cousins were scandalized that Father would let me read the Hebrew, but the Megillah isn't as sacred a scroll as the Torah. Anyway, the hotel party in one of the private dining rooms was very nice, but not like the celebrations at home in Bombay, when Khansamah Sahab [Cook] and I would bake the Sephardic sweets——baklava and *hadji badah* cookies (I loved the cardamon smell in the house)—and Mama's recipe for *haman-taschen* shaped in triangles like Haman's ear and filled with poppy seed. I was always so happy that you went with me to take baskets to the Jews in Bycullah and the little children in the kindergarten at the Sassoon School.

Our relatives here are nice enough but very much on edge because of Cousin Edward's troubles. My birthday dinner was the first large gathering of the family since Father and I arrived, and, though he tried hard to make it merry, no one was much in the mood for celebration. In truth, nor was I, as Maya's death continues to plague me. When I think about Queen Esther risking the favor of her husband—maybe risking her life—to make her plea for justice, I wonder if this story is just a myth—or if there really was such a woman who could take such a risk with a powerful man and succeed. What is it about the relationships between men and women and the customs practised in societies that makes such treatment as Maya suffered acceptable not only as a wife's duty but also as a daughter's lot? In Judaism there are many things men can do that are prohibited to women, but every Shabbat husbands recite the *Eshet Chayil* prayer, Woman of Valor, for their wives. Maya's marriage bed amounted to a place of rape and violent torture, yet even her parents refused to protect her. Death became the only escape route she could see. How can we avenge her death in a positive way to try to change the world for the betterment of women? Easy to say, isn't it, Mena? But we must, somehow.

It is tiresome and gloomy to write of such things, but, believe me, there is also plenty of injustice to be seen on the streets of Shanghai. Here, as in Hong Kong, the Chinese natives generally are the underdogs, except for the rich Chinese, and they don't have much official power. Shanghai is a colonial city in a country that is not totally colonial (unlike India). Here, in the heart of China, the city's government is controlled by foreigners, who live in the International Settlement divided mainly among the French, English, Germans, and Americans. Cousin Edward sits on the Municipal Council and, though a Baghdadi Jew by tradition and British by passport, he's actually the first China-born member! But the scandal with his brother, Judah, will soon force his resignation, Father says. I can't figure the whole thing out but I hear baseball and opium in the discussions. Very strange combination.

Cousin Edward does own this wonderful hotel. (Again, for how long?) The Astor House is elegant, located on the North Bund (pronounced like "bun" with a "d"), the main promenade in Shanghai overlooking the Huangpu River. Though it's only a short distance from the dock to the hotel, Cousin Edward met us with his motorcar, a Rolls Royce he bought just before the war. Father was appalled by Edward boasting that it arrived on time, even though the fighting had started. Our baggage went by rickshaw, and I pitied the poor driver, who was very stooped even when standing up.

The Astor House has about 250 rooms, all with their own bathrooms and telephones. The main reception area is very English with heavy mahogany chairs and tables. There are small staircases on either side of it, one leading to the elevators and the other to a dining room. The ballroom is called the Peacock Room—there's a giant stained-glass peacock on one wall.

On my few trips out I've seen familiar sights of poverty along even the nice streets, sights we'd see in the worst areas of Bombay but not so much on our streets in the Fort area or Colaba. (Am I so homesick I'm forgetting or deluding myself about the truth at home?) I've never before seen people drop from hunger and illness right onto the pavement. They lie there until a horse-drawn cart comes and the driver pitches their bodies up like they're twigs for a fire. I saw this happen on Joffre Avenue, the street in the French Concession where Cousin Edward lives in a grand mansion. I mean, grand like Versailles, with antique furniture from France and a large garden in back—twenty-three acres.

Many poor Chinese smoke opium openly. Of course, my relatives both here and in India make most of their living from this disgusting addiction. Father is the only Ezra male of two generations not in the business. One of my Calcutta boy cousins, cast out of university in England, lies around in his room attached to a hookah like the umbilical cord.

I sound prudish. But these sights give a different view of Shanghai compared to the stylish men and women who dine here at the hotel before sauntering off to cabarets and clubs to dance and drink the night away.

I am only an observer of both the ugly underside and the glamour of this "Paris of the Orient." It's not the lot of a Sephardic Jewish girl to participate much in the latter.

With love from
Miriam

Shanghai
16 June 1919

Dear Mena,

How wonderful to hear about your voyage and arrival in London! You might be the only woman in your class at the university but you will be the star. I can't wait to be there myself. Father still says "just" another year. By then this "untidiness" (his word) in the family here will get sorted out and we can resume normal life. Little by little he's shared with me details of the "untidiness." From what little I know, it's hard to foresee a positive resolution.

Cousin Edward, still in his 30s, was a "boy wonder" in business and in the Jewish community, between the hotels and other properties he has built and owned. He's not without virtues, as he's been active in the community, including a society among the Jewish "elders" that tried to help revive Jewish life in Kaifeng, where the synagogue and observance have dissipated. Kaifeng is a city far west of Shanghai, and the Jews who live there are descendants of Silk Road traders who first married Chinese women about a thousand years ago. This society was started by another Ezra, Nissim Elias Benjamin, N.E.B., also a well known personage (and opium dealer), editor of *Israel's Messenger* magazine and a proponent of

Zionism—the dream for a Jewish country in the homeland of Palestine. No one can tell me if he is related, or how, but he also came to Shanghai from India, Lahore to be exact, so he must be.

Back to Cousin Edward. He's first and foremost an opium trader, so opium is the currency financing all the rest. There's a Shanghai Opium Combine, an open and legal organisation of peers, and he was its first president. With his position on the Municipal Council, some saw conflict of interest, but that was tolerated. Amazingly, the Calcutta and Shanghai branches of the family in the so-called "legitimate" opium business can no longer do business with each other. It's outlawed in China to import opium from India. Before we arrived, there was a burning in Pudong, across the river, of what was supposedly the last stock of Indian opium.

The current problem, however, sounds ridiculous but it's possibly the beginning of the end. Last year Cousin Edward's brother, Cousin Judah (who has a twin, Cousin Isaac), paid a baseball team at the Shanghai Race Club to lose against the team Judah had bet on. Judah was thrown out of the club. Generally, Judah and Isaac are less talented in business than Edward, and therefore dependent on him. Now some of their other foibles are coming to light. This reverberates on Edward's position, and he's just had to resign from the Municipal Council.

Although the hotel business appears to be booming, Father says Cousin Edward is losing money. We have moved into his mansion on Avenue Joffre. This doesn't make either Father or me happy, but it's more practical than establishing a temporary home in Shanghai, plus a relief from hotel life. We have two very large and comfortable rooms with bathrooms. Our Torah we keep in a fancy cabinet in Father's room, so he and I can read from it in private. Not exactly a Holy Ark—authentic Louis XV instead. Cousin Edward has his own Torah, which he keeps in the parlour on the first floor, and he teases Father for having brought ours from Bombay. But Father reminds him that our Torah was written in Baghdad more than 100 years ago when Chacham Eliyahu Chaim was chief rabbi, and blessed by his son, the famous Chacham Yosef Chaim, known as the Ben Ish Chai, a highly revered Torah scholar and master of Kabbalah. When Father says, "This is Miriam's Torah," Edward pooh-poohs the Ben Ish's "crazy ideas about educating women and mixing with the Ashkenazim."

As for my activity, I'm taking Chinese lessons! I wasn't proud not to know more than a few words in Hindi as an Anglo there. But with school who had time? In Shanghai I have way too much free time so I'm studying with an old gentleman named Master Lu, who introduced me to another student, a Chinese woman who doesn't know the highest form of Chinese either. Her name is Mei-ling Soong, or Soong Mei-ling (Chinese way). She's mysterious about her exact age, but I suspect she's a year or two older than us. She's Christian and westernized, having studied in the US for ten years, at a couple of schools in the South and then at Wellesley College near Boston. She returned to Shanghai to live with her mother since her father's death. She has brothers and two older sisters, both married and quite prominent here. One, Ching-ling, is married to Dr. Sun Yat-sen, the founder of the China Republic who's much revered, though the Republic has faltered, and the Chinese government has lapsed back to a chaotic mess of feudal warlords in control. The other sister is married to a very rich businessman.

Mei-ling is smart and certainly has an advantage in Chinese, despite her years abroad, but we get together to practise conversation. Often, though, we slip back into English, which she speaks with a drawl from the American South. Her religion and time away from China make her very conscious of the poverty surrounding us. Mei-ling has not been shy about expressing her opinions about conditions in the silk factories, where the women literally work their fingers to the bone and their children are absorbed into this unhealthy environment without education or medical attention. She's just been appointed to a position on the Shanghai Municipal Council's Child Labor Commission, the first woman to serve. She does charity work at the YWCA. (This is the Young Women's Christian Association. I think some of our English schoolmates belong to the one in Bombay). I admire Mei-ling. She is like you and me—a young woman who wants to change bad conditions. I told her about Maya, and she was a very sympathetic listener who agrees that men, especially husbands, should treat women with respect and dignity.

It is rare among the Jewish women I've met—my cousins and their friends—to know any Chinese people, except servants. The men have Chinese business associates, but socially they don't mix much.

All this to tell you that I was surprised to be invited to a party at Mei-ling's home and more surprised that Reuben Joseph was a guest. He is a tennis chum of one of her brothers and another young man, Zhao Yue (again stated the Chinese way, surname first), who recently returned to

Shanghai from the University of Michigan. He got a doctorate there in philosophy, and he and Reuben argue in jest about whose degree will be more useful. Yue has adopted the English name Joe, which, Reuben teases him, matches Yosef, the Hebrew version. The four of us have even played mixed doubles games at the Jewish Recreational Centre, probably the only courts where this <u>very mixed</u> foursome can play.

It is hot now, more like Bombay, which is fine with me. London in the summer is likely cooler. But your new life will make even fog bearable. Do write soon.

Love,
Miriam

Shanghai
28 January 1920

Dear Mena,

I received your letter with New Year wishes three weeks ago and regret I haven't answered before this. Your letters mean so much to me. To know you are thriving in your studies and life in London reminds me what I'm missing. Right now, though, that's hardly my only source of loss and pain.

Father passed away on 29 December. I am devastated. How one's life can change in one year, even in one month. Father fell ill with bronchitis the second night of Chanukah, 17 December. The weather had turned cold overnight, and he came home from a particularly long day in court feeling chilled all over, yet running a high fever. He was put to bed here at Cousin Edward's house, as our relatives have no faith in the conditions at the General Hospital, and the doctor did not dispute their opinion. Two nurses were employed to minister to him day and night. Of course, I barely left his side when he was awake. Some days he appeared to rally, and I read to him. On Shabbat we even took out the Torah and spread it onto his bed to look over the weekly parsha [Torah portion].

Throughout this time Cousin Edward came to his bedside daily for advice. I've come to know there are two types of opium trading—legitimate (sanctioned by law and treaties) and underground (illegal). It seems that Cousin Edward, the supposedly upstanding founder of the legitimate Shanghai Opium Combine, also operated an illegal operation, managed by the hapless twins, Judah and Isaac. To call them hapless is far more polite than the more accurate stupid, unethical, and immoral.

All of their machinations and these troubles of the Shanghai Ezra cousins have weighed so heavily on Father since we arrived that I just know his strength was drained to the point that he had none in reserve to fight his illness. The coughing sounded like a volcano erupting in his chest. Bronchitis apparently degenerated to pneumonia, and the treatment included hot packs to the chest and morphine for the cough. The last two days he slept most of the time, and his breathing sounded raspy as it slowed down until the end. He was buried the next day, according to the Jewish custom of expediting this ritual. Returning his body to Bombay, where my mother is buried, wasn't even discussed. My parents remaining apart in death grieves me almost as much as the reality of losing both of them.

Cousin Edward and his brothers are totally to blame for this calamity. Had they conducted themselves and their business honorably, my father—the wisest, most ethical cousin and, as a lawyer, neutral and neither a participant in nor beneficiary of the family businesses—would not have been called upon to untangle the mess here. You can imagine how unpleasant it is to remain in this house, this grossly ostentatious house, which has become my father's death place. I had to observe the shivah for seven days alongside the relatives here. Since they barely know me, or only as Miriam, "Nathan's spoiled daughter who reads Torah and has Chinese friends," the condolences are mostly paid to Edward. As a woman, I can't be counted in the daily minyan (group of ten required for Jewish worship) but every morning and every night I say the kaddish [prayer for the dead] on my own, weeping next to Father's empty bed within sight of the Torah cabinet.

As you can imagine, I long to leave. I know Father intended to return home this winter to help me prepare to join you in London for my studies at University College. I've expressed this to Cousin Edward and to Uncle Elias in Calcutta, who is now my guardian. I had a letter from Uncle stating that it would be unsuitable for an Ezra daughter to go abroad to university and, anyway, there is no money in Father's estate for this purpose. I was astounded by this fact as I know Father saved all the money Mother had inherited from her parents, as well as a significant sum from his earnings every year, in a special fund for my education in England. Apparently, a few months ago, in October, he'd "loaned" the lion's share of that money to Cousin Edward—there is a note signed by Edward in the locked box of papers Father kept. Only he and I had keys. The note states Edward's pledge to repay in full—<u>without interest</u>, Father typically being way too generous—by 15 January 1920, when Edward was to receive a large sum due him from a Chinese associate. By then Father was dead, of course. I don't know if Edward received that money, but he claims not to have it and operates on the theory that Father's death cancelled the note. Uncle Elias offers to pay my passage back to India to live with his family in Calcutta. It was torture living in that house even passing as a guest. I won't do it. Staying here in Shanghai in this ghastly house with Edward and his family feels like living with my father's murderer. Yet, it's my only option for now. There are great-aunts, Aziza and Aline, who live together in a large flat with plenty of space. That could be like living in a tomb, as between them there is never a smile nor any sign of humour or compassion. Besides, they haven't offered. I am an untouchable in a gilded cage.

Mei-ling, Reuben, and Joe all came during shivah. Also, Joe's new wife, Yanlai. (I went to their wedding party last month. Yanlai is a graduate of Oberlin College in Ohio. So, you see my friends here are a bright lot! I do think Mei-ling would have liked to become Joe's wife, but she keeps up a gracious attitude toward the newlyweds, who met through friends in the States). You can imagine the look of horror on these great-aunts' faces when the three Chinese walked in the door and sat down to speak with me. Reuben's parents also came. I hadn't met Mr. Benjamin Joseph before, although I had glimpsed him with Reuben at synagogue during the High Holy Days. Reuben's mother, Mrs. Malka Joseph, I met at the Jewish School, where she teaches music and I have been helping the students as a tutor. Perhaps she will help me find actual paying work at the school. Or another job, so I can save money on my own to join you in London and begin my university studies. I wish I could rely on my family, but that is not possible.

So, for now, Mena, wishing me good health and good luck are the most relevant portions of your New Year greeting. Happiness—who knows when that will return? At least I have an elegant roof over my head, though it is a blighted roof with an uncertain future, and I am grateful that Cousin Edward and his wife, Mozelle, are not turning me out and still seem to have enough money to feed me, as well as their sons.

Happy New Year, 1920, to you and your family, too. So enveloped in my own misfortune am I that I haven't even asked about them. People hear talk about India 's turmoil—the Amritsar Massacre last summer and demonstrations when the Prince of Wales visited. Revolution is brewing. Do you think Gandhiji's approach is effective? Fasting, praying? You don't write about how you are treated as an Indian woman in London. I hope this isn't anything you have to worry about. I've not forgotten about all that's important in the world view and about changing conditions for the better. Even if I can't pursue my education now, I know Father supported the positive, helping work—mitzvot (commandments literally, but good deeds in practice)—I've pledged to do. He lived his life that way. Now mine is dedicated thus to fulfill his legacy and make his memory a blessing.

> With loving gratitude
> for your friendship,
> Miriam

Shanghai
2 July 1920

Dear Mena,

How nice it must be to finally go home again after completing your first year of study. No doubt, your parents are delighted with your return for the summer. The news from India is of so much unrest and foment for independence. I know your father is active in Congress, so your home must bustle with conversation about all that goes on.

Here in Shanghai the fortunes of Cousin Edward continue to dwindle. He and Mozelle stay at home most evenings, which I take to mean that their formerly busy social life is no more. The only people who come to dinner are relatives. The household is quiet. Some servants have been dismissed. Where they can find new jobs I don't know, as the women, especially, leave weeping.

But I have become a working woman! Mr. Joseph, Reuben's father, invited me to their office one day a few months ago to ask if I'd like to work as an assistant to the trading department. Why, I can't imagine, because I hardly have a head for figures or the intricacies of buying and selling shares. The Joseph operation is one subsidiary of the Sassoon trading company, but Mr. Joseph is really the boss and an owner. Reuben, with his training in economics, works in the business, too, and seems to be heir apparent to take over from his father.

What I do all day is match buy-and-sell orders on companies as they come in and at the end of the day I tally totals and issue confirmations and bills to buyers. Most shares traded on the Shanghai Exchange are for Chinese companies—banks and rubber producers, mainly. But Mr. Joseph and some clients are beginning to become interested in companies abroad. They see the American stock market as the next big opportunity. Reuben analyzes foreign companies and writes opinions on them based on what he can glean from the foreign press, corporate annual reports, and personal contacts, including business people who come through Shanghai. His work is very intense and detailed, with charts and earnings reports spread over his desk, but he loves it, and is generous about explaining it. So, between his work and mine, I'm finally getting some education beyond QMS, but it's not university. Alas, that's still my dream, if I can save up the funds before I'm too old!

My social life is limited. As an Ezra, I'm apparently stigmatized by the broad brush of their scandals. In fact, I was quietly asked to stop tutoring at the Jewish School. Mrs. Joseph—she's asked me to call her Malka— was horrified by this, and I believe she was instrumental in her husband's offering me a job. Reuben, along with Mei-ling and Joe and Yanlai, remains a constant friend, but that's all. Malka, by the way, is Russian, and came to Shanghai after living briefly in Harbin, a city in northern China close to Siberia. So, she's an Ashkenazic Jew like my mother, which makes her more flexible and more understanding about the snubbing from the Baghdadi community, even my own relatives. She suffered from it when she got married. Her in-laws came only grudgingly to her wedding, but the ice melted when Reuben was born the next year. I am fortunate to have her take me under her wing. And the job is interesting, besides getting me out of this poisonous house and making me money, which I save as much as possible.

The house has lapsed into disrepair, and every day it becomes more disheveled. I can almost smell disappointment and desperation. Cousin Edward continues to go to his office and each evening returns looking older and older. He is only in his thirties but appears at least twice that. Mozelle harangues him at dinner about their lost position in society and the bill collectors who have actually begun to call at the house during the day. The two sons, Cecil and Denzil (12 and 5), tear around the house like bandits with no one paying attention to them and, even so young, are abandoned by friends.

Fortunately, I'm escaping soon. Malka Joseph ('Malka" means queen in Hebrew, and that she is to me) has arranged for me to board with her sister and brother-in-law, Rose and Sam Kadushin. Sam is a doctor, also Ashkenazi, whose parents took him from Russia to Tientsin, a city closer to Peking. Their flat is a few blocks away from here in the French Concession, obviously less grand than my cousins', but I will have a room and WC all to myself. Rose and Sam have two small children, Inna and Aaron, and I'll look after them a bit to pay some of my board. Sam's surgery takes up two rooms on the street level floor just below the living quarters.

I told Edward and Mozelle I want to take the beautiful cabinet that houses my Torah, and they've given their blessing on this, which surprised me. Maybe they're feeling guilty. As they said, it's one less thing to forfeit to their creditors. They tell me it is an authentic Louis XV dark wood piece with ornate bronze handles on doors that open outward on the top (where the Torah is) and three shallow drawers underneath. It will be the finest article of furniture in the Kadushin household and will barely fit in my room, but I'll make it work. Not so independent as you in London. But a start.

Love from your working
girl friend,
Miriam

Shanghai
4 January 1922

Dear Mena,

It's hard to believe that three years have passed since I left India with dear Father. I wish you a Happy New Year, as 1922 will make us 22 years old, with you closer to your goal of becoming a doctor and me your uneducated, but still aspiring (and hard working), friend stuck.

Living with the Kadushins has helped me escape the stigma of being an Ezra, but all that pain came back recently when Cousin Edward died. This happened almost two years exactly since Father's death. Edward was not yet 40, but his health had failed along with his fortune and position. He'd suffered a cerebral hemorrhage at this office and died a few days later at a rest home. Only a few close relatives appeared at the burial and throughout shivah, a pittance, compared to the business associates and social friends— Jewish and Chinese—of Edward's past life. Despite the foibles that landed him in dire circumstances, he had some remarkable accomplishments to his name. The Society for the Rescue of the Chinese Jews (from Kaifeng), the Shanghai Zionist Association. The properties and some of the opium trade were prosperous, legitimate businesses, and he admirably used some of the profits to help the community. Between his brothers' bungling and his own greed, it's all fallen to naught. Mozelle and the boys are moving to Hong Kong. The house is already closed up.

The Joseph family never left my side during the ceremony and mourning. Mr. Joseph's standing in the community, despite Malka's "sin" of non-Baghdadi origins, shielded me from the venom of my old great-aunts and those disgusting scoundrels, Cousins Judah and Isaac, who seem oblivious to accepting responsibility for their actions that contributed to the collapse of the "House of Ezra" and to the honor of our family's name in Shanghai.

My position at Joseph & Company has been elevated to chief clearing assistant, so I now oversee the operations of buying and selling, a job that came with a generous raise in pay. The business is growing so much, in large part due to Reuben's reports promoting American shares. I have saved half the money needed just for the journey from Shanghai to London. If I continue at this pace and gain university admittance, who knows? Maybe I can join you in London by my 25th birthday.

My friends the Zhaos have a baby daughter named Suling, so their life has taken a quieter turn. My friend, Mei-ling, remains active in charities, and I try to join her when I finish work. She lobbies the Municipal Council for better conditions for the women laborers and for their children to be sent to school, instead of the current practice of staying all day in the factories with their mothers. We hope to open a school for these children, but finding the money for this enterprise is not easy. The people who have money are consumed with making more and spending it on themselves and their entertainments. One would think that the Soong family could undertake this, but since the patriarch Charlie's death, its finances are officially the province of Mei-ling's sister and brother-in-law, the Kungs, whose interests are hardly altruistic. I surmise that funds also go to maintaining the political prospects, not to mention the living expenses, of the other brother-in-law, Dr. Sun, whose power has diminished so much that he and sister Ching-ling live in virtual exile in Canton. If you think politics in India are complicated, you should learn about China. There are Dr. Sun and his KMT party (Kuoming-tang), the real government in Peking, warlords, Communists, and out and out criminals involved. Within the foreign community in Shanghai there's a sense of cocoon and wonderment that the Chinese struggle among themselves to rule their own country. And, when Chinese protesters take to the streets and damage foreign businesses and homes, you hear shock and outrage in the offices, hotels, and clubs. "Why aren't these people grateful for what we've done for them?" Like the Raj in India.

Alas, I no longer have time for regular Chinese language lessons. Really the only groups of Chinese-only speakers I encounter are servants and the factory workers and their children. They delight in my efforts to try to communicate with them, although I'm not sure if we're always speaking the same dialect. Just by trying I like to think these poor women realize I care about them. Their children are so adorable. It's hard to accept that all they have to look forward to in life is the same mix of abuse, poverty, and misery they and their mothers have now. Even though the mothers are mostly illiterate, they want more for their children and understand that learning how to read and write is important. Our few Chinese volunteers try to teach both the mothers and the children, but only a few hours a week when the factories are closed.

At the Kadushins I'm shedding some of the strict religious ways of my upbringing. They keep kosher but attend the Ashkenazi synagogue only on holidays. Their friends and activities revolve around Shanghai's theatres and concerts. To me, it's always seemed the Sephardis socialize only among themselves. Rose and Sam help other Russians settle here, as since the Revolution their numbers are growing. Many newcomers speak Yiddish, as well as Russian. Yiddish is a combination of Hebrew and German, a folk language Ashkenazic Jews speak in Eastern Europe and Russia. We Baghdadis don't exactly have such a language, though the Sephardi from Spain have Ladino (a mix of Hebrew and Spanish). There are Yiddish journals, plays, songs—a whole different Jewish culture I knew nothing about before.

The revolution in Russia has also brought an onslaught of non-Jewish refugees—White Russians, they're called—to Shanghai. Many of them were aristocrats in the Czar's court. Not only have they never worked for pay, they've barely ever picked up their own clothes from the floor. They're generally unfriendly to Jews. Yet, they come to Sam Kadushin for medical treatment, and he treats them the same as anyone else, despite nastiness and payments that only trickle in, if at all. I've heard more than a few snarling *"zhid,"* a derogatory Russian word for Jew, when I've passed them downstairs. Many women receive treatment for diseases that come from supporting themselves as prostitutes. Their sole possessions are fancy clothes and furs that look increasingly shabby as they lurk on the streets or in disreputable clubs looking for customers. They have neither aptitude nor interest in working as maids, nannies, or governesses, possible jobs to least try. In the morning when I go to work, I see them slumped on the pavement or dragging along Avenue Joffre—their satin evening dresses stained and sometimes ripped, gold high-heel shoes in hand, rouge and lipstick smeared and caked, dyed hair hanging in greasy strings. Sad. But still not as sad as the starving Chinese dropping dead on the pavement or the women in the factories trying to eke out some sort of honest living, even if their employers exploit and abuse them, which certainly the prostitutes' "employers" do, too.

I've gone, dear Mena, without commenting on what you've written about your hours spent with the tenement women on the East End. How universal it is that the poor dwell in such deprived circumstances—lacking good food, air, jobs in pleasant surroundings—that their physical health suffers, even when their spirit reaches for a better life for themselves and certainly for their children. That so many Jews live like this in London shocks me. We who are fortunate that our families have been able to feed, clothe, and educate us have been given the ability and responsibility to help alleviate the bleak future others face. Your commitment to this work spurs me on to do more—and gratifies me, as I have truly chosen a kindred spirit as my dearest, though faraway, friend.

Yours with love,
Miriam

Shanghai

2 July 1925

Dear Mena,

Marie Stopes? Mothers' clinic? The Society for Constructive Birth Control? I expected you'd return to India with your medical credential at the earliest possible opportunity. But I've read about the controversial Marie Stopes. To champion women engaging in sex for pleasure, not solely to bear children, is very brave. The pleasure part, I suspect, is more the interest of wealthy women. Being able to plan when and when not to become pregnant is so practical and much needed among the poor. The factory workers I try to help need it, as they have trouble keeping their children safe and healthy.

Mei-ling and our friend, Yanlai, who were educated in America, talk about a woman in Chicago named Jane Addams who runs a "settlement house," a place in a poor neighborhood that offers shelter, food, and athletics and teaches people English and other skills to help them get jobs and eventually American citizenship. This Miss Addams sounds like your Miss Stopes. How fortunate you are to be able to work with such a pioneer.

One ally in my work is Reuben's mother, Malka, who is so unlike the other Jewish wives. What she calls social work, which is the name for what Jane Addams does, most of her friends think means their social life! I'd like to think that my mother, had she lived, would have been like Malka and her sister, Rose Kadushin, two Ashkenazic ladies whose interests and activities transcend mah jongg, new frocks, and parties. Not that the Baghdadi Sephardic women are uncharitable or frivolous, but their scope is limited to the Jewish community (where, surprisingly, here, too, there are some poorer people). Malka, who like my mother entered the Sephardic group by marriage rather than birth, directs her efforts toward outsiders because she's still one—even among Jews.

Sadly, she has recently learned that she has cancer of the breast, which is a terrible disease with no cure, as surely you know. Her husband, Benjamin, is desperately seeking advice from people he knows everywhere, and there is consensus that her prognosis is not good. They say, if she lives another year, it will be a miracle. Malka is very stalwart about this news, which has brought about a significant occurrence in my life. I've been oblivious to Reuben's fondness for me, thinking it was simply platonic friendship, especially since we work in the same firm. Reuben talks about economics and politics and religion, jousting verbally all the time with Joe and other friends, up-to-date on world affairs, friendly—yet shy in some ways. Two weeks ago he asked me to accompany him to a tea dance at the Cathay Hotel, the only time we've been together just the two of us. Our first dance was very properly spaced—in fact, another whole of me could have fit in between us! Then the music turned to a very slow tune, and he suddenly pulled me closer, leaned his head down and asked, "Miriam, you know I have admired and cared for you for so long, but do you know I love you?" The intimacy of his whisper in my ear and our closeness gave me a physical feeling I've hardly ever experienced. I assume it's sexual arousal. I feel so naïve, Mena, but whom can I discuss this with, if not you? Especially now, as you work with Marie Stopes, I trust that you are learning enough for two of us.

Reuben has asked me to marry him and soon, so that his mother will witness this simcha [happy occasion]. I do care about him very much, but the taste of independence has been sweet and satisfying. Reuben knows and understands my longing for a university education. He says he would see that it happens. His father wants him to open an office in America— in New York—where I can go to a college called Barnard that is part of Columbia University. A lovely plan but obviously not immediate. With Malka's health, Reuben and his father have already put off a preliminary trip there.

It's hard to integrate all this into my thinking after these years of self-reliance, without attachment or obligation to any family, and a routine that is pleasant enough—work, friends—and stable. I cannot imagine myself as a wife or a mother—and how would I manage children and go to university at the same time? But this is jumping way ahead. Here I am, after only a few dates, writing about a house full of children. I definitely need you and your Marie Stopes to advise me on how to avoid that too soon.

In case you are waiting in suspense for my decision, it is a decision not to decide. Reuben and I are now official as an attached, courting couple attending social functions together. In my heart I've made the decision to marry Reuben eventually. Yet, right now marriage feels like surrender and forfeit. Reuben calls me stubborn. What do you think?

Your stubborn friend,
Miriam Ezra

10 December 1927

Dear Mena,

Your professional accomplishments continue to amaze me, but moving to a mining town in the hinterlands of Scotland? It's honorable work to try to improve the health of the families there, but your life in London brings you so much pleasure—theatre, concerts, opera, museums, walks in the great parks. This Dr. Andrews must be Svengali to persuade you to work in his clinic. I hope your marriage plans come to fruition soon. It's funny, but I don't picture your parents, who are so progressive and fair-minded, objecting to your suitor because he is Anglo and not Hindu. Of course, who am I to talk? The division between Ashkenazic and Sephardic Jews is so ridiculous but so extreme in families. Reuben and I claim we are the best of both worlds with Ashkenazic mothers and Sephardic fathers.

My mother-in-law, Malka, confounds her doctors by not only living but thriving and continuing all her activities. Now they say perhaps it wasn't cancer, just a tumor or cyst that wasn't malignant. Thankfully, when told first there was no hope, she refused the terrible surgery that was recommended. Could it be a real miracle? I've always taken the miracles in the Torah with a pinch of salt. Who can believe a great flood receded after Noah built his ark filled with animals? And the Red Sea really parted when Moses led the Israelites out of Egypt? But seeing my indomitable mother-in-law, who in truth has become my mother, perhaps I should start to trust that miracles do happen

Malka's recovery allows us to forge ahead with our plans for the American office. Reuben and his father have just returned from a trip to New York, where Reuben will be in charge of the office that will open at the beginning of 1930. Although I hope to be a mother of at least one child by then, I plan to enroll at Barnard College. In the meantime, I remain at my job at Joseph & Company and continue to learn more and more about different aspects of the business in order to be useful in the New York operation. It's education—although not the subjects I crave to learn more about: literature, history, the law.

Living with Reuben's parents relieves me of running a household. There are servants, but Malka, coming from a less privileged background, is an accomplished cook, especially of Ashkenazic Jewish dishes, which we have often and she's teaching me how to make. Sweet-and-sour cabbage borscht with meat, dumplings called kreplach that are filled with meat like ones the Chinese eat, crepes called blintzes filled with a dry cheese that's hard to find here, noodles mixed with butter and mali [sour cream]. When I smell and eat these dishes, it's as if my mother has returned.

The most interesting news here is the wedding of my friend Mei-ling. She married General Chiang Kai-shek, head of the KMT party since Dr. Sun died. They have courted for a long time, but Mei-ling's mother opposed the marriage, because Chiang was divorced, not a Christian, and is a boor. He has recently obtained a divorce and become a Methodist, like the Soong family, but boorishness is not so easy to remedy. He is uncouth and boastful, arrogant with no apparent attributes to warrant it. When not fawning after people he perceives to be wealthy or otherwise important, he stands away from the group and whispers with close aides, which makes one think he's constantly scheming. Reuben says Chiang owes his position and financial support to the Green Gang leader Du Yuesheng, who's known as "Big-Eared Du," because his ears stick out so prominently. Chiang acts as if he's the designated heir to Dr. Sun, but Soong Ching-ling, Mei-ling's sister and the widow of Dr. Sun, told me before the wedding that is not true. Dr. Sun didn't trust Chiang, she said.

Despite all this, it appears that the Soong family, except Ching-ling, has accepted the match. The wedding was quite posh. First, there was a private religious (Christian) ceremony in Mrs. Soong's home. As close friends we attended, along with Joe and Suling. Then there was a Chinese style ceremony for 1300 (!!) guests in the ballroom of the Majestic Hotel. You should have seen the streets—people stood there to watch their car pass. You'd think it was King George and Queen Mary.

Mei-ling will continue to work in the factory women's center but she will be much busier now as Chiang's wife. The role will suit her well, and she can perhaps add some class and polish to his coterie. No doubt, the Soong money added to the criminals' will feather the nest. I'm afraid the more legitimate businessmen are in his corner, too, as they collaborated with him to squash the Communists' quest to end the foreign rule of Shanghai. Of course, this works in the favor of Joseph & Company and its close affiliates in the Sephardic business community here. But Reuben and his father see this as a portent that the future will not be forever smooth for our kind. Ergo, the New York plan.

I send best wishes for a very Happy New Year. Please send news of life in Scotland and your Dr. Andrews.

With love,
Miriam Ezra Joseph

Shanghai
12 December 1929

Dear Mena,

As I write to wish you a Happy New Year, I contemplate the start of the 1930s with grave reservations about what kind of decade it will be. As you surely know, the American stock market has collapsed with a bang and along with it our plans to move to New York. We were holding tickets to leave here 2 November. But Reuben and his father became uneasy with the trend they observed all summer—that larger investors seemed to be selling their shares, which caused prices to begin to fall. I didn't know that to be safe they themselves liquidated the firm's—and their personal—holdings in late July. They advised their clients to do the same, though some declined to act on this advice. Reuben cancelled our passage. So we remain here.

After all my trepidation about balancing life as both a mother and a university student, I will have to worry about neither. For about two years after Reuben and I got married we used the device you sent me from the Marie Stopes clinic. For another two years we didn't, and nothing happened. Finally, we both went to doctors for extensive examinations and tests, and the conclusion was that Reuben's war injuries rendered him unable to father a child.

And compounding this news, I have lost a dear friend, Mei-ling, Madame Chiang, also for reasons completely beyond my control. Her husband, Chiang Kai-shek, has forbidden her to associate with me because of something my infamous Cousin Edward did during the legal troubles Father came here to solve. It seems Edward testified against a <u>gentleman</u>— an overly flattering term for this man—named Paul Yip, who is an associate of the Green Gang leader "Big-Eared" Du. This led to Yip's going to jail for a short period of time, but he and Du apparently harbor great enmity toward the Ezra family—even a totally innocent member like me—and

Du's enemies would, of course, become Chiang's as the latter depends on Du to provide money for his military and political campaigns against the Communists. Mei-ling herself delivered the news of this breach in our friendship. She phoned and asked to visit our home at teatime, nothing extraordinary about that, and managed to arrive within minutes after we—Reuben, his father, and I—arrived home from the office. Malka made sure a lovely tea table was laid. Mei-ling first helped herself to a plateful of smoked salmon sandwiches and then proceeded to display the most awful behavior you could imagine—screaming and yelling about my nefarious relatives and insinuating that I was no better. She went so far as to try to blackmail Reuben and his father into contributing to Chiang's war chest by threatening to expose their connection to the nefarious Ezra brothers in business circles from New York to Hong Kong. As sad and shocked as I was about this outburst, it was almost laughable to see this perfectly turned out little woman expounding and pointing fingers between bites of sandwich and sips of tea. Reuben and Benjamin simply listened, smiled, and, when she stopped to catch her breath and signal she wanted more tea, walked together over to her chair and each took one arm to lift her up and escort her to the door. It was magnificent. After seeing her out, my husband and both of his parents embraced me tenderly, as I'd erupted in tears from the shock of Mei-ling's performance and the reality I had lost a close friend. News of this visit has reached all of the Joseph business colleagues who, at least to our faces, support the decision not to succumb to Chiang's extortion. What they do privately we don't know. So far this hasn't affected our business or social position. But I'm now barred from the factory women's center, recently renamed the Madame Chiang Center.

I am trying to temper my disappointment about all of these circumstances by focusing on good fortune. I am a woman who, after leaving my beloved home and being orphaned, is loved and valued and protected in a way so many aren't—as we know from our dear Maya and the coal miners' wives you see and the factory women I see who struggle to feed their children a daily bowl of rice. I have been accepted into a wonderful family and not only allowed, but encouraged, by my husband and in-laws to maintain an active role in their business. We didn't lose all our money—in fact, Reuben's canny investment tactics provided us and the clients who listened to him with enough dollars and pounds sterling to last a lifetime. Malka, my mother-in-law, remains healthy and active to the amazement of her doctors, who were so wrong about her condition. (Could the doctors be just as wrong about Reuben's?) Yet, I grieve for the children I will never bear and the formal education I am less and less likely to receive. If only I knew Chinese better—how to read and write—I could matriculate here in Shanghai. I do devour the shipments of books that the English language bookstore orders for me and those you send.

But hard as I try to be optimistic, I can't help but worry about matters beyond my control and my life. What will happen when so many countries are falling into economic depression? America seemed to so strong. Here in China there is civil war between the KMT and the Communists. You write about the miners' strikes that have only resulted in lower wages and worse working conditions.

All one person can do is push on and wish and hope for the best. You are helping to make things better for people who have far less. I've done what I can in a small way but now am searching for another project to continue this work.

Happy New Year! Reuben promises me a trip to India or London in the next year. Perhaps we can meet in one of those places. I can't believe eleven years have passed since we saw each other.

My best wishes to Dr. Andrews—Thomas—and to you as you continue your work together and your romance. Maybe 1930 will bring you together as man and wife, finally.

Yours with love,
Miriam Ezra Joseph

Shanghai
30 December 1932

Dear Mena,

Oh, such sorrow! The news of the calamity in your town made me wish I could run to your side and embrace you and hold you close in your grief. How brave Thomas was to go into the mine only minutes after the first blast. With tears in my eyes I try to picture him almost reaching the top carrying a miner in his arms when the second explosion hit. After our brief but wonderful meeting with the two of you in London two years ago, I could, of course, see why you and he were such a perfect couple, two people overflowing with compassion and selflessness and equipped with the talent and training to administer care and comfort to the needy. My heart breaks for you and for the other women and their children there who have lost their husbands and fathers, the breadwinners of their families.

But my chief concern right now is for you. It was only a few months ago that I rejoiced at your joy and expectation when you wrote all parents had finally agreed to your match and a wedding in Bombay in February. It's good that you're going home, anyway, after this catastrophe. I'm hardly surprised by your plan to stay in the town until summer to help your neighbors and patients get through these first few months of distress. After that, starting a women's clinic in a village? You say that, with Maya and me not there, you have no friends left in Bombay, but surely a hospital job in the city would reacquaint you with people there and introduce you to new ones. Is it necessary—to say nothing about desirable—to isolate yourself to such a degree and choose the tough path you've got in mind? Surely, there are enough poor and otherwise unfortunate women in the city who would benefit from your services?

I understand and respect the influence on you of Gandhiji's teaching on Satyagraha [insistence on truth] with the emphasis on constructive ways to demonstrate it. Yet, denying yourself some comforts of city life in favor of the privations of the village makes no sense to me. Don't you think you would still fulfill his model of surmounting injustice by working toward correcting the evils that cause it even if you don't completely adopt his personal penchant for chastity and poverty? You may think there will never be another man for you. Thomas, no doubt, was exceptional. However, time can bring healing and the hope of another love. Sequestering yourself in a village will isolate you from such possibility. If you must encamp yourself in such a place, it's a relief to hear that it's a totally Hindu village. Then perhaps one virtue of its remoteness will be freedom from the violence the religions are inflicting on one another in India. Like Chinese fighting against Chinese here.

I shall not belabor this point. It's your life. I confess my reaction, while purely motivated regarding your future, is also selfish. You've written the post to and from villages is slow and often non-existent, and our correspondence is a lifeline, as you're my only soul mate as well as an inspiration to me. In the Jewish world your work is tzedekah [justice], ministering to the less fortunate, trying to alleviate injustice in their lives.

I'm continuing the work that I began with Soong Mei-ling, though she is no longer part of my life. Yanlai Zhao has taken my side and joined me in this endeavor. Our husbands remain the best of friends, spending many evenings in discussion about how Jewish and Confucian tenets compare and differ. Joe, of course, is a professor. Reuben only thinks he is! Yanlai and I are practical. She is scholarly but does not work at a job. Now that her daughter Suling goes to school all day, she wants to occupy herself with something useful. We are plotting a new center to be called Malka House in memory of my dear mother-in-law.

I, of course, still work at the office all day, and Reuben has made me a partner since his father died last year. Yanlai will assume management responsibility at Malka House, which will be a place where women in jobs and home situations that could kill or seriously harm them can live in safety, with their children, while we prepare them for work beyond the treacherous silk factories or, worse, the street. Reuben and I have bought a small apartment house (in the Hongkou district) that had only a few tenants. Those that remained have moved to another, newer, building we own nearby. Hongkou was where the first Sephardic Jews in Shanghai built nice homes, but now it is a crowded area of Chinese only. The future Malka House needs repairs, and Yanlai oversees the workers who are performing them. A friend and business associate from Warsaw, Nachman Tanski, visited us recently and generously donated money to help us buy furniture and equip the kitchen. There will be enough space for up to 40 women and as many as four children each. There has been a new influx of Russian Jews from Harbin since the Japanese have conquered Manchuria. Many of these Jews have owned small factories and stores they are establishing again here, so they will need good workers in their businesses and homes. We're approaching them to give jobs to Malka House women.

Despite its Jewish name, Malka House will serve Chinese women only. Of course, there are Jews in need, but Reuben and I do our part to contribute to the community's social work projects for them. There are few places like this set up by rich Chinese, though I hear Big-Eared Du helps the poor. Soong Mei-ling has begun to set up schools and homes for Chinese war orphans—only children of KMT fighters, not the Communists. She calls them "warphans." You'd think, with the Japanese breathing down China's neck and slowly making incursions south, Chiang and the Communists would stop fighting each other and face Japan together to save the country.

We're on the same path, dear Mena, but in different ways and places. Isn't it amazing after being apart so long we share the same concerns and endeavor to resolve the problems other women face?

Be well as you mourn Thomas.

With respect and caring,
Miriam Joseph

Shanghai
18 December 1938

Dear Mena,

A slew of letters and photographs have suddenly arrived. What a Chanukah gift for your Jewish friend! The pictures show the years in the village wore well and easy on you, and certainly the clinic you began looks well tended. How clever to have attracted a corps of doctors and nurses in training and to have convinced their universities to apply service there to their credential process. I feel as if we need to start over getting acquainted again, as the letters from your few trips out of the village to places with reliable post were so brief and sketchy, though welcome when they came. I was also frustrated knowing you weren't receiving mine. But I am very glad you are back in Bombay in close proximity to your parents. They also look well on the photos.

Malka House is thriving, if that is the precise term for a place that absorbs suffering. If there were no more women and children in need of our services, it would make me very happy to close our doors. Alas, as you well know, that will not happen. It would take what we Jews long for—the coming of Moshiach, the Messiah.

Instead of the Messiah, I fear his exact opposite threatens the Jewish people: Hitler. The world turns a blind eye to this tyrant with shameful policies of visas and quotas that keep Jews in his stranglehold unto death. You have heard, of course, of Kristallnacht last month. After this I don't know how anyone can deny there will be more and more pogroms all over Europe. The Jews aside, it's disgraceful the world gave Hitler leave to simply march into Austria all the while making noise about Czechoslovakia. How disgusting it was to see the photographs of Chamberlain waving that piece of paper after he flew to Hitler's home groveling. We here with British citizenship nearly threw our passports in the fire, but there are enough stateless Jews in the world without adding a couple more. For one brief moment Reuben and I even considered trying to claim citizenship in Iraq, now that it's an independent kingdom. That moment passed quickly, as our few cousins still there have written that Nazi propaganda has infiltrated Baghdad. While they've long considered themselves Arabs practicing the Jewish religion, their non-Jewish Arab neighbors now simply regard them as JEWS.

In Shanghai we're on the receiving end of refugees who make it out of Europe by virtue of transit visas issued, some tell us, by a lowly but beneficent Chinese deputy consul in Vienna named Ho Feng-Shan. Our city is in tumult as the arrival of the Japanese has voided any Chinese government influence that might have remained, and the foreign concessions—British, French, American—vie to be the conquerors' favorite. The Germans, of course, take that prize, and are Shanghai's new elite. The Japanese don't seem ill-disposed to the Jews and anyway have their hands full simply keeping order in the city, which makes the port open for the refugees coming from Europe without proper papers or passports.

We in the larger Jewish community sense and WE, Reuben and I, help these people get settled. A few have arrived with some smuggled money or other negotiable assets, but even the previously wealthy are in reduced circumstances. One woman sewed stock certificates into a down-filled quilt, and her son came into our office to sell them. Imagine a stack of paper leaking pinfeathers like an unclean chicken. The young man is quite clever and speaks excellent English, so we've hired him as a clerk in the office, as at 17 his formal education has come to a halt and his family needs him to work.

This young man is the second refugee who has joined the ranks of Joseph & Company. We've also taken on Erich Heilbron, a lawyer from Vienna who recently arrived, preceded by an excellent recommendation from Nachman Tanski, our client and friend from Warsaw, who knows Erich's family. Erich is single, age 33, the only member of his family who's left Europe. His can't understand how his parents can delude themselves into thinking Hitler is a phase that will pass. His sister's husband, a physician, was taken to a concentration camp immediately after the Anschluss and has already died. The sister refuses to leave the parents, which sounds noble, but she's not so naïve as the parents, and has sent her young daughter off on the kindertransport to London, where there is another sister. Apparently, Nachman Tanski, our mutual friend, intervened to secure the child's passage—and likely paid for it. Erich is living with us, and why not, as we are only two still in Malka and Benjamin's big house? Erich is a boon companion, very polite and thoughtful, and fits right into the philosophic discussions Reuben and Joe still have at least once a week. Erich, coming from a very assimilated family, knows little of Judaism in a formal religious sense. Yet, he enjoys going to synagogue with Reuben and indulges me in listening to my reading from my Torah, still housed in its fancy Louis XV cabinet. Is there another Torah anywhere in such a fine Ark?

We have in a sense adopted the daughter of a wretched woman who died at Malka House. Feng Nien, who likes being called Nina, is twelve years old, and has been with us for the past 8 months. Her mother died after an incident perpetrated by a businessman who was master of the house where she worked as lady's maid, dressmaker, and laundress. Feng Nien discovered her mother backed against the wall on a hard marble staircase. She was pushing the man away when she tripped and fell down the steps, landing face down before the girl could reach her. This man, Tang Guang, is an associate of the Green Gang. In order to clean up the mess, he and some of his henchmen loaded mother and daughter onto a truck, drove them to Malka House, and sped away. When our director, Kan Jobing, heard the thump of a body crudely dumped in the doorway, a child crying, and a truck leaving, she found poor Feng Nien crouching next to her mother, who wore a satchel of money hung around her broken neck. The mother didn't last the night. Naturally, there is no legal recourse, as one doesn't act against someone such as Tang or any member of the Green Gang. I only wondered for a moment how he knew to bring Nina and her mother to Malka House, as our address is deliberately not publicized. Dear Madame Chiang no doubt furnished the information. Despite the lapse in our friendship, she's in a position to keep tabs on my activity.

Nina is a sweet child, very anxious to help us, as well as the servants, yet obviously clever and thirsting for knowledge. We were first at a loss about where to send her to school, but we started by privately employing Miss Margaret Hardwell, a young woman from Leeds, to teach her English last year. By the beginning of the fall term, Nina was able to enter the British International School. If I could not have a child of my own, at least I've been able to foster the success of one who might have been left to live on the street—or worse. We have taken her to synagogue, but the Sephardic women in the balcony who pretend not to notice when we walk in to take our seats, whisper and point to us when I glance around during the service. I don't expect Nina to adopt Judaism, but she's fascinated by the Torah when I take it out at home. Perhaps she will revive the Chinese line of Jews, long dissipated from its roots in Kaifeng, which my Cousin Edward Ezra tried to sustain. Speaking of the infamous Ezra brothers of Shanghai, Cousins Judah and Isaac now loll in prison in the States, having imported their degenerate opium business there in consort with American criminal elements—Jews and Italians. I hope they rot to death there. I shall never get over Father's death, a sacrifice to the cause of saving those unsalvageable relatives.

Dear Mena, it is reassuring to know you are back in Bombay within reach by regular post again. Please give my regards to your precious parents. No doubt, their involvement in Congress [Gandhi's political party leading the way toward Indian independence] keeps them vital.

Always yours,
Miriam

Shanghai
7 February 1942

Dear Mena,

We've just heard that the United States is loaning 500 million dollars to China for the war effort. President Roosevelt called Chiang Kai-shek his ally in Asia. Doesn't the president know that Chiang is more concerned with overcoming the Communists and keeping himself in power than ridding China of the Japanese? This sign of trust and confidence will only puff up Chiang and Mei-ling, and the money will land in their personal coffers. The KMT leaders are corrupt. Many retain old allegiances to the warlords—like your maharajahs—that still dominate certain provinces. The troops are ragtag, poorly trained and equipped. China the Asian hope to defeat Japan? Hardly.

There is relief that America has entered the war, but that does not alleviate the fear of war and the pain we Jews feel hearing news about ghettos and mass killings. Hitler seems to be unstoppable, though we can only hope Russia will prove impermeable to him, as it was to Napoleon. In less than two months Japan has surged throughout Asia: Hong Kong, Thailand, Malaya, Singapore, and Burma have toppled over like dominoes. I hope India will be spared, but Japan talks of liberating your country from British colonialism, the same goal as your countrymen. But submission to the Japanese isn't independence.

We go on tentatively with minimal change to our life so far. It's much harder for the Chinese, who have been brutalized by the Japanese for several years. Our relatives in Hong Kong have already been ordered into a camp for citizens of Britain and America. We are under few illusions about our future.

Which is worse—being British citizens or being Jewish? At the moment our passports pose the greater threat here in Shanghai, and we are forced to wear badges with a large "B" on them, not unlike the yellow stars Jews wear in Europe. One assumes the peril of being Jewish would be confined to countries Hitler has conquered. Since the *Farhud* [pogrom] in Baghdad last summer, I know this is not the case. Jews have had their sporadic problems among the Arabs for centuries, which is why families moved to India 150 years ago. India has been a welcoming place with anti-Semitism nil among the natives. Wandering further to China and Hong Kong was strictly for business reasons. Or, in my case, family loyalty, misplaced on the part of my too generous Father. But the *Farhud* brought the Jewish community of Baghdad to a serious questioning of its long history there. The savagery exceeded anything ever experienced before. My cousin Abraham's wife, Zafira, was set upon by a group of men let into the house by their driver, who joined in raping her and slitting open her pregnant belly, which killed her and the child in one stroke. All in front of Zafira's parents as Abraham was skirting around the mobs trying to get home from his office. Where can we be safe? Reuben and I have long favored the Zionist case for a Jewish homeland in Palestine. But Hitler's stampede across North Africa makes this yet another fantasy.

Our friends the Zhaos, Joe and Yanlai, and their two daughters have moved in with us since the Japanese confiscated their house in January to billet officers. The oldest daughter, Suling, is 20, a beauty and so intelligent. Her parents had planned to send her to America to university—to one of their schools, Michigan or Oberlin—but the war obliterated that plan, so she studies at St. John's University here. There is also Yingfan, cute but devilish, who is eight and had started at the British School, which is closed. Our Nina tutors her and a few other children in English and maths in a little classroom we have fashioned out of our library. Yanlai is teaching our cook, Kwong, the kosher versions of some Chinese specialties her family favors, so we have an international household. It is wonderful to have a houseful after so many years as just a couple. How long it will last no one ventures a guess. In the meantime, you can only imagine the horror on the faces of some of our fellow Jews at this setup. In their homes Chinese only reside in the servants' quarters. Kwong and our maid, Bao, are proud, especially since the Zhaos are so unpretentious, and we try to treat all as family. Their own cook and amah chose to return to their home villages.

You write of your friends who've just made it back from Singapore. They're lucky to have escaped, but their bitterness at being unprotected by the mighty Empire is understandable. No doubt, this reinforces India's disposition toward independence, though the priority, I should think, is to remain free of the Japanese and get through this dreadful war.

Oh, Mena, can you believe we have lived nearly 42 years and seen two wars encompass the entire globe? And we fight our own wars in a small way, you in Bombay and me in Shanghai, trying to make a safer and healthier world for women and girls. Malka House hangs on only because Reuben and I pour so much of our capital into its operation. Our income has dwindled, as trading in markets abroad has become almost impossible, and the Japanese have taken over so many of our properties with no thought of paying rent. What will happen to Malka House if we become prisoners of war I don't know. I am glad your hospital clinic remains open and in general just so, so, so happy that you have accustomed yourself anew to Bombay in the bosom of your family.

Thank you for the early birthday wishes. Yes, I shall take out the little Megillah again this year, and Reuben insists there will be a party. Nina loves Purim, and is advising one of the seamstresses at Malka House in the making of little Yingfan's first Queen Esther costume. Life is not all despair.

Love from an aging queen,
Miriam

Shanghai
26 February 1943

Dear Mena,

It's official. Reuben and I are departing for a prison camp for British nationals. There are a few in the city that are quite full. Yangchow about 240 kilometers from here is where we've been assigned. We can take a suitcase each. Since the Zhao family has been with us, we can transfer the title of our house to them; fortunately, it doesn't seem to suit the Japanese. Erich Heilbrun, as a stateless Jew from Europe, remains in the house with them and runs what remains of our business.

It had been rumored the Japanese intended to follow the lead of their German friends by deporting the Jews of Shanghai, especially those who came here to escape the Nazis. A Japanese consul named Shibata last summer informed a group of Jewish leaders of a plan to round everyone up on Rosh Hashanah. Nothing came of this, except the Jews at the meeting were taken to Bridge House, the Japanese headquarters, and subjected to torture and imprisonment for a few weeks, which makes no sense except perhaps the Japanese wanted to impress the Germans by making these poor men pay for participating in Shibata's crime of revealing secret information. Shibata, meanwhile, was removed from his post and sent back to Japan.

Although the Jews skated through, it's still likely there will be some consequences meted out by the Japanese at the behest of the Germans. Erich, having lived in Vienna until the autumn of 1938, sees the handwriting on the wall but is resolved to survive. He is 38 now, 17 years older than Zhao Suling, who is so lovely and quite mature, but there are signs of romance between them. Joe and Yanlai respect him very much, though they'd prefer to see her married to a Chinese man closer to her own age. However, no one begrudges anyone what little happiness and pleasure is possible now. Both Joe and Yanlai know the old order of traditions in China is on the cusp of breaking apart. As Reuben and I know, too, the life we've known here will not last, even if we're fortunate enough to return unscathed from the prison camp.

Mena, since the "Quit India" resolution last summer, it's evident that nothing will be the same in India or anywhere when this infernal war ends, even if the Allies win. This reinforces what I have known always—our friendship is unique in surviving the insanity of events and long years of separation. Having parted when we were barely beyond school, we've lived in parallel. Just as you sojourned to the village (though voluntarily), I depart for the hinterlands, too. As you toil at the hospital, I spend my remaining days in Shanghai at Malka House, which Yanlai, Suling, and Nina promise to keep open to women who now have to worry about Japanese soldiers, in addition to simply keeping their children sheltered and fed. Mei-ling's "warphan" homes run with abundant food, clothes, and caretakers, thanks to her status as "First Lady of China" with American charity pouring into them (and to her own pocketbook, no doubt. Did you see photos of her visit to Washington and her speech to the US Congress? No one dresses like that here anymore.)

I must be going, as we're to report tomorrow to a place on Bubbling Well Road, a central street, and then march to the Bund and board a boat to Yangchow. Access to the post is only one of the uncertainties about what faces Reuben and me. But do know always, dear Mena, whatever lies ahead, you have always been and remain closer than a sister could ever be. I pray for a speedy end to the war with our good health and ability to work intact AND a reunion after so long.

With heartfelt love,
Miriam

P.S. Do you think the Japanese will throw me my usual Purim birthday party? Ha! I'm leaving the Torah and little Megillah safely tucked away in Louis XV's Ark.

Shanghai
18 September 1945

Dear Mena,

How much it meant, returning to Shanghai, to find your letters carefully boxed for me by Yanlai. Such faithfulness is much appreciated. I was, however, sad to read both of your parents have died in the past two years. How fortunate you were to have had them as long as you did, but even with extreme age and illness, death always shocks as a finality that's hard to overcome. I pray you find comfort in memories of two lives well lived. Certainly, you display the active concern and care for your fellow Indians that is your parents' legacy. How proud they must have been of you.

Our experience in the camp I can't forget, hard as I might try. But neither will I write details, as they're best saved for a time when we can sit down with a pot of tea—or a bottle of sherry. Would that such a time come soon.

We are alive, and what we endured pales compared to the news from Europe that daily brings new shock and amazement at the breadth and nature of the inhumanity. Not that the Japanese didn't do their share.

Poor dear Erich Heilbrun and so many others from Europe cling to the possibility of good news, even though the lists of dead are updated, posted, and published, and many of their fellow refugees hear the worst about their relatives everyday. While we with passports from the enemies of the Japanese were confined to camps, the European Jews who came here from 1937 on were forced to live in the crowded Hongkou district soon after we left. This ghetto was the Japanese answer to the Germans' original request for the liquidation of the Jews. Many of the Jews from Germany and Austria were so put out at their exile to Shanghai from Day 1, and I can only imagine how it was for these people when they were crammed into small tenement apartments in close proximity to poor Chinese. Only now, that the full extent of what they escaped is known, is there a modicum of gratitude for life itself among these malcontents, along with their understandable grief. Erich has told us about the lively cultural activities—music, newspapers, a radio station, "salon" discussions, Viennese restaurants— that sprang up in the ghetto. In this sense I want to say "Jews will be Jews," for Reuben and I experienced this in a small way in the camp. The Japanese had no restrictions on our practice of religion, and we crudely celebrated all holidays. Groups of young people created a band and orchestra and football teams. People passed around the few books anyone could bring along, and we had discussions about them in the evening. No restaurants or cabaret clubs. We were lucky to have a cup of rice with a vegetable in it. The meat was untouchable, even if one were to have forsaken the rules of kosher food. In Shanghai supplies were hard to come by, too, but conditions not so spare as in Yangchow, which is quite remote.

Our household remains diverse, as Joe and Yanlai have done their best to maintain the house itself, now with no servants. Nina, nineteen, is proving to be a competent cook, and she enjoys supervising Yingfan. As her schooling suffered and ended during the war, she's resigned to domestic work and caretaking as a vocation. I'm sad about this but unsure how to change that path. To have formally adopted her was bureaucratically impossible, though we tried. Now she is an adult. Her inclination to help people certainly developed through working at Malka House, which is no more. The Japanese raided it, a prospect that had been rumored a few days before, so Yanlai, Suling, and Nina hustled out the remaining few women and children just in time. Some Russian Jewish families gave them shelter.

The Russian Jews here fared best during the war, as they were stateless. This was one time when no passport was better than any, but as we all see the handwriting on the wall and envision leaving China for good, they will have the most problems getting out.

Why leave China, you might ask? The civil war is not going Chiang Kai-shek's way, despite the support he gets from the US. The KMT is tired from so many years of fighting both the Japanese and the Communists. Chiang is arrogant without reason to be and more devoted to the cause of Chiang Kai-shek than to the Chinese people. His nemesis, Mao Tse-tung, is intellectually superior, and has studied Chinese tradition and culture to an extent that gives him credibility among the vast population of peasants when he promises the end of the warlords and the downfall of the capitalists. Obviously, the latter includes us and most Jews who, if they're not now reeking with the capitalist assets and benefits, certainly want to be. Among Jews in general there is traditional sympathy for the plight of the oppressed. But Stalin has proved to be no friend of the Jews, and no one harbors any illusions that Communism in China will foster good things for foreigners, Jew or not.

Our business picks up little by little, as foreigners and Chinese are also selling any shares they have left to help them emigrate. There is commission on the side of selling, too, of course. Wang, our Chinese manager, presided over the office while we were away when Erich and young Ed, the German lad who joined us age 16, lived in the ghetto. In theory it was permitted to leave the ghetto to work outside, but only at the whim of the mercurial Japanese commandant, Mr. Ghoya. We hear Sassoon is paying his employees all wages accrued during the war. We hope to be able to do the same.

The streets of Shanghai overflow with mobs protesting inflation and lack of goods here. People storm the banks to empty their accounts of cash for which there's nothing to buy. The "Paris of the East" is fading fast. These days American soldiers are the most sought after celebrities as they have largesse not seen here in years—cigarettes, chocolate, nylon stockings. Perhaps you have this phenomenon in India, as well?

It seems the pathway to your independence is clearing. Pity it's littered with the bloodshed among the different religions. Hasn't the fight against the common enemies—Germany and Japan—proved how distracting and unnecessary it should be to fight one's own countrymen? I know I'm ridiculously idealistic, but otherwise how am I to summon hope and strength for the next phase? I'm no longer convinced there is a God.

Love from an ex-POW,
Miriam

Shanghai
30 November 1947

Dear Mena,

Well, the sun is finally setting on the British Empire. Whoever coined that phrase couldn't have foreseen the situation today. India independent? The Jews, as of yesterday, getting their own country? A new world? Yet the same old fighting between religions. Just as the violence in India has reached new levels since 15 August, I fear the same happening in the new Israel when the British leave. England itself is devastated, we hear, with Princess Elizabeth's wedding this month the sole brightness in a dismal and austere place.

Here we also have a wedding to brighten us up. Erich Heilbrun and Suling Zhao married two weeks ago. Joe and Yanlai could no longer protest after Erich's return from ghetto life. His health suffered, as did all of ours during the war, but he's improved and has managed the most brilliant organisation of Joseph & Company for its move to Hong Kong. Suling worries that her parents refuse to leave China before the inevitable arrival of the Communists. Joe's sympathies, despite his privileged upbringing and American university education, lie with the tenets of socialism and spreading the wealth among the peasants. Reuben questions whether Mao and his colleagues will follow this path when they actually govern China. Their formerly philosophical discussions have turned political, as Reuben spends his evenings imploring Joe to leave with us. So far to no avail. Yanlai would go to give Yingfan a better life, such as Suling will have, but Joe is adamant.

The wedding was a formality—not religious, of course—in the license bureau, but we managed to host a tea dance for Erich and Suling at the Cathay Hotel. Since the war it's a shabby version of its past glamour, but the party was festive and a brief period for us all to relive the gaiety we used to take for granted.

Reuben and I will depart for Hong Kong on 1 January, with Erich and Suling (and Nina) due to come later in the year. One thing that saddens me is leaving my precious Torah with its petite Megillah tucked inside. No birthday reading of the story of Esther in 1948, as Erich, Suling, and Nina don't plan to sail until spring. Our early departure will help us establish the office and secure housing for all of us. We are only taking with us clothes and leaving the packing and shipping of our household to those who will follow after us. Reuben is convinced the financial aspects of this removal to Hong Kong should be handled as soon as possible. Every day remaining in China is a day that loses more money and potential for future success. Of course, whatever happens on the mainland will also affect Hong Kong when the British leave this favored colony. But by 1997 you and I will be 97 years old. Worrying about 50 years from now isn't a wise use of time.

I have not left the mainland of China since the journey when we saw you in London in 1930. What a long stretch with such turmoil. I'm not eager for sea travel, but it's only a few days to Hong Kong. Those days will bring me a little closer to the precious India of my childhood, though I know neither Bombay nor the atmosphere of that time remain there. Only you. That's enough for me to wish to be there.

I look forward to picking up our correspondence in my new home. We will stay temporarily at the Peninsula Hotel, not a bad place for refugees.

With love,
Miriam

Hong Kong
22 August 1948

Dear Mena,

Hong Kong in the summer is steamier than Shanghai and Bombay rolled into one. There's water in the air. To stay fresh one changes one's dress twice a day, at least, and then again in the evening to stay presentable in decent company. The locals swear the verandahs on our flats get a downdraft of air from the top of the mountain, but I only feel cool when I sit in front of the electric fan. How old and stodgy I have become. When we were girls in Bombay, where the climate is hardly fresh, I never gave a minute's thought to the heat.

Our transient status persists, as Erich, Suling, and Nina are further delayed in moving here and, along with them, our furnishings, including my Torah and Megillah. Suling became pregnant shortly before they were to sail, and she continues to suffer symptoms that make it inadvisable to travel until after the child is born in January. Of course, they will have to wait a few months more, rather than embark with a small infant. This turn of events has forced our hand in renting a pleasant new flat, complete with aforementioned verandah, at Mid-Levels on Victoria Peak, and it came with furniture, not particularly stylish or substantial furniture, but practical. Three months in the "Pen" was lovely, but hotel life isn't normal. In late April we moved, which is why you have not heard from me in a while. Although there was no need to purchase furniture, I did have to acquire other household goods, such as new china for meat and milk, and begin to train a cook to keep them apart. We have also begun to integrate a bit into the Sephardic Jewish community here, which seems less stratified and pompous than in Shanghai, although there, too, the arrogance and superiority has eased. Isn't it remarkable what war accomplishes? We are all united in celebrating the birth of Israel, though we listen to the wireless endlessly for news about the war there.

I long to visit the "new" independent India. What a shock that, after all the strife, Gandhi-ji lost his life to a zealous follower. I'll never understand such acts, especially when the victim is such a saintly figure. However, I'm wondering if you read his view that Jews going submissively into the gas chambers was exemplary as non-violence. Despite this, his legacy is mostly positive and his assassination tragic.

Reuben envisions we will spend considerable time in Israel after Erich arrives to manage the business. We have increased our donations to funds that benefit the new country. Zionism is much more accepted among our peers than it was back in the days when my purported relative, N.E.B. Ezra, campaigned for it in his newspaper. I'm proud that at least one Ezra, besides Father, had a good reputation. I heard that Cousins Judah and Isaac have been deported from the States after serving their prison terms. I hear Israel has a Law of Return for any born Jew. That could be a salvation for scoundrels who make the rest of us Jews ashamed.

As always, I need to worry less about what I cannot control. Such situations have increased as I've aged. For you, too, I suspect. War and politics are at the top of that list. I think about renewing my efforts for women who struggle to survive and raise children safely. There are many at risk here in Hong Kong, too. When I get more settled, it will be time for the New Malka House. Your continuing work impresses and inspires me always.

So, dear Mena, try to stay cool and enjoy the independence of your wonderful country. As you say, nothing is a panacea, and the struggle continues. Yet, it is a major milestone for Indians. I, for one, am content at the moment to live once again as a British subject under British rule, but only as a relief from where Shanghai is headed. And I promise to write sooner again.

With love and respect,
Miriam

Hong Kong
4 February 1949

Dear Mena,

I regret to inform you my darling wife, Miriam, passed away last night in her sleep. The doctor says her heart simply gave up just short, as you certainly know, of her 49th birthday, which we would have celebrated on the holiday of Purim, 15 March this year, close to her original birth date.

You don't know, because she chose not to dwell on the incident, even among those close to her, what Miriam experienced at the Yangchow prison camp during the war. Typically, she came to the defense of a young English girl who was in the process of being abducted by a Japanese soldier.

The intent of the solider was evident, as he was ripping the girl's shirt-waist when Miriam came upon them in a wooded area behind our barracks. Miriam grabbed a loose tree branch and swung at the soldier, which distracted him and gave the girl an opportunity to follow Miriam's scream to run. But the soldier was naturally stronger than my delicate wife, never fleshy but especially thin in the almost starvation conditions we endured there. He grabbed the tree branch and beat her with it and then with the butt end of his rifle. An officer miraculously not only encountered this scene but called off the soldier and personally picked up Miriam to carry her to the infirmary. Her injuries were never completely diagnosed or treated, but they no doubt included several broken ribs, a punctured lung, assaults to internal organs, and fractures in the vertebrae in her spine. As a physician you'd know better than I the level of shock and stress to one's entire system that would result from such damage, especially in surroundings that were unsanitary and lacked clean water, nutritious food, and medication. Mentally and physically, Miriam absorbed it, recovered her functionality and outward good cheer, and afterward vowed not to speak of it. Yet, her health never regained its heartiness—she tired easily and suffered greatly, though in silence—especially when seasons changed. That is the story.

Our sojourn to Hong Kong was pleasant, but the delay our friends, Erich and Suling, and our "adopted" daughter, Nina, have endured before joining us here preyed on Miriam's mind, as on mine. I remain hopeful, as did she, but, sadly, she won't be here to welcome them.

Although I only met you once, in London nearly 20 years ago, I am thoroughly acquainted with the longevity and depth of your friendship with Miriam. Your correspondence has been a lifeline and source of happy memories for her since she left Bombay and moved to Shanghai. You were a blessing in Miriam's life, as I hope I was, too, for she was my greatest blessing and joy. Already I miss her dreadfully.

I send you best regards and affection on behalf of my now departed Miriam and myself.

Yours sincerely,
Reuben Elias Joseph

AUTHOR'S NOTE:

The Truth Behind the Fiction

" . . . Jews are to be found everywhere. This fact is familiar to all, but it is not so well known that Jews in considerable numbers have existed in China from a very remote period."

Edward Isaac Ezra, East of Asia magazine, Vol. 1, 1902.

Western Jews are often as surprised as Lily was about the long and layered history of Jews in China. It is yet another example of the moniker "wandering Jews" and our global Diaspora. Throughout Jewish history two major factors have fueled our Diaspora: persecution and opportunity. The first Jews reliably reported in China arrived seeking opportunity. Persecution drove successive Jews there, but opportunity greeted the most fortunate.

Today, Kaifeng, in Henan Province, is just another Chinese city with a million residents that most tourists have never heard of and, therefore, don't visit. But for centuries it was a destination that may have been the most populous city in the world in the eleventh century, its zenith as a commercial, governmental, and cultural center. Indeed, the city was one of China's Seven Ancient Capitals during the Jin, Han, Zhou, and Song dynasties. Nestling by the Yellow River, however, made it vulnerable to continuous flooding—some wrought naturally but also deliberately triggered, either by invaders or its own government as military strategy.

The 1642 flood was a catastrophic example of a ruler opening the dikes to rid the area of rebel forces. Nearly the entire Kaifeng population was wiped out, between the destruction it wrought and the disease and famine that arose in its wake. The city had to be abandoned for almost twenty years. Unlike the aftermath of previous floods, when Kaifeng rebuilt and thrived, the Kaifeng that emerged from the dregs of the 1642 flood never regained its prominence.

Yet, for centuries Kaifeng's waterside location provided advantages that outweighed the periodic disasters. Chief among these was its connection to the Beijing-Hangzhou Grand Canal, the longest artificial river in the world, more than 1100 miles long. The oldest parts of the canal date back to the Fifth Century BC. This put Kaifeng on the Silk Road, a wellspring of commercial prosperity and renown. Among the Silk Road traders were Jews hailing from the Middle East, Europe, and Central Asia. Their marriages to Chinese women launched generations of Chinese Jews. Despite their isolation from larger geographic clusters of their fellow Jews, some practiced their faith with relative rigor from the 11th century until the early 1800s.

If there had been a Golden Age for Kaifeng Jewry, it, too, washed away in the floodwaters of 1642. Although the synagogue was rebuilt and other communities donated replacement Torah scrolls, the Jewish population, thought to be 5,000 people before the devastation, diminished considerably.

Ironically, intermarriage was both how the Chinese Jewish community began and grew, but also how it declined, since successive generations of mixed marriages ultimately diluted orthodox tradition. By the late nineteenth and early twentieth centuries, there was no synagogue in Kaifeng, and the families who still considered themselves Jewish were no longer well enough acquainted with the rituals of their faith to practice them. After the last local rabbi died in 1810, no one knew any Hebrew. The Jews began to sell off their remaining Torah scrolls to Protestant missionaries. Yet, still they considered themselves distinct from other Chinese, whose Confucian rites they didn't observe either.

Although Miriam and her father are fictional relatives, Shanghai-born Edward Isaac Ezra was a real-life figure, depicted in my novel as Miriam's wretched "Cousin Edward," whose Shanghai career zoomed and ignominiously crashed in scandal by the time he died at age thirty-nine. A business and community *wunderkind* before his downfall, Ezra wrote in the 1902 premier issue of the *East of Asia Magazine*, a quarterly apparently published only for four years, about hosting a delegation of eight self-proclaimed Kaifeng

Jews. They had traveled to Shanghai to ask their co-religionists there for assistance in rebuilding their synagogue and reviving religious practice through education. In my book David Li and his father, Li Wei, portray themselves as descendants of the Kaifeng Jews.

Edward Ezra summed up the two-hour meeting between the Kaifeng and Shanghai Jews:

"They affirmed with frankness that in coming to Shanghai they are not prompted by the hope of personal gain. They are quite satisfied with their lot from a material standpoint. Rather their chief desire is to be instructed in the religion of their forefathers. Their leader closed the interview by expressing a hope that the Synagogue in Kaifengfu may soon be rebuilt and the remnants of the ancient settlement once more rejuvenated. 'And this,' he continued, 'can only be done with the assistance of our foreign brethren. We are desirous of being instructed—teach us and raise us from the dust!'

"From all appearances these men show great sincerity and their honesty was further proved when one of the their number proposed and then allowed his eldest son, aged fifteen years, to be circumcised, which ceremony was successfully performed on the 27th May last. The lad was named Israel and he is now receiving instruction since he remained in Shanghai after the rest of his delegation returned to Kaifeng."

Mr. Ezra's Shanghai-based Society for the Rescue of the Chinese Jews petered out without significantly helping the Kaifeng delegation beyond sending them home with a Chinese translation of the Torah and imploring them not to sell off more of their remaining Hebrew scrolls. The poor lad Israel seems to have sacrificed his foreskin in vain, a factor inspiring the lingering grudge that David and Li Wei harbor against the long-departed Sephardic Jews of Shanghai.

Today, although their bloodlines as Jews are dubious, there are still a few residents of Kaifeng struggling to maintain their Jewish identity through study with a resident scholar. Others have settled in Israel.

We usually think of Sephardim as Jews from Spain (Sephardi means Spanish in Hebrew) and quite different in ritual and tradition from Ashkenazim, who are from Eastern Europe. The Spanish Sephardim basked in their so-called Golden Age of art, music, philosophy, and science for several hundred years, only to be shattered when they were expelled during the Inquisition.

However, the Sephardic Golden Age was not a phenomenon exclusive to the Iberian Peninsula. It was also widespread among Jews of similar practice residing on the other side of the Mediterranean—from Morocco through Egypt to Mesopotamia (Babylon and Persia, now Iraq and Iran). They lived as *dhimmi,* non-Muslim subjects of Muslim states. At scattered times in history, many rose to prominence as government officials, judges, and generals. In Iraq they descended from the original Jewish captives that King Nebuchadnezzar dragged to exile in Babylon after his forces destroyed the First Temple in Jerusalem in 587 B.C. Under Persian King Cyrus, who conquered Babylon later, Jews could return home and rebuild the Temple, and many chose to follow the prophet Ezra on this journey. Those who remained were able to practice their faith through long periods of tolerance in Baghdad and other regional cities. Indeed, Jewish scholarship and culture flourished: the Babylonian Talmud is the defining treatise of Jewish law. But persecution certainly cropped up from time to time, and perverse changes in government led some Baghdadi Jews to decamp to India in the early nineteenth century. Our fictional Miriam's grandfather had made that move, bringing with him the Torah blessed by Chacham ("a wise man" and the Sephardic equivalent of Rabbi) Yosef Chaim, known as the "Ben Ish Chai," a noted scholar and spiritual leader in Baghdad in the nineteenth century.

Opportunity awaited these businessmen in India and, later, in China. By the mid-nineteenth century most were subjects of the British Empire, which positioned them to reap the benefits of England's defeat of China in the Opium Wars. Their Orthodox Judaism did not preclude engaging in the profitable trading business that addicted many Chinese to opium, derived from India's poppies, while simultaneously extracting tea, silk, and other resources out of their newly adopted country.

Some of the Baghdadi Jews stayed in India, founding Sephardic communities mainly in Calcutta and Bombay, while others moved on to China in short order. The real Ezra family had branches in both places.

To their credit, the Baghdadi Jews in Shanghai invested their talents and ill-gotten profits into real estate and other economic development that built the city. And they stayed, establishing a thriving, though insular, Jewish community, equipped with synagogues, schools, and hospitals.

Shanghai itself was more an international city than a Chinese one, divided as it was into districts known as the International Settlement (governed by British and American officials) and the French Concession that surrounded squalid all-Chinese zones. Although a few prosperous natives occupied seats in municipal government, the majority were wealthy non-Chinese. British dominance gave their Sephardic Jewish subjects considerable political influence. China's brief stab at democracy, under Dr. Sun Yat-sen, benefitted from Jewish support, and one community leader, Silas Hardoon, was a close associate of Dr. Sun.

The last quarter of the nineteenth century brought the first wave of Russian Jews to China—to Harbin and Shanghai, as well as to other northern Chinese cities. These Russian Jews fled czarist pogroms and then, after World War I, the Communist Revolution. Many prospered as merchants and professionals. They introduced to China the cultural flavor of Ashkenazic Judaism, including Yiddish theatre and publications, as well as more synagogues and schools and Zionist organizations similar to those operating in Europe and the United States. Miriam's mother-in-law, Malka, is Ashkenazic, and comes from this settlement stream. Miriam's mother was also Ashkenazic of Russian descent, making both Miriam and Reuben half-breeds of sorts, the offspring of a unique form of mixed-, yet-all-Jewish, marriage.

What happened later is probably the most widely known chapter of Jewish Diaspora history in China — the ultimate wave of Jews who came to Shanghai escaping the Nazis from 1937 to 1940. By the time they arrived, both the Baghdadi and Russian groups had laid the Jewish communal infrastructure that provided what we call today a "social safety net" for the new immigrants. Shanghai became a proverbial "port of last resort" for German and other central European Jews lucky enough to scrape up the fare for passage, especially in the face of closed doors in most other countries around the world. The Japanese had already occupied Shanghai by this time, contributing to a generally chaotic atmosphere that enhanced the city's normal access to stateless travelers lacking passports or visas.

While some of these refugees lived through the charity of the resident Shanghai Jews, others managed to arrive with a few concealed tangible assets. Some found work appropriate to their abilities and enjoyed at the outset a relatively comfortable existence living wherever in the city they could afford. The fictional Erich Heilbron, Lily's uncle and Ruth's father, was one such fortunate refugee from Vienna who not only worked in his legal profession, but also formed a close friendship with the Josephs.

Ultimately, however, as a concession to the pleas of its German allies, the Japanese confined all European Jews who had arrived after 1937 into a crammed ghetto life in a squalid district of Shanghai. Despite its privations, Hongkou was no death camp. Fictional Erich moved there. The Josephs, like real British citizens, went to a Japanese prisoner-of-war camp.

After World War II most Jews left China headed for the United States, Israel, Australia, or back to Europe. As the Chinese Communist takeover became inevitable, the urgency to leave intensified. A few "true believers" of idealized Marxism stayed, however. Like the fictional Miriam and Reuben, many real-life Shanghai Sephardim re-established themselves in Hong Kong, where some remain even since the 1997 hand-over of that former British colony to the Peoples Republic of China.

Today, the Jewish presence in China rests almost entirely with expatriates studying and working there.

Something that seems unrealistic in *The Lost Torah of Shanghai* I read about in Hannah Pakula's biography of Madame Chiang Kai-shek, *The Last Empress*. As a young woman, the former Soong Mei-ling, influenced by her American education, returned to Shanghai as a socially conscious crusader for improved conditions for female Chinese factory workers and their children. Her fervor for helping the less fortunate possibly waned during her marriage to the Generalissimo. She did live more than a century, and her greed and her husband's ties to powerful Shanghai criminals are well documented. But her complicity in a plot to acquire and resell a Torah is fiction.

At least, I assume so. Just when I thought I had made it all up, a November 2013 news report featured a Chinese family in possession of a cache of 2,000 books that had been stored in their Shanghai home since the

1940s. A German-Jewish refugee had entrusted them to a grandfather now long dead. The family's house was slated for destruction to make way for new development in Hongkou, site of the Japanese-imposed refugee ghetto. The family sought to return the books to the owner or his heirs. I have not heard that the owner's family has been found, and the books have been transferred to a library in Shanghai.

Similarly, in the spring of 2014, I was contacted by a Jewish educational institution in Brooklyn. Its leaders were actually seeking a Torah that had been brought to Shanghai by the Mir Yeshiva, a group of scholars and students who escaped the Nazis aided by the visas issued by Japanese consul in Vilna, Lithuania, Chiune Sugihara. Its whereabouts after Shanghai are unknown.

Linda Frank
San Francisco
March 2015

Glossary of Foreign Words
Used in *The Lost Torah of Shanghai*

Yiddishkeit: Of the Yiddish culture

Frume: Yiddish word for religious

Ashkenazic: Jews who lived in and/or emigrated from Germany, Russia, and Eastern Europe

Sephardic: Jews who lived in and/or emigrated from the Iberian Peninsula, North Africa, and the southern Mediterranean, many of whom later settled in southern Europe, including Turkey, Greece, Rumania, and Italy, as well as India and China

Yordim: Israelis who live outside Israel

Refusniks: Russian Jews who applied unsuccessfully for visas to leave the USSR in the 1970s and 1980s before the collapse of the Soviet Union

Meshugenah: Yiddish word for crazy person

Xie xie: Chinese for thank you

Guanxi: Chinese word for connections, good (and useful) relationships

Shamash: Hebrew word for guard or caretaker

Cheongsam: Tight-fitted Chinese dress usually with Mandarin collar and slit in skirt

Tschotchkes: Yiddish word for knickknacks, not necessarily high quality

Ferbrente: Yiddish word for fervent, impassioned

Yad: Hebrew word for hand, also the name of a pointer used in Torah reading in lieu of human touching of the Torah, which is forbidden

Nihao: Chinese word for hello

Shao bing: Chinese pancake

Shivah: Hebrew word for period of mourning lasting seven days, from the Hebrew word *shevah,* which is the number seven

Al fresco: Italian word for outdoors

Mench: Yiddish word for a person of good character

liǎo buqǐ: Chinese word for amazing

Mezuzah: Hebrew word for small container of a prayer ritually hung on the doorposts of Jewish homes

Kippot: Plural of the Hebrew word *kippah,* or scull cap known in Yiddish as a *yarmulkeh*

Acknowledgments

A 2010 volunteer role coordinating "Jews in Modern China," an exhibit brought to San Francisco by the China International Culture Exchange Center (CICEC), a cultural arm of the Chinese government, deepened my knowledge in the subject. It also introduced me to a number of former Shanghailanders who contributed information and, in some cases, treasured personal mementoes to the exhibit. Several of them became friends.

During—and beyond--the three-month run of the exhibit at the Presidio of San Francisco, I was privileged to moderate a traveling panel of "personal historians." This introduced me to Rabbi Ted and Gertrude Alexander, Leah Jacob Garrick, and Inna Mink, representing the Nazi refugee, Sephardic Baghdadi, and Russian streams of Jewish settlement in Shanghai, respectively. Matook "Mat" Nissim, a Baghdadi Sephardic native of Shanghai, gave me a prized copy of his limited-edition memoir and provided hours of conversation, often joined by his equally gracious wife, Jackie, about his early life there and in a Japanese prisoner-of-war camp. A longtime friend, the late Rena Krasno, unfortunately did not live to contribute to the exhibit and its programming. But her books and personal recollections about life in the Shanghai Russian-Jewish community inspired me to delve into this subject matter many years before "Jews in Modern China." Based on Rena's recommendation, I served for several years on the board of the Sino-Judaic Institute, which charged me with marketing the exhibit the SJI had curated, "The Jews of Kaifeng." Special board colleagues, including Dr. Albert Dien, Rabbis Anson Laytner and Arnold Belzer, and Professor Steve Hochstadt, enhanced my education about and interest in that early history of both

Jews and Chinese. I've come to treasure friendships with Tess Johnston—an iconic forever-young "old China Hand," historian, and author long-based in Shanghai--and Manli Ho, whose father was Dr. Ho Feng-shan, a "righteous Gentile" Chinese consul in 1930s Vienna, who risked his career by issuing transit visas for Austrian Jews desperate to escape from Europe.

Successive consuls-general and consular staff members of the Peoples Republic of China in San Francisco have adopted us as "friends" of their country, and our *guanxi* with them and their families are precious personal relationships that have deepened our understanding of their lives and, I hope, given them a unique look into Jewish family and community life. I have also appreciated the friendship and support of the CICEC team who came to San Francisco for the exhibit and welcomed us in Beijing. In addition, Chen Jian, curator, and his colleagues at the Shanghai Jewish Refugees Museum have become valued friends.

From the writing standpoint, I have benefitted once again from the developmental editing of Alan Rinzler, this writer's personal literary *éminence grise,* whose advice and counsel influenced the creation of this book behind the scenes—literally all the scenes—as the plot formulated. Another friend, Susan Pittelman, shared her professional wisdom with publishing tips geared to improve the book's presentation.

Given my peripatetic life style, some of this book has been written thousands of feet in the air, and a good chunk of it at a second "personal Yaddo," the Midwestern branch, offered by our friends, Paula Simon and Howard Schoenfeld--the Fairchild Road Writers Retreat. As grateful as I am for these vacant and quiet spaces, I will somehow manage the next book without either this refuge, which they hope to sell, or the Santa Rosa location that helped incubate *After the Auction* and where they actually live now.

Like my protagonist Lily, I have a Chinese relative, my daughter-in-law, Li Xuebai, also known as Amy Li Ansfield. Through her and during the years that her husband, Jonathan, has lived and worked in Beijing, our family life has been greatly enhanced and enriched by the China connection. Thank you, Amy and Jonathan, for providing me with a degree of authenticity and for so much more, including sharing with us Amy's family and your interesting, accomplished, gracious, and fun friends.

Our other children, Jon and Rachel Frank, add enthusiasm and inspiration to what I do, and they are excellent promoters among their own wide circle of friends and their Friendship Circle organization.

My husband, Eli Frank, supported me on this book, as always. His contribution included wandering all over steamy Shanghai in the summer of 2013 to take photos of locations in the novel. On that trip to China, my eleventh and his ninth, we brazenly weathered frequent stares--and near confiscation of a nice camera across the street from the original Edward Ezra home, where a guard signaled no photos! I love our adventures and hope they will continue for a long time. Thank you.

Linda Frank is a local and national volunteer advocate and leader retired from a business career. A lifelong passion for twentieth-century Jewish and world history has motivated and inspired her novels, *After the Auction* and now *The Lost Torah of Shanghai.* Using journalist-protagonist Lily Kovner and her cohort, Frank crafts a fictional plot into a framework that encourages the reader to explore some of this history through the investigations and experiences of an identifiable character.

In addition to her novels, Frank has written business, travel, and advocacy articles for publications such as *The Asian Wall Street Journal, The Forward, Jewesses With Attitude* (a blog of the Jewish Women's Archive), and *Corporate Report Wisconsin.* She has also hosted her own cable television show that highlighted business topics, particularly as they related to women.

CPSIA information can be obtained
at www.ICGtesting.com
Printed in the USA
FSOW01n1510161015
12258FS